The One Who Knows Me

JOAN EMBOLA

THE ONE WHO KNOWS ME

SOVEREIGN LOVE. BOOK ONE

JOAN EMBOLA

THE ONE WHO KNOWS ME

Love Qualified Press

Manuscript edited by Michaela Bush

Blurb edited by Abigayle Claire

Cover designed and illustrated by Elle Maxwell

For more information, contact;

www.joanembola.co.uk

ALSO BY JOAN EMBOLA

Fiction

The One Who Loves Me: Sovereign Love Book 2

The One Who Sees Me: Sovereign Love Book 3

The One Who Holds Me: Sovereign Love Book 4

Devotionals

Outpourings Of A Beloved Heart: A 30 Day Poetry Devotional About God's Love

The God Who Knows Me: A Companion Devotional & Journal

Also check out the merch store for cute faith-based t-shirts, stickers, notebooks, mugs, and so much more.

Trigger Warning: This story involves sensitive topics such as characters dealing with depression, anxiety, the death of a loved one, and references to suicide. I have done my best to treat these issues with the care they deserve. However, if these topics are triggers for you, I suggest you please pray before going any further, knowing that my intentions for choosing to address these topics are not to plunge readers into darkness, but to point them to the light and hope we have in our Lord and Saviour—Jesus Christ.

To my Heavenly Father, the One who knows me

But He knows the way that I take; when He has tested me, I will come forth as gold.

— JOB 23:10

1

TEEYANA

I need to get out of this building before Olivia sees me. If I can escape her dirty looks, her taunting, and my usual daily dose of embarrassment, then today will mark the end of my bullying story.

Olivia Hastings is the most popular girl in Boston's Coverton High; and unfortunately, myself, and my best friend—Amara, have been one of her bullying targets for the past two years. But even though my time in Coverton High has felt like an endless struggle to survive, I've always known the bullying would end someday.

Today is that day. It's the last day of high school, so when I get out of this building, Olivia will no longer exist to me. She'll become a memory buried deep inside my brain alongside all the other memories which keep me awake at night—the ones which make me wonder how my life turned out to be like this.

Today is not about Olivia, though. It's about me finally taking control of my own life—without the watchful eyes of my parents. All I need to do now is graduate, do my summer internship, and I'll be off to New York to start graphic design school in the fall.

I wince as the school bell rings above my head; the sound ricocheting off the white walls of the empty hallway. The former stillness vanishes and in its place, there's loud chattering, thumping of bouncing balls, and banging of metal lockers. The hallways are now flooded with students who can taste freedom.

As the classroom doors fling open and the crowd presses into the hallway, I take a step aside, dodging a bouncing basketball heading in my direction. I run my fingers against the long row of green lockers and my mouth curves into a broad smile. I, too, can taste the freedom.

Placing my backpack on top of my feet, I glance over my shoulder to check for Olivia before putting in my locker combination. I pull out my denim jacket and empty my locker before taking one last look at my face in the mirror. Mom bought me her most talked about foundation in shade toffee caramel, and I love how it makes my skin glow today. Sometimes, Mom knows exactly what I need, and so does Amara.

"Oh, shoot!!!" I press the home button on my phone to check the time. I planned to meet Amara outside fifteen minutes ago.

This is why I need to stop using my phone while I'm on the toilet.

Slipping the gadget into the back pocket of my jeans, I put on my purple beanie and adjust my fish tail braid to sit on my shoulder. But as I slam my locker shut, I pause when I spot Olivia half a mile away. She has tied her perfectly brushed blonde hair up in a ponytail, making her flowy curls hard to miss—even in an enormous crowd like this.

Olivia struts past the crowd as she heads for the bathroom, and I breathe a sigh of relief. But my relief is short-lived when Olivia turns her head in my direction and locks eyes with me. I freeze in my spot, paralysed with fear as Olivia walks towards me. All the false confidence I had a few minutes ago quenches inside of me.

Please, not today. Surely not today. A sweat breaks on my forehead and I gulp, my chest heaving as a slight wheeze escapes my lungs. *Move, Teeyana. Move now.*

Turning my face away, I pick up my backpack and slide into the crowd. I clutch my notebooks tight against my chest and make my way towards the exit with one goal in mind—to get out of the building.

With a tightened grip on my backpack, and shuddered breaths escaping my mouth, I channel all my energy into my walk, giving it everything I have. As I round the corner to get out through the double doors, I collide with someone. The impact is so strong; I lose my grip on my notebooks and they drop onto the smooth tiled floor.

"I'm sorry. I'm so sorry." My hands tremble as I stoop to pick up my notebooks without looking at the person I bumped into.

"No, I'm sorry." A gruff voice replies from above my head, forcing me to look up. "I didn't see you there. Are you okay?"

Phew!!! I thought I bumped into Olivia.

"Hey, Jimmy." My shaky voice steadies as I shove my notebooks into my backpack.

"Are you okay?" Jimmy asks again, his head lowering to meet my gaze as I stand up.

I nod and glance around until I spot Olivia again. She's now talking and laughing with her group of friends at the opposite end of the hallway. I breathe another deep sigh of relief.

"Hello?" Jimmy waves his hand in my face before lifting his skateboard up to his chest.

"Oh, I'm...sorry, Jimmy. What did you say?" I turn my head to face him.

"Are you sure everything's alright?" He raises a brow before glancing in Olivia's direction.

"Yeah...of course." I tuck loose hairs behind my ear. "I'm fine. What were you saying?" I huddle close to him as we walk outside the building.

"I said I wanted to speak to you after class, but you left early. Are you still happy for me to DJ at your birthday party on Friday?" He rakes his fingers through his silky hair.

"Yeah, that would be great. I'm looking forward to it." I smile at him.

"Sweet!!! I'll see you and Amara on Friday then." He jumps on his skateboard and glides away with no care in the world. Little does he know that he just saved me from my last torture at Coverton High.

I jog my way through the school courtyard to the front entrance, where Amara is waiting for me. As I near the parking lot, her silver braids come into full view. She's sitting on the bench where we usually have lunch together, hunched over, and typing away on her phone.

I place my backpack on the bench and plop down on the sidewalk next to her. "I'm such a coward." I bury my face in my palms.

"Whoa, slow down, girl. Who's a coward?" Amara straightens and places her phone on the bench.

"Me!!! I'm a big coward." I groan. "I just saw Olivia and—"

"Whoa, you saw Olivia?" Amara jumps to her feet. "Girl, where is she? What did she do to you?" Amara adjusts her African print headband and hoop earrings, as if she's getting ready for a fight.

"I think she's still inside or something." I wave a dismissive hand towards the school building. "She didn't do anything. I saw her walking in my direction, and I assumed she was coming for me. I felt so petrified and defenseless. It was a good thing I bumped into Jimmy. I used him as an anchor to help me get out of there without looking as if I was being chased." I look up at Amara. "It's not fair. Why do *we* have to deal with this?"

Amara flicks her braids to the side and sits down again. "Girl, I'm so sorry. I should have waited for you inside. I know we've always been stronger together." She places her arm around my shoulder and leans her head on mine.

"No, it's not your fault, Amara. This has nothing to do with you." I sigh. "It just sucks that one person can make me feel so afraid, so insecure, and so weak." I cross my arms against my chest.

"Aww girl, we both know you're not weak." Amara straightens. "And you're not a coward either." She stands up and pulls me up with her. "Sitting here and complaining means we're giving Olivia the victory."

Amara grabs hold of my face. "Listen to me, girl. We can't let her have the victory. We've come too far, and we know better. Look on the bright side. God sent Jimmy to help you get out of that sticky situation, didn't He? He's always got our backs, remember?" Amara tilts her head and smiles, hope radiating from her voice.

Yeah, right! Just like He had our backs all the other times when Olivia got her way, huh?!

"I...guess so." I return a half-hearted smile, looking so unconvinced, I know Amara can tell. She looks at me for a few seconds before opening her mouth to speak, but she closes it again and resumes her seat on the bench.

"Anyway, I have something for you." Amara reaches into her navy blue bag lying next to her. She pulls out a wrapped present and hands it to me. "I know your birthday is in three days, but I wanted to be the first one. My best friend is special like that." She winks at me and I sit next to her on the bench.

"Please don't let whatever happened with Olivia ruin your

day. Your party is going to be amazing and girl, she ain't gonna be there." Amara waves a finger in my face.

I chuckle and start tearing off the wrapping paper when a car honks at us from the parking lot. We both snap our heads in the direction of the sound, and Amara springs to her feet.

"Ooh, come on. Our ride is here." Amara nods in the car's direction and drags me up by my arms.

"Hello, Mrs. Ikezie." I wave to Amara's mom as we approach her grey Hyundai Sonata. Mrs. Ikezie closes her car door and walks towards us, the rhinestones on her matching African print blouse and headscarf sparkling in the sunlight. Mrs. Ikezie's love for colour has never failed to speak volumes through her beautiful cultural outfits—a love she has certainly passed down to Amara.

"Hello, my dear." Her heavy Nigerian accent comes through. "How are you and your parents?" She takes off her sunglasses and brushes the mole on the side of her chin.

"We're doing great." I smile at her.

Mrs. Ikezie turns to Amara and moves the silver braids covering a quarter of her daughter's face to the side. "*Adamma*, my beautiful daughter, how was your exam?" she asks, but doesn't wait for Amara to respond before adding, "*Ahn ahn*!!! I always tell you not to wear your hair down if it is going to cover your entire face like this. Tie it up so the world can see your beautiful face." She tilts her head and tries to sweep Amara's braids away from her face.

"My exam was fine, Mom." Amara moves her head away from her mother's grip. "My braids are fine too." She adjusts the braids herself. "Can we go now, please? Teeyana needs to open her gift and try it on." Amara and I share a smile before she grabs my hand and pulls me toward her mom's car.

2

TEEYANA

I lean my head against my bedroom window pane as the sun disappears behind the tall tree in our backyard. The warm summer air brushes against my skin as images of my future encircle my thoughts.

But not long into my moment of complete solitude, a familiar wave of doubt and anxiety breaks into my thoughts. The unsettling feeling that ensues forces me to long for the days when sunsets were a source of inspiration to unleash my creativity.

Back in our house in L.A—where my desk sat close to my windows—sunsets were my motivation for my after-school drawing sessions. They were an example of one thing which made my life perfect. Dad had a good job, we had a cool house, Olivia didn't exist to me, and I had no doubts about God.

But after Dad lost his job, we lost all our privileges and had to move in with my grandparents in Atlanta. It was then that sunsets became nothing but a distraction from the raging sea of questions in my head.

And now, the sunsets here in Boston mean nothing to me—they only remind me of the days I feel I can't talk to anyone. But even though life has been unfair to me, I have to give myself a reason to keep going.

For two years, this spot right here has been my thinking spot, my crying spot, and my *"clear my mind"* spot—as I like to call it. Today, I choose to think about college. It'll be the beginning of a new adventure for me. It's the only thing I'm looking forward to —my only reason to keep going.

Loud vibrations from my phone interrupt my thoughts and I turn my head towards the gadget on my bed. I push myself away from the window and walk across the room to find Amara's name flashing on my screen.

The perfect person to put me in a better mood.

I smile and bring the phone up to my ear. "Hey, you." I plop down on my bed, pressing my free hand against my soft, sheeted mattress.

"Hey, birthday girl!!!" Amara screams from the other end of the line. "We go'n have a part-ay. Woo!!!" Her shriek is so loud, I have to take the phone away from my ear for a second before bringing it back.

"Oh my God, why do you *always* have to be so loud? I can hear you perfectly fine, you know?" I tap my ear to make sure it's still working properly.

"Oh, whatever." Amara ignores my question. "How's my birthday girl feeling today, hmm?" I can imagine her wiggling her eyebrows right about now.

"*Ugh*, Amara, it's not even my birthday yet. Stop it." I whine.

"Girl, I don't care. There's no difference between today and tomorrow. But since you're so particular about time, you have exactly eight hours, twenty-three minutes and sixteen seconds left before you become an adult and officially older than me." She mocks. Our birthdays are only a month apart, but Amara loves teasing me about being older than her.

"Whatever." I roll my eyes. "Age is only a number after all."

"If that makes you feel better, baby girl. Don't come crying to me when your hair starts greying, and your teeth start falling out, okay?" She jokes.

"*Ugh*, you're so annoying. Go away." I laugh.

"Nuh-uh. You can't get rid of me that easily. I'm here to stay." Amara giggles. "But how are you *really* feeling about tomorrow?" Her tone turns serious.

"I'm only turning eighteen, not joining the army." I lay on my back. "I'm excited for the party tomorrow."

"Now, that's my girl. I'll come in early to do your hair, makeup, and sort out any last-minute issues. Girl, you sure ain't ready for my inner hairdresser persona. I'm gonna have you looking *real* good."

I chuckle. "Thanks, Amara. I don't know what I would do without you. You're the best."

"I know!!!" Amara screams again. "That's why I'm your B.F.F." She adds and I giggle at her overconfident response. She's right, though. We know each other so well, I can't agree more with her statement.

"Teeyana!!!" Mom calls out from the bottom of the stairs, forcing me to sit up. "Your grandma and grandpa are on Skype." Mom announces.

I move my phone away from my ear. "Okay, Mom. I'm coming."

Saying goodbye to Amara, I drop my phone on my bed and dash out of my room.

"Danny? Granny is on Skype." I call out to my little brother, and he rushes out of his room, where he'd been playing with Dad.

"Yay, Granny!!!" Danny runs into my widespread arms and I carry him down the stairs as Dad follows close behind us. Nothing excites us more than Skype calls from our grandparents —especially on our birthdays.

"Hey Grandma. Hey Grandpa." I balance Danny on my lap and smile at my grandparents on the laptop screen in front of us.

They're both sitting on their favourite grey couch in their living room—the same one I used to fall asleep on until Dad woke me up and guided me back to my room.

Grandpa is wearing his favourite shirt—the blue striped one Grandma loves. She says it makes his grey hairs pop and Grandma has a special love for her greys. She sits beside Grandpa with her back straight, hands on her lap, knees together, and looking twenty years younger even though she has a full head of kinky coily grey hair.

"*Happy birthday to you*." My excited grandparents sing with big smiles on their faces. They've been talking about this all year because I'm the first grandchild to become an adult.

"But my birthday is tomorrow." I say after they finish singing.

"Yes, we know, honey. But your grandpa and I couldn't wait to give you your gift." Grandma rubs her palms together like a three-year-old waiting to open Christmas gifts. She loves buying gifts for others, and if you ask me, I'd say that's her love language for sure.

When we first moved to Atlanta, Grandma wasn't pleased with my constant moping and refusing to get involved with the new youth group. To cheer me up, she got us tickets to Disney World for my fourteenth birthday. I had wanted to go for a long time, but Mom and Dad had been too busy to take me. That was the best birthday gift ever.

"Wait, what gift?" I look up at Mom and Dad, who are standing behind us. They move to one side and reveal a parcel wrapped in purple paper in the corner of the living room.

Putting Danny down to sit beside me, I rush to the gift and tear off the wrapping paper to reveal the MacBook Pro I've wanted to get for Graphic Design school.

I can't believe my grandparents got it for me. I mentioned it in passing last Thanksgiving when we visited them in Atlanta, but I didn't think they were *actually* going to get it.

"Thank you so much. This means a lot to me," I say after getting over my disbelief.

"You're welcome, honey." My grandparents respond in unison as they hold each other's hands.

"I never thought you could beat the Disney World tickets, but I think this comes real close." I nod.

"Oh, sweetie," Grandma jumps in. "We love you so much and that's why we shower you with all these gifts." She pauses. "But remember, the most valuable of them all is the gift of knowing God."

And here we go again. There can never be a gathering without Grandma mentioning God, and Jesus, and salvation, and blah...blah... blah.

"This gift is even better," she continues. "It's free, and the Giver is our Heavenly Father who loves us very much." Grandma tilts her head and looks at me. "You still have that Bible I got you for your baptism, right?"

I straighten in my seat, tightening my arm around Danny's torso. "Erm...yeah...of course." My heart pounds in my chest. "I always keep it in a...uh...in a safe place." I swallow to get rid of the dryness in my throat.

Oh, shoot. I hope she doesn't ask me to get it. I can't even remember if I brought it to Boston with me when we moved.

"Okay, good, because I made sure to put it in your suitcase before you left." Grandma smiles.

Phew. I better find it after this in case she asks me next time.

Grandma arranges Grandpa's collar to lie flat around his neck before turning to me again. "I know you children use Bible apps on your phones these days, but nothing beats the good ol book. Right, honey?" She smiles at Grandpa.

"Yes, of course. You listen to your Grandma, Teeyana."

Grandpa winks at me and I flash him a nervous smile as heat rises to my cheeks.

"Now you be a good girl when you get to college and when I see you at Christmas, I'll give you your birthday hug." Grandma blows me a kiss. "And you too, Danny boy. You have grown so big. You're not a baby anymore." Grandma leans forward with her hands on the sides of her face.

"Yeah. I'm four." Danny waves four fingers in front of the laptop screen. "I'm a big boy." He nods in confidence.

"You are a big boy indeed. Grandma has a special present for big boys too." She winks at Danny, and he lets out a cute chuckle. Danny was fortunate to get Grandpa's unforgettable infectious laughter. I used to laugh easily too, but now it takes a lot to get me smiling. At the moment, Grandpa's kind face, coupled with Grandma's graceful presence, is enough to make me forget my groanings for a few minutes.

"Teeyana, even though we can't be with you on your special day, we want you to remember that we're always praying for you." Grandpa adds.

"Thanks, Grandpa. I can't wait to see you at Christmas. I miss your pies, Grandma, and I want to play with your hair too." We both laugh as I touch her greying, kinky coils on the screen. I still remember when she did her "big chop" and rocked her teeny weeny afro. Now her curls are grazing the top of her shoulders.

"Those pies and this head of hair will be right here waiting for you if the Lord lets me live till then." Grandma smiles and her eyes sparkle. "Honey, we have to head to church now, but can we say a prayer for you?"

My smile fades—but not so much that anyone takes notice. "Erm...of course." I hold hands with Mom and Dad, Danny wraps his arms around my waist, and Grandpa prays for us.

It's been a tradition for my grandparents to pray for us on

our birthdays. It used to be one thing I looked forward to, but I'm not into this whole routine anymore. I'm a hypocrite saying amen to this prayer when I know deep inside that my heart no longer believes in the God we are praying to.

~

"Hurry up, girl. Everyone's waiting for you." Amara yells at me from the bottom of the stairs as our living room fills up with students from Coverton High.

With one hand resting on her hip and the other holding onto her silver clutch bag, Amara taps her foot as I do my snail-walk down the flight of stairs, counting every step as I go.

"I told you these heels were too high. I can't walk in them." I stare at the three-inch stilettos on my feet.

"Nuh-uh." Amara shakes her head. "Girl, you go'n learn today." She replies, before climbing up one step and holding my hand.

Okay, Teeyana. You can do this. Come on, it's not that hard.

I let go of the rail, my hand aching from my previous tight grip. Grabbing the hem of my black dress, I make my way down the last few steps, holding on to nothing but Amara's hand.

"Yay, you made it." Amara cheers as I let go of my dress, the hem gently sweeping the floor behind me. She adjusts my off-shoulder neckline before taking a step back to admire. "Now that's my best friend. You look beautiful. Breath-taking. Phenomenal." Heat rises to my cheeks as she spews out her exaggerated compliments.

"Your curls are lit." Amara fluffs my hair, which she helped me curl earlier. It looks different from my usual straight hair-style, but I love it.

New age, new me. I guess?

"Thanks, girl. You look beautiful too. Breath-taking.

Phenomenal." I throw Amara's words back at her. There's no way I'm letting her off without a compliment.

"Aww, tell me something I don't know." She twirls and shows off her purple one-shoulder jumpsuit, which has a massive bow attached to the sleeve. The jumpsuit hugs her wide hips in the right places and the purple complements her beautiful skin tone, which is darker than mine. She's also wearing her silver three-inch heels which match her clutch purse and braids.

Today she tied her braids up in an "*umbrella bun*," which means she listened to her mom and didn't let the braids "cover her beautiful face."

"Wow, you're very modest, aren't you?!" I chuckle. "Come on. Let's check out this party you won't shut up about." I wrap my arm around her shoulder as we walk into the living room together.

I gasp when I see the bright coloured lights hanging around the room, and my mouth waters as the smell of sweet chilli sauce and onion tartlets fills my nostrils.

"Wow, that's a tall cake." My jaw drops as I stare at the four tier cake on the central table. Purple cascading roses run from the top tier to the bottom, and a huge number eighteen sits at the top, also wrapped with a string of smaller purple flowers.

I bet Amara had something to do with this cake decor. But at least she used my favourite colour.

We meander through the crowd of approximately twenty people holding their cups of fruit punch, and moving their bodies rhythmically to the music coming from the speakers.

"Hey, Sally. Hey, Tammy. Thanks for coming to my party." I smile at the twin brunette sisters from psychology class as Amara and I walk past.

"No, thank you for inviting us." Tammy responds with a broad smile.

Close to one corner of the room, ten more people are

hunching over a long table lined with silver trays of all kinds of food, but the Buffalo wings, hot fries, and mozzarella bread sticks catch my attention.

On the opposite side of the room, six more people are gathering around a chocolate fountain, dipping their fresh strawberries into the running chocolate. Jimmy is standing behind a DJ booth, which is pitched a few yards away from a giant speaker, and he is bopping his head to the loud music. Amara and I wave at him, but he is too lost in the music to notice.

My gaze falls on Danny running across the room towards us, my parents following behind. He latches onto me and I pick him up from the ground—being careful not to twist my ankles in these heels.

"So? What do you think, honey? Do you like it?" Mom asks.

"Like it? Are you kidding, Mom? I love it. This looks amazing." I put Danny down and he wraps his arms around my legs. "I don't know why I worried when you guys said you would handle everything. I should trust more, shouldn't I?" I nudge Amara's arm.

"Yeah, you dang well should, girl." Amara rolls her eyes and I laugh.

"Yeah, I have to agree with Amara on this one." A familiar voice comes from behind Mom, and I tilt my head to look past her shoulder.

"Aunt Bella!!!" I gasp, my heart fluttering in excitement.

"Hey, partner." She winks at me, before putting down the gift bag she's holding to hug me. Her warm, furry coat tickles the skin on my face, and the scent of her expensive, strong-smelling perfume wafts into my nostrils. "You didn't think I was going to miss my favourite niece's birthday, did you?" She grins.

I arch an eyebrow. "I'm your *only* niece."

"Well...you never know. Things can happen." Her mouth curves into a cunning smile before she turns around and wiggles her eyebrows at Mom and Dad. They both shake their heads in disagreement, drawing laughter from all of us.

"Bella, I thought you were working today." Mom asks after Aunt Bella makes her round of hugs.

"Well, it turned out I was wrong." She shrugs. "It was my day off, so I thought I'd make my way down here to give this pretty girl her birthday gift and also to take this little man home with me. It's your turn to have a sleepover at mine, isn't it, Danny?" She bends down and hugs him before lifting him up to sit on her hip. "We're going to have fun watching *The Lion King* tonight, aren't we?" Aunt Bella rubs her nose against his.

"*The Prince of Egypt*." Danny objects.

"Alright then. The man has spoken." Aunt Bella nods, before leaning close to Mom and whispering something into her ears.

Even though Aunt Bella is eight years younger than Mom, they've always looked like twins to me. They have the same caramel complexion and long face, but Aunt Bella is two inches taller, and while Mom loves wearing straight black wigs, Aunt Bella prefers coloured, big, curly hairstyles like Amara. Both sisters also have an exceptional eye for make-up, with accentuated high cheekbones and sleek eyebrows.

We haven't spent much time with Aunt Bella since she got promoted to merchandise team manager at Macy's, so Danny is the fortunate one today. Aunt Bella and I are having our girls' day out in two weeks though, so it's all good.

"Okay, who's ready to part-ay?" Aunt Bella grins at Danny before heading towards the stairs.

"We'll be right back, honey." Mom and Dad follow Aunt Bella up to Danny's room to get him ready for the sleepover.

I tuck some hair behind my ear and look around the room again, still baffled by the number of people who have come. Olivia once tried to make me believe that everyone at Coverton High hated me. Well, I think I can say she was wrong.

"Olivia was wrong." Amara's voice startles me, and I turn around to face her. "These people have come to celebrate with you because you're amazing. You have friends because everyone can see you have a kind heart."

My eyes widen in disbelief. "How...how did you know I was thinking about Olivia?"

Amara places her hand on my shoulder. "Because I'm your BFF and...I just know." She laughs.

Sometimes I think this girl can read minds.

"Happy birthday, Teeyana. I know the past two years have been tough on you, but here you are, still standing tall. I'm so proud of you, and I hope you've had an amazing day. I love you so much, girl." Amara wraps her arms around my neck.

"Aww, I love you too." My voice breaks as tears form in my eyes.

"Uh-uh." Amara shakes her head and holds me at arm's length. "You're not allowed to ruin this make-up I spent hours trying to perfect. We need to cheer you up, come on!!!" She drags me towards the dance floor when the music changes and everyone else follows.

"Amara!!!" I try to resist her pull. "I can't dance."

"Nuh-uh. Girl, you're not sitting out of this one. It's your birthday. Come on, shawty." She moves my arms around until I give up and let my body flow to the rhythm of the music. I smile and shake my head at her. "I don't like you."

She laughs out loud before twirling. "But you just said you loved me a minute ago. You can't take that back now."

3

JAYDEN

"T*hat's some wicked awesome music, Jay.*" Tyler would have said if he was sitting next to me right now. In four months, it'll be five years since he died, but every time I listen to his favourite songs, I still expect him to walk into the room and sing along with me.

It's ironic that I never listened to these songs when Tyler was alive. But now that he's gone, they're the only songs I listen to. At first, I only listened because they reminded me of him. But as the years passed, the truth in the lyrics came to mean so much more, and every day, I wish for a chance to tell Tyler how God used his favourite songs to save me from depression.

I bop my head to the soft music radiating from my mobile phone. The guitar chords, drumbeats, and piano notes all blend into one beautiful sound which fills the air in our front porch. Our porch swing creaks, swaying back and forth as I tap my hands against the bench to match the drumbeats of the song "Whom Shall I Fear" by Chris Tomlin.

I reach over to turn up the volume as our neighbour's cat struts past our front door—its orange furry coat glistening in the sunshine God has blessed us with. A sweat breaks on my temple, reminding me of the heat of the Boston summer weather, and I palm it away before returning to tapping my hands and feet.

Then, I hear faint footsteps coming from behind me. My senses tingle, and I adjust in my seat. I wait a few seconds and... 3...2...1....

"Boo!!!" Mom shouts in my ear before wrapping her arms around my shoulders.

"Hey, Mom." I laugh at her pathetic attempt to scare me.

"But...but..." She stutters before dropping her shoulders in disappointment. "But you didn't even flinch. How did you hear me over this loud music?" She sends a sullen look to my phone on the bench.

"Hey, what can I say? My Spidey senses tingle." I cringe at my cheesy comeback, before turning the music off.

"That's not fair." Mom crosses her arms and pouts.

"Aww, maybe you need to find new ways to try and scare me. I'll be nineteen in November, Mom. I need adult scares now." I grin.

"Oh, come on." A dimpled smile creeps on her face, and she presses her lips against my forehead. "Maybe you're right. My baby boy is all grown up now." She brushes my cheeks before sitting next to me on the porch swing, causing it to squeak under our weight.

"So what book are you reading now?" Mom peers over my shoulder, her gaze focusing on the book lying next to my phone.

"Oh, this?" I pick it up and bring it closer so she can read the title.

"Hmm, that looks interesting. What's it about?" She pushes her glasses close to her face.

"Erm...I don't know." I scratch my head and give her a sheepish smile. "I haven't started reading it yet. I found it in Tyler's room and it looked interesting."

"Ah, of course." Mom nods. "You love spending time in his room, don't you?" She reaches for my hands and squeezes them. "You boys have always been so alike, and now you do exactly what he used to do." Mom sighs and meets my gaze. "As long as you come back to me at the end of it all, I'll be fine." She lowers her head and kisses my hands. "You're all we have left, Jayden." When she brings her head back up, her eyes glisten with tears waiting to drop.

The all-so familiar pain in her voice is back—like it never left. I put the book down and place my arm around her shoulders. "I know, Mom. I'll always be here for you and Dad. I promise." I catch a lone tear gliding down her cheek.

I know it's not up to me to promise I won't be going anywhere because only God knows tomorrow. But I have to do everything it takes to comfort my mom—at least for this moment.

"Hey," I squeeze her shoulder and stroke her cheek with my thumb. "You promised me no tears today, remember?"

She nods. "Yes, I promised—at least not while you're watching." She laughs and holds my hands again. "I want you to know that Tyler would have been so proud of you. Your dad and I are proud of you too, Jayden."

"I know, Mom. I'll finish what Tyler started. By God's grace, I will." I reassure her.

"Please, Jayden. Promise me you'll keep in touch when you go off to college? I don't want to be a clingy mom, but I want you to know you can talk to me about anything." She pauses. "And always remember that we love you." She touches my face.

"And I love you too, Mom." I press her hand on my face. "Now, stop worrying and go enjoy your date with Dad. Please?" I nudge her with my elbow until she stands up.

"Right. Let me see if he's ready this time." She rolls her eyes and turns around. "And I better fix my makeup since these stupid tears have ruined it." She fiddles with her fake eyelashes, which no longer look symmetrical.

"You look beautiful, Mom. As always." I smile at her.

"Thanks, baby." She returns my smile before disappearing into the house.

I lean back on the swing and let it rock me. Now that my music is off, it's quiet enough for me to make out the high pitched shrills and shrieks from our neighbour's children on the other side of the fence. They're having water fights like Tyler and I did when we were younger.

As far as I remember, we used to fight about anything and everything—a chair to sit on when we had supper, who should hold the clicker when we watched TV in the parlor, and who should have the last grinder in the lunch box.

Tyler drove me crazy, but I'd do anything to bring him back to us. I want to go back to the days when I was naïve and didn't know any pain or sorrow. As much as I'm grateful for where I am now, I still wish in my heart that things had turned out differently.

~

It hasn't been long since Mom and Dad left for their date night and I'm back inside the house. After closing our front door, I climb up the stairs and head toward my room, but I slow down to a halt after walking past the first door on my right.

Turning around, I stare at the door for a few seconds before approaching it. Each step I take causes memories to flicker in my head—memories of the countless times I stood outside the room and bopped my head to the music blasting from the other side.

Tyler used to play his guitar for hours without remembering

he had to eat, so Mom used me as a middleman, to draw him out of his little world and back into reality.

He never heard me knock, and he never knew I always listened outside his door. He had a wicked awesome voice and I still can't believe I'll never hear it again.

Taking a deep breath, I stretch my hand out to touch the doorknob and the illusion of Tyler playing and singing "Blessed Be Your Name" fills my thoughts.

I turn the doorknob and step into his room, expecting to find him sitting on his bed, holding on to his guitar. I want to see him wearing his favourite blue t-shirt which reads *Free Indeed*. I want to hear him laugh and see his hazel brown eyes twinkle. I want to hear him beckon to me to sit next to him so he can play the newest song he has learned.

I want to see his face again and hear his encouraging words telling me everything will be okay. But all I'm staring at is the emptiness of his room—the emptiness he left behind.

A fresh breeze blows in from the open window, leaving the room cold and eerie. I shut the window and step away from it, tripping on a black guitar case. It was Tyler's favourite guitar—his only guitar.

I smile to myself, thinking about how annoyed he would be if he knew I knocked his guitar over. Picking up the case, I take out the guitar and sit on his bed.

Tyler and I had many deep conversations on this bed, like the one we had the day I came home from school after having a horrible day. Mom drove me home that day, but I mentioned nothing to her.

When I got home, I heard Tyler singing upstairs and without hesitating; I ran up to his room. I didn't know he was back from college, so it was a pleasant surprise to see him.

"*What up, kid?*" Tyler wrapped his arm around my shoulder

as we did our special handshake. I tried to mask off my worries, but he could tell something was wrong with me.

"I hate school." I threw myself on his bed. *"I wanted to try out for the basketball team today, but the boys in my class made fun of me because they said I look small."* I raised my skinny arms and showed them to him. They were nothing like Tyler's. He was over six feet tall, had a neatly trimmed beard, and he was muscle-built with broad shoulders. He was the sort of guy who got all the attention every time he walked into a room.

"Have you ever heard the saying that bullies are the most insecure people ever?" He asked.

I shook my head. *"No. Bullies always have the upper hand and they do whatever they want because they can."* I replied.

"Jay, listen to me." He said in a firm tone. *"We're all different in our own way. Take you and me, for example. We are brothers but we have our unique differences too."*

"Yeah, that's the whole point." I crossed my arms in frustration. *"You've always been the cool, funny one and I'm the annoying younger brother, right?"*

"No, silly." He elbowed me. *"You're Jayden Williams and you're unique—with all your flaws and imperfections."* He nodded. *"God is not stupid, Jay. In fact, He knew exactly what He was doing when He made you and I look so different. If everyone looked the same, it'll be a boring world. But hey, you're only thirteen and you have a long time to grow. You won't look like this forever—hopefully."* He snickered.

"Jay, you'll change, and you'll grow, so I want you to love every bit of your growth and your journey. Don't wish to be like someone else or allow anyone to put you down. If you want to try out for the basketball team, do it. Nothing is stopping you. It's better to fail than not to try at all." He rounded up his pep talk and leaned closer. *"Because no one else in the world can make an awesome Jayden Williams like you do."*

He flashed a cunning smile before dragging my head in and

pretending to have me in a headlock. I had to fight my way out of it, and of course I won. Or maybe he let me win. I'll never know. I'll also never know what his reaction would be if he sees me now. He was right. I changed, and I grew so much to look like him.

It was good having him around that weekend. When he went back to college, he checked on me every day and kept encouraging me until I tried out for the basketball team and got in. He told me he was working on a surprise for me, so I was looking forward to seeing him again for Thanksgiving, and my fourteenth birthday.

Little did I know he was never coming back home.

I still remember when Mom got the phone call. I had never heard anyone scream so much in my life. Her words eluded her and all she did was bang on the table as Dad tried to calm her down.

Paralysed with pain, she laid there with her head on the table for hours, crying her eyes out. I waited for her to stop crying and tell me it was all a joke. That she had heard wrong. That Tyler was going to come back home. But she didn't.

And now, almost five years later, the stinging pain remains. It has left a scar in my heart—a scar that has refused to go away.

I run my hands down Tyler's guitar, just like he did every time he was about to play. I strum a few chords and finally settle on the chords for "Blessed Be Your Name."

I open my mouth to sing, but I swallow the lump in my throat instead as I fight the tears that blur my vision. I strum the strings, and then I strum some more, the words getting heavier and heavier as they come out of my mouth. And then, when I get to the bridge of the song, instead of singing it, I recite the Bible verse.

"The Lord gave, and the Lord has taken away. Blessed be the

name of the Lord." I stop strumming. "Lord, blessed be Your name." My voice reduces to a whisper as the tears break free.

I press the guitar tighter against my chest and the tears fall down, drop after drop, onto the wooden body of the guitar.

The pain—I can't explain it and I can't make it go away. There's only so much strength I can fake in front of my parents when deep inside, my heart is still shattered.

"I love you, Tyler." I whisper again, looking around his room and admiring the posters from all the concerts he had been at. "I miss you—every second, of every day."

4

TEEYANA

I place my cold fingers on the computer's mouse, clicking the buttons, and sucking on the honey-tasting lozenge in my mouth. *Ugh,* I wish I could sleep right now, but I promised Kevin I'd get this project done in time for our annual youth day service next week.

I close my eyes, breathing in through my nose and out through my mouth. The truth is, when I agreed to take this website revamping project alongside my summer internship programme, I never thought I'd struggle to balance it all. Now my creative pangs are suffering and nothing is coming together.

I have to do this though. I need this experience to prepare me for Graphic Design school. *Come on, Teeyana. Stop complaining and get the work done.*

I shake my head and focus even harder, dragging and dropping images on the screen as the small wooden clock ticks next to me. But the more I try to focus, the more the strokes throw me into a hole of distraction. Finally, I let out a frustrated sigh and push against the desk, wheeling myself to the centre of the church office room.

I press my feet against the floor and force the chair to spin me around. Closing my eyes, I tip my head back and keep my feet off the floor as I wait for the chair to stop spinning. But when it stops, I don't move. Instead, I sit with my eyes still closed and let the ticking sounds fill my head.

Tick Tock

Tick Tock

Tick Tock

It sounds like Grandma's alarm clock. She never trusted my phone alarm to wake me up on Sunday mornings, so one day, she set up the alarm clock for eight a.m without telling me. When it was morning, the screeching sound jerked me out of my slumber, and I almost fell out of my bed.

I still remember seeing Grandma's sly smile through my half-open eyes when she strolled into my room, humming "This Little Light of Mine." She opened up the window drapes to let the light in, and the scent of her perfume filled my nostrils so much, I could taste it at the back of my mouth.

"*Rise and shine now, baby girl.*" Grandma's voice echoed throughout my room. "*You don't want to be late for church now, do you?*" She threw her rhetorical question at me before walking out of the room again, leaving me to moan about how much I didn't want to go to church.

When we lived in L.A, I had many friends in my teenagers' group at church. We grew up together in Sunday school, where we learnt about Noah and the ark, and Jonah and the big fish. I used to enjoy going to church then; but this all changed four years ago when everything I believed about God turned out to be a lie. It was then I realised I needed more than a bunch of cute-sounding stories to make sense of my life.

The move was hard on me because I left all my friends behind. I couldn't connect with anyone at the new church group in Atlanta, and it was during that time that I started losing interest in everything.

We lived in Atlanta for two years before moving to Boston, and we've been living in Boston for two years now. Whenever I meet new people at the youth group, I never fail to notice the enthusiasm written all over their faces—the same enthusiasm I once had.

But do they have questions for God too, like I do?

Am I the only one who feels dissatisfied with life?

Am I the only one struggling to understand?

A soft knock on the door forces me to open my eyes, my gaze resting on the ceiling fan hanging above me. I shake my head and yawn before wheeling myself back to the desk. "Come in, the door is open." I click random areas of the screen with the mouse pointer.

"Hey, Teeyana, do you have a minute?" Kevin, our youth pastor, pops his head into the room.

"Yeah, sure." I glance at the little clock and gasp. "Oh wow, I didn't realise it was eight p.m already."

Ugh, I can't believe I sat there for thirty minutes.

"No, that's alright." Kevin sends a warm smile my way. "Time flies when you're having fun, right?" He adjusts his glasses to sit on the bridge of his nose.

"Yeah...I guess." I save my work and shut down the computer. "Is Bible study over? Has everyone else gone home?" I ask.

"Yup. It's just you and me, kiddo." He looks over his shoulder to confirm. "But hey, before I forget, I thought I'd drop this off with you." He hands me a little book.

Taking the book from his hand, the title jumps at me in bold white letters, *How To Stick To Your Faith At College.* I stare at the front cover for a few seconds before turning it over and pretending to read the back cover blurb.

"I've seen many young people go off to college from this youth group over the past few years, and I'm glad God has given me the opportunity to be a part of this significant step in their lives. I was once in college too, and as much as it's a place to explore new opportunities, it can also be a place where many young people get distracted from their faith. So please, if you're ever struggling, I'll be more than happy to help in any way I can." Kevin smiles at me.

I try to think of the perfect response and the only thing I can come up with is, "Thanks, Kevin." I smile back at him.

Kevin is a patient and understanding man. He is the reason I still come to Bible study. Sometimes, his wife Isabel joins in his teaching too. They're both down to earth and approachable, but I don't think I'm ready to ask questions.

"You're welcome. Let me know when you're ready so I can lock up, and if you don't mind, I'd like to drop you off at your house. Izzy is cooking my favourite meal tonight and I can't wait to get home." Kevin rubs his palms together as he walks out of the room, displaying his excitement for whatever his wife is cooking.

I stare at the front cover of the book again before slipping it into my backpack. If I put the book away somewhere and never touch it, no one will know.

But perhaps someday, I'll need it.

Perhaps someday it'll be useful to me—although, I highly doubt that.

~

I wake up to the sound of the loud roaring of thunder, and as I roll onto my side, my gaze rests on my alarm clock. It's two a.m. and it's pouring outside.

I forgot to pull my curtains shut before going to bed, so the light from the street lamp outside is shining into my room. I rub my eyelids with the back of my hands before dragging myself out of bed and walking across my room to the couch next to the window.

Sitting on the couch, I pull my purple fleece sheet over my legs and stare outside, observing the raindrops trickling down my window. Just like that, I'm back to my "*clear my mind*" spot.

I used to watch the rainfall in Atlanta too, but Grandma always cut my time short whenever she came in to check on me on the way to her room. It was the same routine of her prodding me to tell her what was on my mind, and me never finding the right words to express how I was feeling.

She always led me back to my bed, covering me up with my duvet and sometimes singing me to sleep even though I reminded her many times I was fourteen and not three. Her favourite lullaby was her favourite song—"Be Thou My Vision," and I usually fell asleep after the first verse.

Be thou my vision, oh Lord of my heart
Naught be all else to me, saved that Thou art
Thou my best thought, by day or by night
Waking or sleeping, Thy presence my light

Grandma's soothing voice fades into the background of my thoughts as the tree branches in our backyard bend and move from side to side under the influence of the wind. The trees have no choice but to do that. The force of the wind is too strong to keep them staying calm. It's out of their control and they can do nothing about it.

That's *exactly* how I've been feeling—like these trees, bending helplessly under the influence of the wind. Except in my case, it's not the wind bending my branches. It's God. I don't want Him bending my branches anymore. I want them free to grow.

I tip my head back and my gaze slides up to the black sky stretched out above me. When I sat at this same spot a few nights ago, I was staring at a blanket of a million stars which were twinkling in all their glory; but not tonight. Even though I know the stars are still there, the storm has made them less visible—the same way my own storms have thrust me far away from God's presence.

Another roar of thunder and a flash of lightning interrupt my thoughts, so I stand up and walk back to my bed. As I near my bed, my door knob twists and my door opens, the squeaking sound travelling across my room.

"Who's there? Mom?" When I take a few steps towards the door, little hands appear on the side and Danny pokes his head through the narrow gap.

"Danny? Are you okay?" I kneel next to him. "Did the thunder wake you up?"

He throws his arms around my neck when another clap of thunder rages through, so I carry him to my bed and cover him with my duvet.

"Teeyana?" Danny speaks. "Can you pray for me, please?" He holds my hands together and brings them close to his chest.

Mom or Dad always pray with him before bed and I wished for a moment he wouldn't ask me to do that. But looking at his adorable little face right now, I can't say no. I mean, what kind of big sister would that make me?

"Okay, big boy, but promise me you'll go to sleep if I do?" He nods before closing his eyes. I stroke his dark, short, kinky hair and keep my eyes focused on him.

"Dear God," I start, the words heavy in my mouth. "Thank you for Danny, who is a big and strong boy. Please help him have a good night's sleep tonight, despite the horrible rain outside. Amen."

I kiss his forehead and continue stroking his hair until he falls asleep. As his little chest rises and falls, I'm taken back to when he was a baby. I still remember like it was yesterday. Mom and Dad had been praying for another child for many years after they had me, so getting the news of the pregnancy was a huge blessing.

We couldn't wait for Danny to arrive, but Mom's pregnancy journey wasn't an easy one. Her frequent visits to the hospital made me think at one point she was going to lose the baby. Danny came two months early, and I remember going to the hospital every week to see him.

He was the tiniest baby I'd ever seen, and they strapped him to so many wires—some of which were connected to loud beeping machines. I used to sing to him and read him stories from my favourite books. I promised I would be the best big sister he could ever ask for, if he came home with us—alive and well.

Right there in the hospital, by his incubator, holding on to his little hands, I promised I would protect him and live my life setting a good example for him to follow. Every day, I hoped Danny would pull through so I could shower him with all the love I had to give.

One Friday afternoon after school, three months after Danny was born, I wondered why Dad didn't drive me to the hospital to see Danny like he'd been doing. When we got home, Mom was there too, standing next to Danny's cot.

"Come closer, honey. We want to show you something." She beckoned to me.

Moving closer, I looked into the cot, and there he was. Danny was home and having a peaceful sleep. For the first time since he was born, he wasn't strapped to any wires and he looked like a healthy baby. I was so overwhelmed with joy that I broke into tears. My brother had come home, alive and well.

So now it's time for me to fulfil my promise to him and be an example for him to follow. But I can't lead him when I'm not sure about my own path. I can't lead him when I have no clue about what I'm doing.

5

TEEYANA

I take a long look down the street, searching for a sign of Dad's car, but like the last ten times I've checked, nothing comes into view. Adjusting the sunglasses on my face, I step into the cool shade again, hiding away from the scorching sun over my head. "Oh please, can he come quick?" I mutter while fanning my face with a folded sheet of paper.

Then, looking down the street again, Dad's Chevrolet Cruze appears in the distance and I breathe a sigh of relief. He drives a few metres past me and parks close to the curb so I can jump in.

"Hey, Dad." I lean over and kiss his cheek, before strapping on my seatbelt and taking off my sunglasses.

"Hey, honey. How was your last day?" Dad twists the car key and drives off again.

"It was amazing!!!" I lean back in my seat. "You remember the design I told you I was working on, right?" I ask and Dad nods. "Well, I showed it to Mira today, and she loved it. She said she'll consider printing it on her next line of t-shirts." I sink deeper into my seat, satisfied with my accomplishments this summer.

"Really? That's great. I told Mira she wouldn't regret taking you on this internship. I knew you would do a great job." He smiles at me before focusing on the road again.

"Thanks, Dad. I can't believe it's over. I'm going to miss the team." My smile fades.

"I know, honey. But Mira is a good friend of mine and she has promised to have you back anytime you want." He grins. "I'm glad you loved your experience, but you have something much bigger coming your way, don't you?"

"Yeah, you're right." I turn my head to face the window as Dad takes a left turn.

"So how are you feeling about that?" He asks.

"Huh?" I turn away from the window to look at him. "Feeling about what?"

"College." He shrugs. "Move-in day is next week, remember?"

"Oh, yes." I smile as *my* idea of college comes to mind. "I'm excited. It'll be nice to make new friends and earn my place at the Google internship."

"Yes, you're a hardworking young lady, but remember that only one Person can lead you to where you need to be." Dad pauses. He doesn't need to add more because I know he's talking about God.

I avoid his gaze when he turns away from the road to look at me. I can tell he is observing my facial expression and waiting for me to say something.

"Right." I smile and meet his gaze. His hazel brown eyes tell me there's more to this conversation than meets the eye.

"It's a beautiful day, isn't it, Dad?" I attempt to change the subject.

"It sure is, honey. A beautiful day the Lord has made. We will be glad and rejoice in it." He grins as the air grows thick with tension and we remain silent for the rest of the journey.

In a few minutes, Dad pulls into our driveway and I open the passenger door, gearing up to run up the stairs when he calls my name. "Teeyana?"

I stop in my tracks and turn around to face him.

"Please, have a seat." He lowers himself on to the stairs on our front porch and I plop down next to him.

"I'm so proud of you, Teeyana Joy Sparks." Dad squeezes my hand. "Since you were a little girl, I've watched you put your heart into everything you do. I can't thank God enough for giving me this opportunity to raise a beautiful daughter like you."

Heat rushes up to my cheeks and if not for my dark skin, they would've been as red as a tomato now. "Aww Dad, you've said this a thousand times already."

"I know that, honey, but I need to tell you all the time so you never forget how much I love you." He maintains the seriousness in his voice.

"Forget?" I raise my eyebrows. "Oh, come on, Dad, of course I'll never forget how much you love me. I love you too."

"I know you do." He grins and playfully shoves me. "And your Mom does too. In fact, she has a special way of showing it by worrying about you kids—worrying all the time." He shakes his head.

I sigh. "O—kay, spill the beans, Dad. What's Mom worrying about this time?"

I knew it. I knew there was something else he wanted to say.

Dad clears his throat. "So last night, I was lying on my bed and reading my Bible, you know—minding my business." He starts recounting as if he's reading a story from a book. "Your Mom was sitting in front of the mirror, plaiting her hair into cornrows—you know, the way you girls spend hours getting your hair ready to wear a new wig." He grins.

I shake my head. "Dad, you know I've always preferred braids."

"Yeah, but you still have to spend hours washing and blow drying your hair before you get braids, don't you?"

I tilt my head. "Yeah, you make a good point."

Dad rubs his palms and grins. "Anyway, so all I could hear were deep sighs coming from this distressed damsel—"

I feign a gasp. "Oh no, not a distressed damsel! What did you do?!"

"I walked over to her and used my special skills to get her to tell me what was troubling her so I could rescue her—you know, as her knight in shining armour?" He winks at me.

"And by special skills, you mean you kept asking her until she gave in?" I laugh and rest my head on his shoulder.

"Heey, I'd like to think that's a special skill. Don't judge me." He laughs too.

"Whatever makes you happy, Dad." I surrender. "So what did this distressed damsel say was on her mind?" I ask, now interested since he has made a big deal out of his story.

Dad's smile fades. "You." He responds.

I pull my head away from his shoulder to look at him. "Me? What did I do?"

"Well," he starts, "she's worried you'll drift away from your faith at college." Dad gives me a look as if to say, "*Well, what have you got to say for yourself, young lady?*"

I don't want to talk about my feelings now. I want a chance to figure things out on my own.

"Have I done anything to make her think that?" I stall.

Dad leans in closer. "She said you used to love doing things for God when we were in L.A. But now she's noticed you seem more withdrawn—almost distanced from everything. She's convinced there's something bothering you and you're trying not to worry us by not telling us."

Ugh!!! Why does Mom have to be so good at figuring me out?

"I promised her I'd talk to you and get answers for myself. So is it true, honey? Is there something bothering you?" Dad's eyebrows furrow.

I shake my head. "Hmm. Hmm. I'm fine, Dad." I lie.

Dad holds on to my hands. "Are you sure, honey? You know you can talk to me about anything, right?"

I gulp. "Yes, Dad. I know that. There's nothing wrong." I shake my head, hoping to shake away the guilt rising in my chest.

He faces forward. "You know how I said I'll always love you? Well, someone else loves you *way* more than I do."

I chuckle. "Is that Mom? I know you guys always argue about which one of you loves me and Danny more." I try to dissuade him from mentioning God—even though I know he'll do it anyway.

"No, honey." He maintains his serious tone. "God does. He's always loved you more and He always will." He nods. "I know the past few years have been rough on us, but God has never stopped being a good Father."

See, this is my problem. How can Dad still call God a good Father when the people who ruined his life are walking free? They robbed us of our luxurious life in L.A and because of them, Dad has to settle for this church job he has now. I know Dad believes these words with all his heart, and I want to believe them too—but I don't. I can't. Not after everything that has happened.

I put my hand on top of his. "Dad, I believe that too." More lies roll out of my tongue.

Dad looks at me for a few seconds before kissing my forehead. "That's all I wanted to know, honey. We're excited for you and we want you to go out there, make new friends and have a great time. Even though your mom and I won't be there with you, God will. You want that job at Google? Tell Him about it, trust Him, and He'll get you there."

Hmm. Nah. I'm sure I can get there by myself.

"It's so easy for us to carry on with our lives thinking everything is our doing and then realise later that we had no strength all along." Dad concludes.

I have no strength? I beg to disagree, Dad.

This is where I don't see eye to eye with my parents. I don't have to depend on God. I want to do things my own way. That's not too much to ask, is it?

"Thanks, Dad. Kevin gave me a book a few weeks ago." I attempt to change the subject. "It's called *How To Stick to Your Faith At College.*"

"Sounds like a good read. Have you started?"

"No, not yet, but I'll start reading it soon."

Or perhaps never.

I stand up and give him another kiss on the cheek before going into the house—still thinking about the statement he made.

I have no strength? Pfft. Yeah right!

Let's see how I get that Google internship all on my own then. Failing is not an option right now. It's not part of my plan.

6

TEEYANA

"So is Nigerian jollof rice better than Ghanaian jollof rice? Or is that a thing all Nigerians say?" I ask Mrs. Ikezie, who is sitting on the sofa in front of the TV.

"*Ahn, ahn!!!* Is that even a question?" She turns away from the TV to look at me. "Of course it is better. My dear, this is not a joke *o*. Jollof rice originated from Nigeria and every other country's recipe is a phoney. A counterfeit. *Obi m,* am I lying?" She leans close to her husband, who is sitting beside her.

"Yes *o*." Mr. Ikezie turns away from the Nollywood drama on the TV to look at us. He is wearing a white vest top with his ankara wrapper tied around his waist—low enough to reveal his well rounded belly. "*Adamma*, your mother is right. We are the originals." He pats the newspaper resting on his lap before turning back to the TV.

"Mom, I don't think there's a difference between the two." Amara tries to rain on her mom's parade. She knows how passionate her mom is about Nigerian culture and food, but she sometimes tries to get on her mom's nerves for the fun of it.

"*Ahn, ahn!!!* Look at your mouth." Mrs. Ikezie retaliates.

"There is a big difference *o*. Nigeria is the best. Always and forever." She beats her chest with pride.

"Okay, okay!" Amara raises her hands in mock surrender. "I get it. Nigeria forever! Woo!" She pumps her fist in the air before putting another spoonful of the yellow spicy rice into her mouth.

Amara leans over and whispers in my ear. "I've tasted Ghanaian jollof rice. It's very delicious." We both giggle, drawing the attention of Mrs. Ikezie.

"What is that?" Mrs. Ikezie adjusts her ankara wrapper around her chest to cover her white blouse underneath.

"Nothing, Mom. Just telling Teeyana how much I agree with you." Amara grins at her mom, who gives her a suspicious look.

"*Eheeh-eh*? So you think I was born yesterday, *abi*? It's okay. When you go and taste all the other counterfeit jollofs and they fail you, you can always run back to your mother's original, *eh*? It will be here waiting for you." She sucks air between her teeth from behind pursed lips, making a kissing sound.

After two years of being around Amara's Nigerian parents, I can say with confidence that I know what the *"kissing teeth"* gesture means. Amara's mom uses it when she's irritated, tired, impatient, or when she has given up a fight. The first time I heard Amara kiss her teeth, I was so fascinated by the sound I asked her to teach me how to do it.

Mrs. Ikezie turns her attention back to the TV and joins her husband to watch the Nollywood drama. Amara stifles a laugh, so she doesn't choke on the spicy rice. We've had this jollof rice conversation a million times before, but I can never get over Mrs. Ikezie's sense of humour.

Mrs. Ikezie makes her special jollof rice for me without making it too spicy because the first time I tried it, it took five glasses of water and half a carton of milk to calm down the burning sensation in my mouth. I don't know how Amara has coped with so much spice her entire life.

"Thank you so much for the jollof rice, Mrs. Ikezie. The food was delicious as always." I smile at her as I help Amara clear the table. "Oh and thank you for my dashiki dress too. It's beautiful." I rub my hands on the colourful garment I'm wearing. I first saw Amara wear a dashiki dress to church one Sunday last summer, and I begged her to ask her mom to get one for me too. Mrs. Ikezie bought one for me during her recent trip to Nigeria.

"You're welcome, my dear. Enjoy the magic work of talented Nigerian tailors." She smirks. "And make sure you wash those plates *o*, Amarachukwu." She yells at Amara from the living room as we both carry our plates to the kitchen.

"Yes, Mom, that's what I'm *about* to do." Amara yells over her shoulder and rolls her eyes before placing the plates inside the kitchen sink. I've had the pleasure of watching Amara and her mom bicker for the past two years. It's funny because they don't realise they are more alike than they think. They have the same bubbly personality, the same round face and full lips, and the same commanding presence when they're serious.

"Girl, you need to help me wash my hair today." Amara says as she runs tap water over the plates in the sink.

"Wait, what do you mean? You took off the silver braids already?" I raise my eyebrows.

"I sure did. Why do you think I'm wearing this headscarf?" She points to the yellow ankara scarf on her head, soapy water running down her arm.

"You always wear headscarves, Amara. How was I supposed to know?" I shrug.

"I got bored with wearing the braids and my hair was screaming to be washed. I swear if *Frolita* could talk to me right now, she would tell me off."

"You named your afro *Frolita*?" I chuckle.

"Heey, it's a cute name. Don't laugh." She splashes water on me.

"Alright, if you say so. Don't ruin my beautiful dashiki dress." I laugh.

Amara smiles and shuffles close to me. "Sooo, you'll help me wash my hair then? It won't take long, I promise."

I roll my eyes and check the time on my phone. It's seven p.m. now. The last time I helped Amara wash her hair, it took us well over four hours.

"But...but I loved the silver braids. I didn't know about this. I wasn't ready." I try walking away, but Amara stops me.

"Well, now you know, so we better get started. It'll be a fun evening, I promise." Amara rinses the washed plates one last time and places them on the drying rack before pulling my arm.

"I should've known you were bribing me with that jollof rice. Let me take off my dashiki dress first." I sigh as I run up the stairs after her. "Can you just relax your hair, please?"

Amara stops midway up the stairs and scowls at me. "I've told you I'm never going back to that creamy crack. Never!!!" She stamps her feet the rest of the way up the stairs while I celebrate my success in teasing her.

~

Two hours have passed and all we've done is detangle Amara's hair and wash it with shampoo. We've now lathered it with a deep conditioner and Amara has wrapped it with a plastic bag. She insists on using a plastic bag instead of a shower cap because she says the plastic bag does a better job.

That's my best friend for you.

"You see this, right here, is the reason I won't be growing out my natural hair anytime soon." I sigh as we both lay on our backs on Amara's bed. "Washing this hair of yours is a total arm workout. I can't subject myself to this labour. Never!!!" I shake my head.

"Oh, come on, it's not that bad. You should join the squad. You get used to it with time and natural hair is beautiful." Amara presses.

I shake my head again and stare at Amara's chandelier, hanging up from her ceiling. "Nah, girl. I'm good. Last Thanksgiving, my grandma spoke to me about transitioning to natural hair, but I told her I'd think about it."

Amara gasps and sits up. "Oh. My. Gosh. Your grandma's hair is hashtag goals. I hope mine is that beautiful when I get to her age." She places her hands over her chest and closes her eyes. I bet she's imagining what she'd look like at sixty-one.

"Maybe you should follow us to her house this Christmas so you can gawk at her hair the whole time." I tease.

"Heey." Amara slams her pillow in my face before laying next to me again. After our chuckles die down, Amara speaks again, sounding more serious this time. "Teeyana?"

"Yeah?"

"Do you ever worry about the future?"

I turn to look at her. The easy way out would be to lie—the same way I've been lying to my parents. But if there's one person I can be vulnerable with, it's Amara. I have to tell her the truth. "Yes, I do." I respond. "A lot, actually." In fact, I worry so much that sometimes I have nightmares about losing everyone I love and everything I've worked for. But Amara doesn't need to know about that.

"Really? Me too." She sighs. "But I think you're in a good place. At least you know what you want and you're determined to get it. Nothing is going to stop you." She smiles at me.

I shrug. "Yeah...I guess. You're the only person I've told about being worried. You'd keep it between us though, wouldn't you?" I plead.

"Of course. That's why I'm your B.F.F." Amara lets her favourite phrase escape her lips again.

We've been friends since I started school at Coverton High two years ago. On my first day of school, I noticed Olivia and her group of friends taunting and teasing Amara in the cafeteria.

I didn't know Amara at the time, and I'd never spoken to her, so I didn't see the point in getting involved. To me, it was watching yet another kid getting bullied. It happens all the time, so I had to make sure I didn't get involved.

Many weeks passed and still, I watched from a distance, as these girls put Amara on blast. I watched the sneers, the insults, the shoving, and the poor girl who acted brave in front of the bullies but who was too afraid to report them. I wanted my last two years in high school to go as smoothly as possible, so I turned a blind eye.

But one Tuesday afternoon, I was eating lunch outside in the courtyard when I saw Olivia and her friends walk up to Amara and take away her lunch box. When Amara tried to fight back, Olivia's friends restrained her and Olivia threw Amara's jollof rice into the trash can.

"You don't belong here." Olivia said. *"Go back to the ghetto where you came from. And if you don't like that, how about you board that ship back to Africa where you belong?"*

Olivia's words hit me like a knife driven straight into my heart. It was then I knew I was a hypocrite for staying silent. I had to make a choice, and in the end, I stood up for what I believed was right.

After they left Amara alone in tears, I walked up to her and gave her half of my sandwich. It tasted nothing like her mom's tasty jollof rice, but she accepted it anyway, and we've been inseparable ever since.

I encouraged Amara to report Olivia and her friends to the principal, but she didn't think anything would be done. Then, I showed her the video I had recorded of the incident and this gave her the confidence to stand up for herself.

After reporting Olivia, the principal summoned her to his office and soon, everyone else was summoned, including Amara's parents and Olivia's parents. My parents were also involved because I was an eyewitness and I had the evidence.

Our plan worked. Olivia and her friends were suspended and they stopped teasing Amara. When they returned to school, they found a new target—me. It's funny how I encouraged Amara to report them, but couldn't do it myself. I ignored Olivia's subtle antics to belittle me and convinced myself if I could only survive high school, I'd never have to deal with bullies again.

Amara is like my sister now, and we get along well with each other. She can be a worrier too, like my mom, and when we face challenges, I'm good at showing how in control I am—well, at least I thought so, until fear paralysed me two months ago when I thought Olivia was going to approach me in the hallway.

Ugh, I hate feeling out of control.

"Do you think there'll be people like Olivia in college? Or even worse?" Amara's bottom lip juts out.

"Even if there are, you'll be fine." I reassure her. "You've got this. I know I won't be there with you, but girl, I got your back all the way from New York."

"I don't feel I'm strong enough to fight like you. You put in your one-hundred percent and I struggle with giving twenty percent." She drops her hands and lets out a deep sigh.

If only Amara knew about all the times I've struggled to keep going, she wouldn't have this much faith in me. But if she sees strength in me, then I have to act strong.

I sit up and playfully push Amara's leg. "Girl, what are you talking about? You're going to be an amazing NICU nurse. You're going to grace Spelman College with all your black girl magic—

crowned in *Frolita* and all. They don't know what's coming. They better call the fire department because Amarachukwu Ifeoma Ikezie is about to blow the roof." I pause and laugh at my horrible attempt to pronounce her full name with a "Nigerian accent." It makes Amara laugh too, so I count that as a victory.

"You're one of the coolest people I know. You're a blessing to me and you have to believe that." I elbow her again.

Amara sits up and throws her arms around me. "You're a blessing to me too. You're the only one I can count on to help me wash this thick hair of mine." She squeezes me tighter. "Speaking of hair, it's time to wash out the deep conditioner. Come on."

"Please tell me we'll be done after that?" I whine as I drag myself out of bed.

"Nope. We have to moisturise and seal it too. And then twist it for the night." Amara winks.

"You're kidding, right?" I roll my eyes for the umpteenth time. "You might as well kill me now." I grumble and follow Amara to the bathroom.

"Oh, you've done this before. You should have learnt by now. Come on, mate. Chop, chop." Amara claps her hands to quicken my strides.

"Erm, dude, why did you switch to a British accent?" I chuckle.

"Because I think it makes me sound cool." She grins and turns to face the mirror.

As Amara removes the plastic bag from her head and hunches over the bathtub, it hits me that today is the last day I'll be spending with her before I leave for college. This will be the longest time we'll be spending apart since we became friends. I won't be able to run over to her house whenever I want to speak to someone. I'm about to venture out into this world—all on my own.

7

TEEYANA

The view from my dorm room window is nothing compared to my "*clear my mind*" spot back in Boston. There are no beautiful trees like the one in our backyard, but countless brown buildings stand tall across the vast college campus.

At the campus entrance, a long queue of cars stretches from the car park and down the road that leads to the highway. Hundreds of students, relatives, and friends are rushing back and forth, carrying suitcases and bags with the help of student volunteers wearing bright blue t-shirts.

My room is on the second floor, but it's still within hearing distance of the sirens going off on the main road. I hope it won't be too noisy to sleep at night. *Man, I need to buy earplugs.* I make a mental note of that and take a deep, long breath—as if the air in New York is better than the air in Boston. It's probably more polluted, but that's not the point.

I'm gonna be studying in Queens!!! In New York!!! Now I know how *Prince Akeem* felt when he first came to Queens in the movie *Coming To America*. I just won't be shouting at my neighbours in the morning unless I want everyone to think I'm weird.

I turn away from the window and scan my room, inspecting the beige coloured walls, which are stained with remnants of sticky notes and blue tack. My roommate hasn't arrived yet, so I can choose which side of the room I want to be on.

Taking another deep breath, I close my eyes and take in the dusty smell of the place I'll be calling home for the next year. I can't wait to put up my decorations and make it smell better.

Mom and Dad come rushing in, huffing and puffing as they drop the last of my suitcases at the centre of the room. The journey from the parking lot to my dorm involved meandering through the crowd of sweaty relatives, disengaging from the interesting conversations with the student volunteers at the Mental Health Awareness stand, and even resisting the free ice cream stand so we could get away from the commotion.

"Thank you so much. We appreciate your help." Dad extends his gratitude to the student volunteer who was assigned to help us. The girl is two inches taller than me with a long neck, and curly blonde hair which flows to her mid-back.

"It's my pleasure." She smiles and fans herself with a leaflet.

"Welcome to St. John's University." She turns towards me. "My name is Ellie, and I'll be your resident assistant this year. If you have any problems with your accommodation or if you need someone to speak to about *anything* at all, I'll be the one to contact." She hands me a small card. "Here are all my contact details and since I'm in my junior year and majoring in Graphic Design, I'll be more than happy to help you with any tips and advice."

I must say that Ellie's red lipstick and blonde hair remind me of Olivia Hastings, but Ellie is nothing like Olivia. She's nice— at least that's what it seems like so far.

"Cool. Thank you so much. I'll hit you up." I put the card away in the back pocket of my jeans.

Ellie smiles and nods. "Oh and don't forget our *Freshman*

Welcome Barbecue tonight at six o'clock. It'll be a great place to make new friends. Hope to see you there. Trust me, it'll be good fun." She smiles again before turning around and leaving the room.

After choosing to take the right side of the room, Mom and Dad help me put up my posters, stickers, and fairy lights while I sort out the stationery for my desk.

After two hours, we get to a point where I'm happy with the way my room looks. It's now five p.m. and it's time for Mom and Dad to leave.

Even after reassuring Mom that I'll be fine, she still sheds tears as I walk them to the car. I can't blame her though. This will be the first time in eighteen years I'll be living away from home. Even though I'm only three hours away from Boston, it'll still take a lot of getting used to.

All I want to do now is hold Mom and not let her go. I want them to take me back home so I can have Mom's mac and cheese, hug Danny, and watch movies all night. But I have to do this because this is what I want.

I bite my lower lip to fight back my tears and I look over at Dad, who is doing a good job of keeping himself together. "I promise I'll call home, okay? I'm going to be fine. Dad, please tell her I'll be fine." I squeeze Dad's hand, hoping he'll come up with the right words to calm Mom down. Dad always gives off the same calm, reassuring presence that Grandpa has. That's why the two men get along so well.

"Sweetie, she'll be okay. Let's go home so she can make some new friends." Dad helps Mom release her hold of me.

Then I wrap my arms around Dad's waist, burying my head in his chest to hide my watery eyes. "Please tell Danny and Aunt Bella I love them." I whisper as my tears soak his shirt.

"I'll do that, honey. I promise." He kisses my forehead and opens the door for Mom to get into the car.

"We love you, honey." Dad says before entering the car. I wipe the tears rolling down my cheeks as the car drives out of campus. I stand there and wave at them until the car disappears from my sight.

It's done. I'm all on my own. All alone in New York City.

There's no going back now, Teeyana. No going back.

I glance around the campus again, taking in the sight of the emerald green lawn, and the last of the summer flowers fading away as they give in to the cold weather. This is where I'm meant to be, so it doesn't matter how rubbish I feel right now. I need to start enjoying it.

You can do this, Teeyana.

As I turn around to go back to my dorm room, my gaze lands on a red-haired girl struggling to carry her suitcase up the stairs. I walk over to her and pick up the suitcase from the other end. "Here, let me help you." I say, but the girl pushes my hand away.

"No. I'm fine" She scowls and her face goes pale.

"Are you sure?" I raise my brows. "We're going in the same direction."

"I said I'm fine. Are you deaf?" she snaps, and it takes me by surprise.

Her green eyes burn into my skin, and I take my hand off her suitcase, but she keeps staring at me. I stare back, my gaze moving from the thick eyeliner going across her eyelids, to her septum piercing, and to her black choker necklace, which *definitely* looks too tight.

As if her hair isn't red enough, she had to wear a red cropped leather jacket as well. This girl sure *loves* the colour red.

When she stops staring at me, she takes one look at her suitcase, and then screams at the top of her voice. "Dad!!!"

I cover my ears as she storms off, abandoning her suitcase on the stairs. She power walks towards the car park where an auburn-haired man is bringing out more suitcases from his car.

They exchange words for a few minutes before he puts all the suitcases back into the boot of the car and walks away. The girl chases him across the street to the fountain on the other side of the campus, and everyone stares at them.

Wow, what a spoilt brat. The words move to the edge of my tongue, but I don't say them. It's my first day, so I won't let someone I don't know put me in a bad mood.

I shake my head and turn around to head back to my dorm room, hoping that the next person I speak to isn't going to burst my eardrums. It's almost time for the freshman barbecue, and I hope I can meet some nicer people.

~

I stare at my reflection in the mirror and adjust the two jumbo cornrows I've been working on for the last half hour. Picking up the toothbrush designated for styling my baby hairs, I dip it in hair gel and smother the gel all over my edges, working the baby hairs back and forth until I'm satisfied with the laid down look.

Outside my window, smoke is rising from the grills and students are walking into the courtyard, chattering and laughing out loud. As the smell of barbecue hits my nostrils, I grab my phone and my keys, and head out the door.

My first sight as I near the courtyard is a group of boys standing in a circle next to the grills, each of them holding a white plastic plate with at least two burgers. The group of girls on the opposite side are giggling and whispering to themselves as they look over their shoulders at the boys.

Walking past a St. John's University banner, I grab a plate and put a bun on it, before getting in line to get a burger.

"Teeyana?" A familiar voice calls out my name and I turn in the direction of the voice.

It's Ellie—the one friendly person I've met today.

"Oh wow, you remembered my name?" I smile and walk up to her.

"Yes, of course." She hugs me. "I don't always remember names, but your parents were so sweet and couldn't stop talking about you." She replies cheerily.

"Oh no. I'm so sorry you had to listen to their non-stop talking."

"No, don't be silly. They weren't complaining about you. Everything they said reflected how proud they are of you." She leans closer and whispers. "You know, I wish my parents could talk about me like that too."

Okay, when she puts it that way, then I have to admit that I miss my parents, and I miss Danny too. He was feeling under the weather today, so he stayed home with Aunt Bella, who was visiting us for the weekend.

"Have you had anything to eat yet?" Ellie's voice breaks me out of my thoughts.

I shake my head. "No, I just got here."

"You see those boys over there?" Ellie nods in the direction of the group of boys standing next to the grills. "They've already had three burgers each. You should have some before they're all gone." She laughs. "Go, go, go, and then you can come over and I'll introduce you to my friends." Ellie gives me a gentle nudge towards the barbecue grill.

"Thanks, Ellie." I smile at her before she walks back to her friends sitting on one of the benches.

My stomach rumbles, and as I inch closer to the food table, I spot the last burger on a silver tray. Quickening my steps, I move towards it, but one of the boys cuts in front of me and I lose sight of the burger for a split second. When I get to the table, the last burger is gone.

"Nooo!!!" I let out a frustrated cry, unaware of how loud I

was. I turn around and kiss my teeth—a habit I copied from Amara.

Great! I haven't eaten since we left Boston this morning, and now I have to wait an extra ten minutes.

"Uh, excuse me?" A finger taps on my shoulder and I turn around. "Did you want that last burger?"

My eyes meet gorgeous hazelnut brown eyes and a charming dimpled smile which stuns me into silence. I open my mouth to speak but I'm not sure what to say, so I stare at the over six foot tall guy standing in front of me.

"Hello?" He waves his hand in my face, still smiling, his dark brown skin glistening in the light lighting up the courtyard.

"Huh? What?" I shake my head and open my mouth to speak again, but I can't find the right words.

"I took the last burger a few seconds ago, but my friends and I have already had two each." He points to the group of boys Ellie was talking about earlier. "You seem to need it more than I do." He shrugs his broad shoulders and hands the burger over to me.

"Oh I see. No, that's fine. I'll wait for the next one." I manage to make full sentences.

"Are you sure you don't want it? It's mayo and cheese." He leans closer, his dimples forming on the sides of his clean-shaven face.

Looking at the tempting burger in his hand, what I want to say is, *I'll wait it out*, but my rumbling stomach throws me under the bus.

I place my hands over my belly and exhale. "Actually...I think I need a mayo and cheese burger right now."

"I was hoping you would say that." He chuckles as I take the plate from his hand without hesitation. "And I see your stomach agrees with you."

My cheeks warm up as I walk over to the nearest empty bench and start devouring the burger one bite at a time.

Instead of the nice guy leaving, he occupies the space next to me on the bench. "Wow. You must've been really hungry." He says, adjusting the sleeves of his white t-shirt.

"Yeah, well, I surprise myself when I'm hungry." I try not to laugh with food in my mouth.

"Oh really? I like people who are full of surprises." He smiles.

"Thanks again for letting me have your burger. You don't have to sit here with me though." I try to push him away before I end up embarrassing myself.

"I know that, but I'd like to sit here if you don't mind. After all, this barbecue is about meeting new people, isn't it?" He shrugs and leans back on the bench.

Yay!!! I was hoping he would say that. Of course I don't want him to leave, but I don't want to come across as desperate either.

"You make a good point." I use my napkin to wipe the mayo from the corners of my mouth. "So what's your major?" I ask before taking another bite.

"Graphic Design." He responds.

"No way!!! That's mine too." My heart flutters at the possibility that I might see him again.

"Wicked!!! So I'll be seeing you around more often. At least now I know I have one interesting person I'll be having classes with. Are you looking forward to it?"

"Yes, I am. I did an internship over the summer and it was a wonderful experience so I can't wait to start." I clap my hands together in excitement, but I stop when I remind myself he's not Amara, and he might think I'm weird now.

But instead of weird looks, he gives me an even bigger grin. "That's great." He says. "You're very keen. Let's make that the second thing I like about you already."

Oh gosh, he said he likes me? Is...is it hot in here?

"So, what's your na—" I try to ask, but I'm interrupted by his ringing phone.

He takes it out of his pocket and stares at the screen. "Oh, I have to go now. Duty calls. It was nice meeting you. I hope to see you around. Have a good night." He jogs over to his group of friends, greets a few of them, and then turns back to me and waves.

Within a split second, this gorgeous new friend of mine disappears from my sight the same way he appeared.

"Nice meeting you too. Have a good night." I try to respond before he disappears around the corner of the nearest building.

Aww, man. I don't even know his name.

But that's okay. I have a feeling I'll be seeing him again. In the meantime, I'm going to post-up in the corner with Ellie and her friends.

8

JAYDEN

Bounce. Bounce. Bounce.

The ball ricochets off the floor and flies into my hands as I fix my gaze on the hoop at the opposite end of the court. Endless beads of sweat slide down my spine and soak into my t-shirt. I wipe my forehead before running across the smooth brown tiled floor, which reminds me of my high school basketball days.

Clutching the ball close to my chest, I take my stance as the boys from the opposing team approach me—determination written all over their faces.

Go on, Jayden!!! You can do this!!!

Tyler's voice echoes in my head and I glance over at the stands to see if he is standing there and yelling out to me, or if my mind is playing games again.

One boy from the opposing team, who is wearing a lime green t-shirt, runs towards me and reaches for the ball in my hands. Without hesitation, I turn around and dodge his attempt before passing the ball over to my partner standing in the corner of the court.

A few metres away, Coach Simpson is pacing on the sidelines, watching our every move and making notes on his clipboard. I take another glance at the clock and there's less than a minute left till the end of the game.

Lord, please help us make another basket.

I sprint to the other side of the court, running over the giant words *St. John's* plastered on the floor. When I get close enough to the hoop, I raise both hands over my head, signalling to my partner to throw the ball.

My partner bounces the ball again before throwing it toward the hoop. As it flies through the air, I take a leap and catch it in mid-air before redirecting it through the hoop—a few seconds before the final whistle blows. My legs dangle in the air as I hold onto the hoop for a few seconds, finally jumping off to land on both feet.

Loud cheers erupt from the few people sitting in the stands. I narrow my gaze to the front row seats, where I imagine Tyler would sit—if he ever got the chance to watch me play.

As I expected, Tyler's not sitting there, he's not waving his arms and jumping around telling the people sitting next to him I'm his brother. Instead, some students are sitting in the seats, clapping and cheering. I smile at them before turning away.

They're not Tyler, but I'm grateful for the support, anyway.

Coach Simpson jogs towards us, clapping his hands. I grab a bottle from the table and empty the cold water into my mouth, appreciating every moment of the refreshing feeling in my throat. I turn around to face Coach Simpson's grey head of hair and moustache, which makes me think of Morgan Freeman with glasses.

"It's the end of the tryouts, boys. Thanks for coming today." He moves his glasses from the bridge of his nose to his head before looking at his clipboard again. "The list of those who made the team will be out before our first practice session next Friday here at Taffner Field House from five p.m to eight p.m.

Keep an eye out for that." He puts his clipboard under his arm and continues. "Until then, I'll see you around."

"Thanks, Coach." Everyone mutters as the crowd disperses.

"Williams!!!" Coach shouts, and I turn around to face him again. "That was a good game. You should be proud of yourself. I'll see you next Friday, son." He winks at me before turning around and walking away.

Wait, did he say he'll see me next Friday? Does that mean I got in?

"Thanks...thanks, Coach." I smile as he gives me a thumbs up without looking back.

"Hey, man. That was sick!!! You play so well." The guy with the lime-green t-shirt from the opposing team approaches me. He is about three inches taller than me, with high top cornrows and shaved sides. His beard frames his jawline the same way Tyler's beard did his.

"Thanks, man." I nod at him as we walk towards the pile of backpacks on the floor.

"I'd do anything if you can teach me to play like that." He rubs his palms together, a broad smile plastered on his face.

"Sure, man. We can play together anytime. My name's Jayden, by the way, and you are?"

"Warryn." He replies as we pick up our backpacks and head for the locker room. "I'm a pre-physician associate student."

"Oh, wicked!!! I'm a graphic design major." I push open the locker room door and we walk into the steamy, moist air.

"So how long have you played ball?" Warryn asks as we meander past the other boys.

"Since high school." I respond, lowering myself onto a bench.

"Me too. It's such a stress reliever for me." Warryn rubs his beard.

"Me and you both, man." I add.

And by stress, I mean all the pain in my heart that has refused to go away.

"I almost never tried out for basketball in high school, you know. The boys weren't very nice and told me I'd never make the team." I shake my head and smile as the story replays in my mind.

"Oh really? They were so wrong, man. What made you try out in the end?" Warryn asks.

I pause and look at him—trying to gauge if this is the right time to divulge any personal information. "My brother." I bend over and take off my sweaty trainers. "The coolest dude I've ever known."

"Ah, sweet!!!" Warryn concurs.

"So what you doing after this?" I change the subject, robbing him of any opportunity to ask any more about Tyler.

"The guys and I are thinking about checking out *Times Square*. We'll be taking the subway there. Wanna come?"

"Of course. There's no point living in New York and never seeing *Times Square*, is there?"

"Yeah, brother. You know it." Warryn pumps my fist.

9

TEEYANA

"I'm telling you, girl. Her hair was so red, I wondered if the colour was getting to her brain." I describe my recent encounter over the phone to Amara. "I don't understand why she was mad at me like, dude, all I wanted to do was help."

I place my phone on top of my drawer behind the green and yellow ribbon I got at the Mental Health Awareness stand yesterday. It's a cute ribbon, but green and yellow aren't my colours. I'd still love to find a good place for it, though.

Putting my phone on loudspeaker, I straighten in front of my mirror and refocus on my conversation with Amara. "Imagine if I ever had to live with someone like her. It would be a nightmare." I unravel the two jumbo cornrows I wore over the weekend.

"Well, it's a good thing you're not living with someone like her." Amara says. "But quick question, where is your roommate anyway?"

"I messaged Ellie last night, and she said my previous roommate bailed last minute." I respond. "But she promised to find someone else, so I'll have to wait and see." I use my fingers to separate the wavy curls in my hair formed by the cornrows.

"Ooh, I wanted to tell you about this guy I met at the freshman barbecue." My mouth curves into a smile as I fluff my curls.

"Ooooh, girl. Now that's the type of news I like. Start spilling."

"Well, don't get too excited because he—" I jump when loud banging from my door echoes across the room.

"Teeyana? What was that?" Amara asks.

"Erm, can I call you back? Someone's at the door." I walk to the door, my hand on my chest as I wait for my heart rate to slow down.

"Nuh-uh, girl, keep me on the line. I want to make sure you're alright before hanging up." Amara squeezes in before I take her off loudspeaker.

As I get to the door, there's another loud bang and I swallow before taking a deep breath.

This is a building full of students. Surely, it can't be anyone harmful.

"Who's there?" My voice comes out sounding like a whisper, but nobody responds.

I creep towards the door until I'm close enough to look into the peephole, and my eyes fall on *her.*

Oh, crap!!!

I step away from the door. "You've got to be kidding me." I blurt out before putting my hand over my mouth.

"Teeyana? Who is it? Teeyana?" Amara's voice projects from my phone.

"It's the red-haired girl." I whisper into my phone.

"What does she want? Oh, no!!! She's a stalker. Does she have a weapon? Call the police. Now!!!" Amara panics.

"Shh!!! Amara, she's a student at this university too. I'm sure there's a good reason why she's banging on my door at eight o'clock in the morning." I take a deep breath and step forward again.

"No. Wait. Teeyana. Don't open the—" I ignore Amara's plea and swing the door open.

I know I'm not a morning person, but I'm sure my eyes aren't deceiving me right now. The red-haired girl is indeed standing in front of me, with the same green eyes, the same blinding red leather jacket, and the same nasal septum ring. My gaze washes over her, sliding down to the two suitcases by her side before resting on the backpack slung over her shoulder.

"Erm, excuse me? Are you lost?" I glance around to see if there's anyone else with her. *Please say you're lost. Please!!!*

She rolls her eyes and places her hand on her hip, revealing a tattoo on her inner wrist. "No, I'm not lost." She snaps. "This is my dorm room."

My jaw drops open as her words replay a million times in my brain. "I'm sorry, what?" I ask again, hoping I heard her wrong the first time. She doesn't respond, but instead, she pulls the two suitcases into the room, forcing me to move out of her way. She throws her backpack on the floor and it crashes into one of my empty suitcases.

I put the phone back up to my ear and step outside. "Hello? Amara? There's an emergency. I'll call you back in a few minutes." I end the call and step into the room again.

"Wait, I don't understand." I inch towards the red-haired girl as she pushes my suitcases to make room for hers. "If this is your room, why don't you have the key? And when I saw you on Saturday, you were already moving in, so why are you only bringing in your stuff this morning?" I question.

"The last time I checked, I owe you no explanation." She straightens and folds her arms across her chest. "If you don't like this arrangement, go speak to that annoying blonde girl downstairs—whatever her name is. She was the one who told me to come to room 202."

I turn around and look at the number outside the door, hoping I read it wrong the last time. But no, it still says 202.

Okay, this went from 0 to 100 real quick.

This girl is going to be a pain in my backside. I can feel it in my bones. She may be red-haired, but her very presence and demeanour depicts Olivia Hastings.

Can this day get any worse?

The girl moves her clothes from her suitcase into her closet and I'm not sure what annoys me more—her appalling attitude, her red hair, or the fact that I can't do anything about this situation.

I have to admit though, her boots are kinda cute. No!!! Focus, Teeyana.

What I want to do now is hold her by the arm and shove her, and her stupid suitcases, out of my room. But I can't. This is her dorm room, and she has as much right to be here as I do.

Okay, be nice, Teeyana. Be nice so she'll be nice to you.

I expel a quick breath and force a smile. "I'm Teeyana, by the way."

She doesn't respond and my smile fades.

I walk up to my drawer and pick up my backpack from the floor. I also grab the green and yellow ribbon and pin it on my backpack strap without thinking about it. "Do you need any help unpacking your stuff?" I say to her before vivid images of what happened the last time I offered to help flash in my brain.

She still doesn't respond.

"You haven't missed much." I try one last time. "We didn't have classes yesterday, so you can still enrol by the end of today. I can show you around the campus later if you want. I went on a tour yesterday and—"

"Look, let me make something clear here." She cuts me off.

"The fact that we'll be living together doesn't mean we're going to be best friends, okay? I've already told you I don't need your help, so why are you still talking to me?" She frowns.

Wow!!! How can someone be so rude?

"Okay, then. Suit yourself." I turn away from her. Taking one last glance at the mirror, I fluff my wavy curls again before heading for the door.

"Oh, and by the way, the blonde girl who helped you find this room? Her name is Ellie, and if you get to know her, you'll find that she's nice." I smile, but my roommate reciprocates with nothing but irritation in her green eyes.

"Have a good day." I shut the door and shoulder my backpack before walking down the hallway. I know what this is. It's another opposition, but I won't let it get to me.

So what if the green-eyed, red-haired girl doesn't like me? My world would never revolve around her. I've craved control for so long, and now I choose to keep my head high. I've come too far to let anyone discourage me. Olivia might have gotten her way, but this red-head girl won't.

Keep your chest up and chin high, Teeyana.

As I round the corner of the hallway and make my way down the stairs, I meet the same auburn-haired man my new roomie was arguing with on Saturday. He smiles at me as I brush past him.

"Excuse me, I'm looking for room 202." The man says as I turn around to face him. "My daughter sort of left me behind when I went to find out information about her enrolment. Am I going the right way?" he asks.

I stare at him for a few seconds. He has the same pointed nose and green eyes as his daughter, but his attitude is nothing like hers. "Yes, you are." I smile back at him. "That's my dorm room."

"Oh really?" He raises his eyebrows. "Have you met Heather, then? My daughter?"

"Red jacket, red hair?" I pull on my own hair.

He laughs out loud and shakes his head. "Yup, that's my Heather for you."

"She's already in there, unpacking her stuff. It's a few doors down the hall on your right." I point above his head.

"Oh, I see. I think she forgot I had her key, so thank you for letting her in."

"No problem at all."

I step out of the way and the middle-aged man walks up to the top of the stairs and turns right. He acts nothing like his daughter, so I hope he can speak some sense into her.

10

JAYDEN

"Yo, Warryn, wait up." I call out to him as he walks in front of me, alongside Josh and Brian—two other boys I met at basketball tryouts.

Today is the first day of classes and I'm excited about my information design class because I'm hoping to see the burger girl again.

I tried to find her at the enrolment yesterday, but my efforts felt like I was looking for a needle in a haystack. I've met many new people over the past few days, including when I went to church on Sunday. I have a strong conviction that the people at Faith Baptist Church will soon become my second family, but this burger girl is different.

I don't know what it is about her that I find intriguing, but our conversation ended abruptly and I need an opportunity to at least apologise.

Oh God, I don't even know her name.

I resist the urge to do a facepalm. I better not call her "*burger girl*" or she'll never be speaking to me again, that's for sure.

"Do you think Coach will put the list out today?" Warryn's voice presses into my thoughts. "I hope I've made the team. It'll be sick playing with you every week." We turn left at the end of the hallway.

"I know, right?" I turn to face Warryn. "He said it'll be out before Friday, so it could be today." I halt when I see the signs to room 218. "Alright boys, this is my stop. I'll meet you guys for lunch. Warryn, text me if you hear anything before then."

"Of course, man. Take it easy." Warryn pumps my fist, and we part ways, Josh and Brian going with him.

The lecture theatre is much bigger than I expected, with about a hundred seats spread out across the entire room. I shift my gaze from one corner of the room to the other, hoping my eyes will find that familiar face I've been wanting to see again.

After scanning from the back to the front, my eyes fall on her —the burger girl, sitting at the front of the class. Her hair is no longer in neat cornrows, but now in loose curls which fall below her shoulder, complementing her caramel brown skin.

Wiping my palms on my jeans, I exhale and take my first steps towards her.

Lord, please help me. I meander through the crowd of students at the front of the lecture theatre and place my backpack on the table next to her before lowering myself on the chair.

"Hey." I grin at her, hoping she'll remember me.

"Hey." She responds with a smile and tucks a strand of hair behind her ear, revealing more of her high cheekbones and long face.

Okay Lord, she's smiling. That's a good sign, right?

"We met at the welcome barbecue on Saturday?" I manage to make a proper sentence instead of plastering a stupid grin on my face.

"Yeah, I remember you." She nods and adjusts in her seat.

"Sorry, I hope you don't mind me sitting next to you. You're the only one I know." I lie.

"Oh really?" She raises an eyebrow. "Didn't seem like it to me on Saturday with your group of friends." She shakes her head. "Why would you say I'm the *only* one you know?" She crosses her arms and leans back in her chair.

Oh, boy. Why did I have to say that?

"Well, what I meant to say was, I've met many people over the past few days and they've been amazing." I try to redeem myself. "But I wouldn't say I've gotten the chance to know them well."

"Well, I'm sure that two days is not enough time to know someone well." She shrugs.

"You make a good point, but...I have to admit that my roommate, Bob, and I have had awesome conversations—awesome enough to make me say he's a cool dude. But apart from him, I would also like to be your friend." I catch a glimpse of her dark brown eyes.

"Hmm, are you sure you want to be my friend? And are you sure you won't run away this time? Cinderella?" She tilts her head.

I pause for a minute, trying to figure out what she means, and then the events of Saturday come flooding back into my memory.

"Oh right, about that." I rub my forehead. "I'd been thinking about it over the weekend, and it's part of the reason I came over to talk to you. See, the thing is, I had promised to call my parents earlier that night to let them know I was alright."

I forgot to do that before the barbecue so I had to rush off when I got a text from my Mom. She...uh...gets a little worried sometimes so I had to make sure I didn't add to her worries. But I know it was rude of me to leave like that, so I'm sorry." I let out the words all in one go, hoping she wouldn't think I'm nothing else but a Mama's boy.

"No, it's okay. My mom is a worrier too, so I understand. A

boy's gotta do what a boy's gotta do." She gives me a reassuring smile.

"Great!!! Now that we've cleared the air, I have to say that I went back to the barbecue, but I couldn't find you." I add.

"Oh, you did?" Her eyes widen. "I didn't know you were coming back, and I was tired, so I left early."

"That's okay. It doesn't matter now, because here we are again." I grin. "I didn't get the chance to ask for your name, so can we try this again?" I extend my hand to her. "Hello, my name is Jayden Williams. It's nice to meet you."

She stares at my hand and smiles before taking it into hers. "My name is Teeyana Sparks. Nice to meet you, Jayden."

My gaze slides down to the green and yellow ribbon on her backpack strap and the muscles in my jaw tense up. A knot tightens in my chest and memories of Tyler force their way into my mind again. The memories themselves are pleasant, but the emotions that accompany them prick me like a thorn in my flesh.

"I like your ribbon." I clear the lump building in my throat when Teeyana catches me staring. "I still can't decide where to put mine." That was partially true. My own ribbon has been sitting on my desk in my dorm room since the student volunteer gave it to me on move-in day.

To everyone else, it's just a ribbon to help spread mental health and suicide prevention awareness. But to me, it's a daily challenge to learn how to share my story with others. I still don't know how to do that, and that's why the ribbon is still sitting on my desk.

A broad smile creeps on Teeyana's face as she pulls her backpack closer. "You should put it on your backpack too. We can be twins." She wiggles her eyebrows and I laugh, her relaxing gesture putting me at ease again.

"I'll think about that offer." I wiggle my eyebrows back at her.

We spend the next few minutes talking about what we did over the summer and the people we've met so far. Not long into our conversation, we realise that we both know Teeyana's roommate—or I suppose the girl most of us now know as "the screaming red-haired girl."

"Oh, I can't believe you know her too." Teeyana gasps.

"Yeah, we saw her screaming at her dad in the parking lot on Saturday. It went on for a while and it wasn't a pretty sight." I shake my head.

"So did you see me trying to help her before she started screaming?" Teeyana asks.

"No, I didn't. I was talking to some of the guys on the stairs in front of Donovan Hall. Is she a Graphic Design major too?"

Teeyana shakes her head. "Nooo!!! And thank God for *that.* I glanced at some of the books on her desk this morning and I think she's majoring in marketing and business administration." She pauses and then sighs. "The girl is so difficult to communicate with, and she gets mad at the littlest things. I feel I have to walk on eggshells around her and not step on her toes so she won't explode." Teeyana rolls her eyes.

"Hmm. That doesn't sound like fun." I lean forward and rest my elbows on the desk. The more Teeyana talks about this Heather girl, the more alarm bells ring in my head. "You know, if you don't feel safe, you can always tell the RA—Ellie. You've met her, right?"

Teeyana nods. "Yeah, she's very nice."

"Good. I'm sure she can arrange for you to move somewhere else." I pause, before letting myself go on a tangent.

"Hmm." Teeyana nods. "Thanks for your concern, but I don't think it's that bad. Besides, doing that will mean I'm letting her have her way. I can't let that happen. I'm just not looking forward to it, you know?" Her dark brown gaze meets mine.

"Yeah." I nod, resolving in my heart not to push her any further. "Well, it's only the beginning. You can't know what the whole journey will be like by looking at the map. I think you come across as a fighter." I smile at her before the professor walks in.

We stop talking and turn to face the front. Teeyana takes out a purple striped pencil case from her bag and places it on the notebook on her desk. The professor hushes the class and everyone quiets down.

"Good morning everyone, and welcome to your first class of your first semester of Graphic Design school." The middle-aged man adjusts his glasses. "My name is Professor McBurne and I'll be taking this class as well as your objects in space, and colour classes. You better get used to seeing my face around." He rakes his hand through his long, dark, wavy hair as he walks to the centre of the room.

"I'm sure you've all had a fun weekend of meeting new people and getting to know each other, but now, I would like to talk about the exciting projects you'll be working on this semester." He flashes his teeth and rubs his palms.

I glance at Teeyana and my eyes wander to the hand-lettered quotes on the front cover of her notebook. The first one by Maya Angelou reads, "Nothing Will Work Unless You Do." I finish reading another one, "You Get out Of Life What You Put into It," when Teeyana catches me staring—again.

She looks down at the object of my attention and then takes her hand away from the cover so I can see all the quotes better. "So you love quotes?" I whisper when Professor McBurne walks to the opposite end of the room.

She nods. "They inspire me."

"I see." I whisper back. "I love the lettering. It's beautiful."

“Thank you. My four-year-old brother—Danny, helped me stick down the letters. He did all the work.” She laughs.

“He must be a talented kid.”

“He is.” She smiles. “Do you have any brothers or sisters?”

“Errm...” Her question catches me off-guard. I’m sure Teeyana is trying to go with the flow of the conversation, but she has no idea the battle going on in my head right now. “Uh, no...I guess.” I reply and resist the urge to facepalm myself for the second time today.

No, Jayden. You can’t guess if you have brothers or sisters. You either do or you don’t.

I breathe a sigh of relief when Teeyana turns her attention back to the different projects Professor McBurne is talking about.

Four years ago, my response would have been different. It would have been something like, *yeah I have a brother too. His name is Tyler.*

And sometimes, those words creep to the edge of my tongue, like they did now. But I have to keep reminding myself that I don’t have a brother anymore. It’s easier, and less painful to say I don’t have one than to explain what happened to him.

But I feel guilty for keeping him away as a secret—as if he’s some sort of skeleton in my closet. These memories were my reality for almost fourteen years, and now I have no choice but to accept that they’re nothing but memories.

This is where I am today, holding on to the shattered pieces of my heart, but also holding on to a hope that God is mending these shattered pieces. So even sitting here, right now, getting to know Teeyana, I’d like to think that God is working and putting the pieces together to form something that He alone knows.

11

TEEYANA

After our last class, Jayden suggested we cruise up to Times Square because he'd been there before and he wanted to show me around. The journey on the subway lasted an hour, but there was never an awkward moment between us.

Jayden took photos of me with the billboards in the background so I could send them to my parents. We watched the entertainers singing, dancing, and playing a variety of instruments. Shops and restaurants lined the streets, and every corner was jam-packed with tourists who stood in awe of the lights like I did.

So many people. So many colours. So much noise.

Jayden and I bowled for hours, and when we were exhausted, we grabbed some tacos before heading back to Queens. My conversations with Jayden have been effortless, and he is so nice, he even offered to walk me back to my dorm.

"I can't believe she didn't realise you were right behind her. That's crazy." Jayden and I walk side by side as he recounts the story about when he pranked his mom.

"Yeah, I know. She can be jumpy sometimes. She has been

trying to get me back since that day, but she has never succeeded." Jayden stops in front of the stairs leading up to Donovan Hall—the same stairs where I had tried to help Heather a few days ago.

"My best friend, Amara, tried to prank her mom when she was younger by laying on the floor and pretending she was hurt. Well, that was a huge mistake, and it did not end well. Her mom gave her a whooping that day and she even used her slipper."

"Oh no, not the slipper." Jayden clasps his hands over his mouth and we both burst into laughter. "I think pranks are silly and I don't like them anymore. The incident with my mom was a one time thing. It was a long time ago, I was young and I've changed a lot since then." He places one hand on his chest.

"I believe you." I lift my head, and our eyes meet, sending my heartbeat into overdrive. "I had so much fun today. Thanks for inviting me."

"No problem at all. Thanks for coming with me." Jayden responds cheerily. "The next places on my list are the Empire State Building, Brooklyn Bridge...oh and 53rd street. I've heard they sell the best street food over there." He rubs his palms and grins.

I open my mouth to reply, but his phone chimes and he takes it out of his pocket, pressing his thumb on the home button to view the notification. "Oh, wicked!!!" He exclaims with a broad smile and brings the phone close to his face.

"What happened?" I raise my brows.

"Oh, my friend—Warryn and I both made the basketball team. Our coach emailed us instead of putting a list on the notice board."

"Oh, wow, congratulations." I smile at him.

"Thank you." He slips the phone back into his pocket.

"I didn't know you played basketball." I say, wishing I knew more about basketball so I can ask him more questions.

"Yeah, I've been playing since high school. We'll be having practice every Friday to prepare for the next season. You can come watch if you're into basketball."

Oh, I'm not into basketball, but I'm into you.

"Of course. I'll check you guys out." I tuck my hands in my jacket pockets. "Thank you for walking back with me."

His face beams with a smile. "Well, as long as you're safe, then I believe my job here is done." He backs away towards his own dorm. "Make sure you rest up and I'll see you tomorrow—God willing." He waves at me. "Goodnight, Tee." He says as he turns around but then stops and turns to face me again. "Can I call you *Tee,* by the way?"

I shrug. "Well, no one's ever called me that before. I guess you'd be the first and I don't mind." I give him a sheepish smile and fiddle with my fingers.

Ugh!!! Why do I get all jittery around this guy? Get a grip on yourself, Teeyana.

"Okay, good." He gives me two thumbs up before walking away again.

"Goodnight, Jayden." I reply as he disappears from my sight. Then, I shiver when the chilly night air quenches the butterfly feeling in my stomach. As I climb up the stairs, I push away the thought of meeting Heather—or shall I say, my roommate from hell. Walking down the hallway, my stomach twists and turns as the sound of my heartbeat fills my ears.

Standing in front of my dorm room, I take out my bunch of keys from my purse, being careful not to make any noise. The door squeaks open as I step into the room. The lights are off, but Heather's desk lamp is on. It lights up her side of the room, but she's not at her desk. I breathe a sigh of relief and tiptoe to my bed, hoping I don't trip over anything.

When I get to my bed, I take off my shoes and shove them

underneath the bed, while shuffling through my things to find my torch light.

"What are you doing?" A voice questions as the lights come on, and I jump back, dropping my backpack on the ground. "You know you don't have to act like a thief in your own room, right?"

I straighten my back to face Heather, who is standing next to the bathroom door with a knee-length black towel wrapped around her body. She's wearing a black face mask and her red hair is sitting up in a messy bun at the top of her head.

"Erm...I didn't want to disturb you, so I thought I'd try to be quiet." I mumble.

"More like you didn't want to talk to me." She scoffs. "Do you think I bite?" She gives me the same cunning smile she gave me earlier this morning. Unlike Jayden, whose smile is heart-warming and welcoming, this smile is repulsive and intimidating.

Ugh, who does she think she is?

"No, of course not." I stand my ground. "I already told you, I didn't want to disturb you." I tuck a stray piece of hair behind my ear and pick my backpack off the floor. "Plus, you were the one talking about not getting into each other's space, so why do you care now?"

Heather laughs and walks towards me. "You're scared of me, aren't you?"

I give her a blank expression. "I don't understand what's funny." I put my hand on my hip, trying to hide the fact that she terrifies me.

"I know your type, Teeyana Joy Sparks. You think you're all high and mighty and can't mingle with people like me, huh? You think you're the smartest, high achieving one?"

I roll my eyes and look away.

I'm so not ready for this nonsense tonight.

"Heather, with all due respect, I have no idea what you're

talking about. I want to sleep in peace because I'm tired." I cross my arms. "And how do you know my name—my *full* name?" I raise my eyebrows.

"Well, what do you expect when you leave all your certificates, awards, and documents lying around? Who do you think will clean up your mess?" She demands.

"Well, I'm sorry I left my things lying around. I was in a rush this morning and I was going to sort them out as soon as I got back. You shouldn't have gone through my stuff, though. You had no right." I snap.

"Wow. I had no right? This is my room too, and you had no right to inconvenience me." Heather snaps back.

"But they are *my* things." I raise my voice. "You could have put them to one side instead of going through all my documents."

"You think you're tough, don't you?" Heather crosses her arms.

"No, I think you're being ridiculous right now. You don't know me, Heather, so can we stop this right now, please?" I bring my voice down. "You and I may have our differences, but can we try to co-exist, please?" I beg.

"Co-exist?" Heather stares me down. "We'll see about that." She turns the light off again, restoring the room back to its partial darkness.

"Please, don't go through my stuff again. I'm sure you wouldn't appreciate it if I did the same to you."

Heather doesn't respond, but instead, she—or rather her silhouette, turns around and walks into the bathroom, before slamming the door shut.

My fists tighten and my jaw clenches as I resist the urge to scream out my frustration. Tears creep to the edge of my eyelids and threaten to fall, but I wipe them away.

Breathe, Teeyana. Just breathe.

Heather's annoying escapades won't get to me. I refuse to let them get to me. *Breathe, Teeyana. Come on, breathe.*

I can't believe I've found myself here again. This is a replica of my life during my last two years of high school. College was supposed to be fun, so why am I still living in fear and looking over my shoulder? Why am I back to the life of cowardice I thought I would never experience again?

I just want to have it all under control in my own world. Is that too much to ask? Why does there have to be someone, or something, trying to make things hard for me? Can't things go ahead as I plan them out in my head?

My phone vibrates in my pocket and when I take it out, a message from Dad pops up on my screen. He and Mom have been taking turns messaging me to make sure I'm alright. I want to tell them how much I'm struggling already. I want to ask them how to deal with my annoying roommate, but I won't.

This is *my* journey. I chose this. Therefore, I have to figure it out for myself. Plus, it's only been three days, so I'm sure it can't get any worse than this, can it?

My fingers hover over my keypad as I read Dad's message.

Hey honey,

I hope you're okay. We miss you so much but I think Danny misses you the most. Please call us if you need anything.

We love you.

A small smile forms on my lips when I scroll up to a photo of Danny wearing the lion onesie I got him for his fourth birthday. Mom and Dad are cooped up behind him, both of them pressing their cheeks against his. The longer I stare at the photo, the more my urge to bawl increases. A lump builds in my throat, but

I swallow it all the way down to where I've been piling up my feelings for the past four years.

Climbing up on my bed, I lean my back against the wall and bring my knees up to my chest before burying my face in my palms.

You have to be strong, Teeyana.

You'll soon have the upper hand.

You'll make things turn out in your favour.

12

TEEYANA

The reality of being away from my family has hit me harder than I expected; and living with Heather has only made my worries worse. Despite all this, I've kept on top of all my classes, and spending time with Jayden has kept me distracted.

Today, Jayden and I are in one of the discussion rooms in the library, and we are working on our projects from our Objects in Space class. Professor McBurne challenged us to make a normal day-to-day object ten times bigger than its usual size. I'm making a giant button and Jayden is making a key.

"Tee, what you doing on Saturday?" Jayden asks, as he draws his key outline on a large piece of cardboard paper.

"Erm...studying, I guess. Why?" I say, my attention glued to the frisbee in front of me. I press it down into the piece of wood laying on the table, before drilling the last hole into it.

"Well," Jayden speaks again when my drilling stops. "My church is organising a youth group social in the evening. My youth pastor—Anton, is having us over at his house in the Astoria neighbourhood, here in Queens. We'll be playing games, watching movies, and eating lots of food. Wanna come?"

Oh great!

A few weeks ago, I found out that Jayden is a Christian because he started talking about church and Bible study. I haven't told him about my Christian background yet. The truth is, I enjoy his company and since I live with Heather; I need Jayden's positive energy around me.

But the problem here is he takes this God thing way too seriously and I don't. How do I decline this invitation or future invitations without sounding like I'm making stuff up?

"Tee?" Jayden's voice shakes me out of my thoughts, and I look up at him.

"Hmm? Oh, right. Saturday." I rub the back of my neck. "Erm...I left my planner in my dorm room. I need to check it's not on the same day as Ellie's party." I lower my head again. Ellie told me her boyfriend's fraternity was throwing a party and she invited all her sorority sisters. She invited me too, and I couldn't refuse. This is the college experience I've been looking forward to.

"Oh, okay. Let me know if you can make it so I can pick you up on my way there. It's only a fifteen minute drive away. I'm looking forward to Bible trivia. It's such a fun game." Jayden picks up a pair of scissors and starts cutting out his outline.

"Yeah, it is." I reply absent-mindedly. "We play it at my youth group in Boston and people always get so competitive." I smile, before realising I just blew my cover.

Ooops!!! Maybe he didn't hear any of that?

Jayden's eyes widen as he sets the pair of scissors on the table. "Wait a minute. You go to church? You're Christian too?" He tilts his head.

Oh darn it, Teeyana.

I could give the perfect excuse and brush everything away, but I don't want to start this friendship with a lie, so I nod and smile.

"Really? That's awesome." Jayden's face beams. "I knew there was something special about you from the moment we met."

I lift an eyebrow. "And...how does being a Christian make me special?"

If he thinks he's found someone to go to church with, go evangelising with, or do Bible studies with, then he couldn't be more wrong because that person sure ain't me.

"Because, when two or three are gathered in God's name, we have confidence that He is with us. So you see, this friendship is already blessed." He shakes his shoulders to show his excitement.

Okay, when he puts it that way, then it sounds kinda special. Clearly, this new revelation has made his day so good for him.

"How come you didn't tell me?" Jayden asks.

"Tell you what? That I'm a Christian?" I was hoping he wouldn't ask me this question. I don't want to talk about it, but since I've already blown my cover, I have to give a reason.

"Okay, here's the thing," I pause, searching for the right words in my brain. "I'm from a Christian family but...that's about it. At the moment, I'm not sure where I stand with my faith. I have a lot of questions, and I'm still trying to figure out what I believe." I purse my lips and pick up my can of spray paint.

I hope he doesn't push this any further.

"Oh, I see. Anything you want to talk about? Or ask me?"

"I think it's a tale for another day." I reply. "Thanks for your concern, though. I appreciate it." I give him a half-hearted smile, hoping I've said enough for him to let it be.

"That's cool, Tee." He returns a warmer smile. "Whenever you're ready to talk, I'll be here. I've left my *Cinderella* days behind, and I won't be running off again. I promise." He chuckles before picking up a pencil and shading in his key outline.

"I'll keep that in mind. Thanks, Jay." I shake the can of spray paint and start spraying my frisbee when my eyes catch the green and yellow ribbon on Jayden's backpack. "Hey," I tilt my head and smile. "You put the ribbon on your backpack too." I point to the object of my attention.

A dimpled smile tugs on his lips and he shrugs. "I...kinda liked the idea of us being *twins.*" He winks at me and my insides turn to mush as the butterflies set off again.

"He's a Christian too? Girl, that's great!!! You found a Christian friend." Amara says from the other end of the phone line. "My mom always says 'as iron sharpens iron, so does a friend sharpen a friend.'" She reminds me of how pleased Mrs. Ikezie was when she found out I grew up in a Christian home.

"So have you guys found a church yet? Is it close to your campus? Do they have Bible study too?" Amara fires questions at me.

"Erm...yeah, he found a church. It's called Faith...something, I can't remember." I stutter. "He invited me to his youth group social tonight."

"Oh, that'll be cool." Amara responds. "It'll remind you so much of Boston, with all the Bible trivia, and charades we used to play."

"Yeah, well...I'm not going."

"No? Why not?" Amara asks.

"I'm busy with assignments." I lie.

More like I'll be busy at Ellie's frat party. I'm in college now, and I can do whatever I want.

I open the top drawer of my bedside table and my eyes fall on the book Kevin gave me. I can't believe I brought it to college. I took it out of my bag on move-in day and put it in my top drawer, but the intention was never to look at it again. Just like I intended, it's still laying here, untouched, and screaming the words at me, *How To Stick To Your Faith At College.*

I rub my forehead before taking the book out of my drawer and placing it on my lap.

"Well, I'm sure there'll be many more socials in the future, so don't worry about it." Amara reassures me.

I'm more worried about what I'll be wearing to the frat party tonight.

"Yeah, you're right. Thanks for always listening to me." I put my hand up to my chest in gratitude, as I would do if Amara was sitting next to me.

"Girl, don't thank me. You're my person, and I'm here for you." Amara brings in her usual reference to *Grey's Anatomy*. "Now I better rush back to my lab partner. We have to finish our lab report in a few hours. Love you, girl."

"Love you too. Take care." I turn off my phone and drop it on my bed.

Opening the book on my lap, I flip past the introductory pages and move on to the first chapter titled, *Stick To Like-Minded People.*

Ugh, I'm already bored. Even God knows I tried.

I close the book and throw it back into my drawer before pushing it shut. Opening up my wardrobe, I scramble through my clothes until I find the pair of ripped jeans and black halter-necked top I bought for this party.

Spreading the clothes on my bed, I walk over to my mirror and take off my purple beanie, revealing the single-stranded twists I did when I washed my hair yesterday. I slowly unravel the twists, leaving well-defined curls behind.

After unravelling all the twists, I use a wide-tooth comb to fluff my hair out until I get the look I want. Stepping away from the mirror, I walk towards my bed to change into my clothes.

I catch a glimpse of my project for Professor McBurne's class peeking out of my backpack. It's due on Tuesday and I was supposed to finish it up today, but I've spent all afternoon getting ready for the party—my first college party. It's a big deal, so my project can wait.

This will be good for you, Teeyana. You're doing the right thing. You're taking control of your life like you've always wanted. Have fun and don't you dare feel guilty about it.

13

TEEYANA

Ellie parks on the street outside the house hosting the frat party. As we squeeze out of the car one by one, I press the home button on my phone to check the time before slipping it into the back pocket of my jeans.

I let out a sigh and suppress a yawn. In high school, I was usually fast asleep at this time because I spent most of my weekends studying. But this isn't high school. Ellie has told me many times that these first few months are crucial for making friends. It's now or never.

Tonight I rode with three of Ellie's friends from her sorority. After spending an eternity interrogating me about my non-existent love life, the girls went straight in to sharing their tips for my first frat party and my first semester of college.

"Okay, Teeyana, remember everything we said," Ellie slams her car door shut and presses the key to lock it. "You have to always stay close, okay? And do *not* leave your drink unattended. Got it?" She raises her eyebrows the same way Mom would to Danny.

"Yeah, sure." Panic settles in my chest and my tongue sticks to the roof of my dry mouth. *Oh darn it, I forgot my water bottle.*

The other girls strut past us and make their way towards the front door, but Ellie lags behind them and matches my hesitant pace. "How are you feeling?" She asks.

I pause to think about her question. If she had asked me that ten minutes ago, before I spent the entire car ride listening to the girls feed me all their frat party horror stories, my answer would have come with a lot more enthusiasm.

"I'm...fine." I force a smile.

Ellie wraps her arm around my shoulder as we climb up the stairs. "I'm sure you'll have tons of fun. Just be careful because not everyone is as nice as they seem."

Okay, all this talk is starting to make me feel sick. Now I wish I had taken the easier option and gone with Jayden. The music gets louder as we approach the front door and the sound of Ellie's heels hitting the pavement soon gets drowned out by the beats.

"You ready?" Ellie turns to me and flashes me her broad, relaxing smile, which eases the tightness in my chest...just a little.

I exhale sharply. "Yes...ready."

We walk through the door and right into the deafening blasts of music coming from the far end of the room. Right away, the smell of alcohol attacks my nostrils and the deepening bass of the music awakens a throbbing in my head.

I cover my ears to adjust to the new volume of sound when Ellie gently pulls my arm, saying what I think is, "This way, Teeyana."

I follow her and the other girls further into the room as the music changes to another upbeat song. A group of boys make their way to the dance floor and start jumping to the beats of the new song.

On the other side of the room, shouts erupt from another group when two boys bite into cans of what I think is alcohol, but they end up spilling most of the cans' contents on the floor as they try to drink.

Jheeze, don't they know wet floors are a trip hazard?

"Would you like something to drink?" Ellie's voice draws my attention back to the group of girls I am now standing with. My gaze drops to the shot glass in her hands and when I look around, all the other girls have glasses in their hands too.

"Eerm...no thank you." I bring my gaze back up to Ellie, hoping she would see the plea in my eyes for her not to push it.

"Come on, Teeyana. There's always a first time." Ellie brings it closer and the strong smell of the brown liquid forces me to scrunch my nose. "We promise we won't tell anyone." Ellie adds and with all the other girls staring at me intently, a compulsive feeling envelopes me.

Okay, just one glass, Teeyana. You want to fit in? Here's your chance.

As I'm about to take the glass from Ellie, my phone vibrates in my pocket. *Oh yes, this is clutch!!!* "Excuse me, I have to take this." I turn away from the group and thread my way through the crowd of sweaty students to the kitchen where the noise is quieter, and the air is cooler.

Leaning against the white wall next to the fridge, I send a quick text to Mom and it takes ten minutes to soothe her worries and reassure her I'm not putting myself in danger. When she finally types goodnight, I breathe a sigh of relief before slipping my phone back into my pocket.

I should go back to the group, but my feet are planted on the kitchen floor. This was supposed to be fun, but I feel like I don't belong here. I sigh and shake my head when two girls walk in laughing out loud and chattering.

"Hi." I force a smile at the girls but they barely notice me. They both grab bottles of water from the fridge and walk out again, as if I don't exist.

Dude, this is harder than I thought. I don't know anyone here. I should have just gone to an event for freshmen.

I yank the fridge open and take out my own bottle of water before sipping on it—the cool liquid soothing my dry throat. When I gather the courage to get back out, Ellie is no longer with the group. She's now sitting on a sofa to the left of them, making out with a guy who I can only assume is her boyfriend.

The music changes again to a faster song, which brings more people to the dance floor. The shouts get louder as everyone takes out their phones to stream on their various social media platforms.

The party has barely started and my feet are already aching in these new shoes I ordered online. *Ugh, I should have just worn one of the shoes I brought with me from Boston. This sucks. I need to go home.*

"There you are!!!" A voice comes from the left of me and before I can turn around to see who it is, strong arms wrap around me as one of Ellie's friends pushes me to the centre of their group. "Teeyana is one of the freshmen here, so she gets to go first." The girl says as loud cheers erupt from the people around me and my heart rate picks up speed.

One guy who I saw drinking from a can earlier brings a glass close to me. He adds a few drinks into it; a yellow one, a clear one, and the dark brown one the girls tried to give me earlier. After mixing the concoction together, the guy thrusts the glass into my hands and everyone steps back. "Go, Teeyana." Ellie screams from the lap of her boyfriend and soon, everyone is chanting my name.

"Teeyana!!! Teeyana!!! Teeyana!!!"

My hands tremble and I tighten my grip around the glass so I wouldn't drop it. I scan the faces of the people around me, all their attention on me. This is it. This is my chance to fit in.

Come on, Teeyana. It can't be that bad. Just drink it.

I hold my breath and bring the glass up to my lips before tipping my head back and downing the liquid as fast as I can. The crowd counts down to ten as the liquid foams in my mouth and runs down my chin, my neck, and my chest.

When I finally finish, the crowd erupts into cheers again and Ellie runs up to me and gives me a hug. "I told you it won't be that bad." She says as the crowd disperses and everyone goes back to their dancing corners. I sway to the music as the girls thrust more glasses into my hands.

As time passes, the room starts spinning and then my legs start to feel like jelly, as if they would give way any second. I place my glass on the table next to me and turn around to find Ellie, but my vision is blurry.

I take a few steps towards the nearest couch so I can steady myself, but sticky brown liquid smears my hands when I lean on the couch. It could be alcohol...or urine at this point. *Eww.*

"Ellie?" I kick away the glasses and bottles in my path as I near the blonde-haired girl who is dancing at the far end of the room. "Ellie?" I reach for her shoulder and she turns around.

"Oh, no. Teeyana, are you okay?" Ellie asks.

I shake my head, and a wave of nausea engulfs me. "I don't feel good." I clutch my tummy as my stomach's contents rise to my chest. Instinctively, I lurch forward and empty the contents on Ellie's shoes.

The singing from the crowd turns to gasps and shrieks as the people standing nearby retreat. I don't know how long I retch for before Ellie hands me a bottle of water. "Come on, I'll take you home."

Slipping in and out of consciousness, I lean on Ellie as she helps me get into the front passenger seat. "I'm so sorry for ruining your shoes." I say for the thousandth time before leaning my head against the window glass. "They didn't spike my drink, did they?" I ask and Ellie laughs.

"No, honey, you're just drunk. You'll be fine in the morning." She pats my shoulder as we pull over in front of Donovan Hall.

As I climb out of the car, Ellie helps me balance and we cross the sidewalk towards the stairs. Incoherent words continue to fly out of my mouth, followed by snorts and then giggles. *What did they put in that drink?*

"Tee?" A familiar voice echoes from behind me and I freeze in my spot.

Oh crap. Don't turn around. Don't turn around. Don't—

My mediocre effort to plant my feet on the ground is thwarted as Ellie's arm strength turns my whole body in the direction of the voice.

"Tee, are you okay? What happened?" Jayden asks as he runs up the stairs. *What is he doing out at this time?*

I open my mouth to respond, but only a pathetic mumble comes out. So I give up and bury my head again in Ellie's neck. It's better this way because I'm sure I look a mess.

"She's fine." Ellie responds on my behalf. "She just drank a bit too much."

"Erm..okay, do you need any help?" Jayden asks as Ellie and I resume our slow ascent up the stairs.

"Nah, I've got this, big guy. You go get some rest. I'll take care of her." Ellie says.

"Okay. I'll...I'll call you tomorrow, Tee." Jayden says again, and a groan escapes my lips when Ellie and I enter the building.

Just great! I'm sure I'll be getting a well-deserved sermon from Jayden tomorrow!

14

JAYDEN

"Baby, you know you shouldn't be staying out this late." Mom's exasperated breath comes through my phone. "It's New York, for goodness' sake."

I rub my temples as I climb up the stairs, trying to get my thoughts away from Teeyana and back to my current conversation. But with every step I take, a new question pops into my already cluttered brain.

Did someone spike her drink?

Did Ellie encourage her to get drunk?

What else did they get up to at that party?

"Boy, are you listening to me?" I wince at the sharp inclination of Mom's voice, and I adjust my headphones.

"Yes, Mom, I'm here." I sigh and take a right turn to walk down the hallway. "I drove to and from Anton's house, so it was all good. It was fun because we watched movies and shared testimonies for hours. That's how we lost track of time." I lower my voice as I near my dorm room. "I was in good company, Mom." I stop and lean against the wall.

Mom pauses for a few seconds before speaking again. "Okay,

in that case, I'm happy you're making friends." Her voice is much calmer now.

"I'm happy too. Besides, New York streets are very beautiful at night. You need to experience it." I tease her as I take out my keys from my pocket.

"Someday we will take a drive, but until then, I'll let you get some rest."

"Oh, thank God. I need to end the call now before my roommate starts thinking I'm a Mama's boy."

Mom snorts. "Oh, but you are."

"Okay, good night, Mom." I laugh and shake my head before ending the call. Turning the key in the lock, I twist the doorknob and open the door into the dark room.

Bob's loud snores fill the room as I walk slowly to my bed. I use the light from my desk lamp to get ready for bed and then climb underneath the covers. Turning my head to face the wall, I force my eyes shut but sleep refuses to come. So I open my eyes again and stare at the ceiling, my thoughts drifting once more to Teeyana.

Since the day she mentioned having doubts about God, I've had an increasing urge to say something or do something to encourage her. But how do I do that when I don't know what her story is?

Being a youth group leader at church, it's much easier to encourage a room full of Christians because they already know the truth. These people *want* to draw closer to God, so all I need to do is remind them about the truth. But how do I encourage someone who wants to move away from God?

Lord, what do you want me to do?

My phone vibrates underneath my pillow, and I sit up before pulling it out. Anton's message comes through the notifications section and I swipe up to read it.

. . .

Hey buddy,

Sorry we didn't get the chance to catch up after the social like we planned.

Should we reschedule for after church today? Annie will make lunch :)

My eyes widen when a probable solution to my current dilemma hits me. I should ask Anton and Annie for help. They seem really cool, so I'm sure they'll have some useful tips. I click on the reply button and start typing,

Of course.
You had me at lunch.
See you soon :)

"Annie, you need to tell me when next you make these stuffed peppers and I'll come running." I reach across the table and grab my fourth one before turning to Anton. "You don't mind, do you?" I smile sheepishly.

Anton laughs and shakes his head. "Buddy, you're welcome here anytime you want."

"Yes!!!" I pump a fist.

Annie emerges from the kitchen carrying a bowl of salad. "Jayden, honey, all you need to do is say the word." She places the bowl in front of Anton before settling in the seat next to him.

"Seriously, I never knew a salad could taste so good." I fill my mouth with more prawns, avocados, and leafy greens.

"Now you can understand how much of this I enjoy every day." Anton winks at Annie.

Annie laughs and takes Anton's hands. "Aww, thanks, my love." She leans over and kisses his cheek before turning to her food again. "So, Jayden, I heard you play the guitar." She says as she chews on some salad.

I swallow the remaining bits of couscous in my mouth before speaking. "Yeah, just a little."

"A little?" Anton interjects. "You're *really* good at it."

Correction; Tyler was really good at it.

I'm nowhere near as talented as he is...I mean, was. But of course Anton wouldn't know that because he never heard Tyler play. I got the chance to tell Anton about Tyler while Annie was preparing lunch earlier. I'm glad I've finally told at least one other person about my story. That's a good start for me. I hope I'll learn to share it with more people as time passes.

"Aww, that's amazing." Annie's voice pierces into my thoughts. "So that means you'll be playing more at church now?"

"Hmm." I nod.

"Seriously, buddy, we're so happy you're doing this." Anton says. "Annie and I think it'll encourage more youngsters from the youth group to get involved too, so thank you for taking the first step."

"I'm glad I can help." I smile at them and pick up my glass of water. The truth is, the more time I spend in church and play basketball, the less time I'll spend thinking about Tyler.

I clear my throat and sip on my water when an image of Teeyana reminds me about my agenda for today. "Oh, by the way," I place my glass down again. "There's this...friend of mine who is a Christian, but who is also struggling with her faith. I want to encourage her, but I don't know where to start."

"Ooh, what's her name? Was she at the social last night?" Anton scrunches up his eyebrows.

I shake my head. "No, I invited her, but she..." I pause when the events of last night come flooding back into my memory. "She had other commitments so couldn't make it."

"Oooh," Annie leans forward, her black cross earrings dangling down each ear lobe. "Do you like her?"

My eyes widen. *Gosh, this woman is so direct. I wasn't ready.* "Errm...what makes you think I like her?"

Annie shrugs. "I don't know, you talk about her in such a...caring way."

Is it that obvious? "I care about her a lot. She's smart, hard-working, pretty, funny, and...."

"Aww, so you *do* like her." Annie's grin widens.

"Well..." I adjust in my seat and rub the back of my neck. "There's...something about her I find very interesting, but I don't know what it is. I just know I've had this overwhelming burden to help her restore her faith in God again. Problem is, I don't know how to do that." My gaze alternates between Anton and Annie. "You guys got any tips?"

"Of course," Annie places her fork down and clears her throat. "Honey, let me give you a little chicken nugget of wisdom." She interlocks her fingers in front of her. "Walk in the fruits of the spirit, show her love, be patient with her, be kind and compassionate to her, and soon, she'll wonder how you do these things. That's when you can tell her about the gospel of Jesus."

"Yeah, buddy." Anton nods. "Also, remember that only God can restore her faith again, and not you. But He can certainly use you as a tool. No matter what happens, keep praying. It will be discouraging sometimes, but you have to keep praying. Okay?"

Keep praying. Of course. If God is truly in this, then I know He'll help me when times get tough. "Okay." I reply with a nod, a feeling of determination welling up in my chest. "It won't be easy, but I'll do just that. Thanks guys."

15

TEEYANA

I suppress another wave of nausea and straighten my back. As I lift my head, my gaze meets the bright lights on the library ceiling and this triggers a shooting pain around my head. *Why did I do this to myself?*

Bringing my head down again, I close my eyes and welcome the darkness. I haven't finished Professor McBurne's project yet, and it's due on Tuesday. I only have the finishing touches left but my muscles hurt and every time I try to pick anything up, I get terrible shakes in my hands.

I've never waited this late to finish an assignment before, so this deadline is stressing me out. It doesn't help that I feel so awful today. I couldn't sleep last night and after two episodes of vomiting this morning, I made a cup of coffee and dragged myself down to the library. I thought the coffee would help because that's what people take in the movies. Well, so far it hasn't worked for me.

Come on, Teeyana. Get up and do your work.

"Hey Tee," A familiar voice forces me to open my eyes. My gaze falls on Jayden's sneakers next to mine on the floor. *Just*

great! Now comes the sermon to remind me about hou hell for getting drunk.

"Tee, you okay?" He pulls a nearby chair close t screeching sound worsens my headache.

"Oh, please stop." I groan and Jayden stops imr lifts the chair and places it gently next to me.

"Sorry." He whispers. "You okay?" He asks agair my head, saying nothing more as I brace myself for

"How are you feeling?" He continues in a hushe

I want to lie to him as much as I want to lie to m handling this well, but who am I kidding? I remember fixing my hair when I left the dorm roo ing. *I'm a mess.*

"My head hurts." Another groan escapes my li my hand up to the top of my head where the pain li

"Did you speak to Ellie this morning?"

I shake my head. "She wanted to come over, bu was okay. I think I've caused her enough trouble an ment already."

Jayden remains silent for a few minutes and if staring at his sneakers, I would have thought he left. I w tell me off, or at least say the words 'I told you so,' but no No sermon. No judgemental or sarcastic comments. No

Then Jayden speaks again. "I'll be right back." H and his retreating footsteps fade in the background.

I lift my head again, catching him running down the ground floor. *Wait, where's he going?* I scru eyebrows as my gaze drops to his unlocked phone or

I know I shouldn't look, but my curiosity gets t me and I slide the phone towards me. I squint so focus on the words. The page shows a list of things when you have a hangover.

A few minutes later, Jayden reappears running up the stairs d I slide his phone back—a little too hard; it almost tips off : edge. I hold my head up with my hands and massage my nples as Jayden settles in his chair again.

"Here," he places two bottles of water in front of me, a choco- e bar, and a flapjack. "They said you need to stay hydrated d get some carbs into you." He reaches into his backpack and lls out a packet of aspirin. Placing it on the table, his hazel- own gaze meets mine. "This should help with the headache." pushes the packet close to me.

"I...I..." The words catch in my throat. What am I supposed say? Why is he being so nice when I'm responsible for this ess? I sigh and take the open bottle of water from him. hanks, Jay."

"You're welcome." His warm smile causes heat to rise in my eeks.

I devour the golden syrup flapjack and chocolate bar within ew minutes and then empty half the bottle of water before pping down an aspirin tablet. "That flapjack was delicious." I ile and Jayden does too.

"I'm glad you like it. Now another recommendation is for u to get enough sleep. It doesn't look like you've had much."

I shake my head and start pulling out my project from my ckpack. "Jay, I need to finish this by the end of today."

He places a firm grip on my hands to stop me. "No, half an ur will make a big difference."

"But..." I protest.

"How much do you have left to do?" He asks and I take out e project to show him.

"I need to finish these design patterns." I flip open my sketch d which has the design for the finished button. "You know I e intricate details, so this will take a while."

"But you can't make the details perfect with shaking hands,

can you?" Jayden lets go of my hands, exposing my tremors. "Okay, how about this? If you rest for half an hour, I'll help you finish it up."

Aww, really? "Jay, you don't have to do this."

"But I want to help. Please, Tee." His pleading finally gets to me.

I need way more than half an hour, but if he's going to help me, then I won't refuse. "Okay, then." I place both arms on the table and rest my head on them. Closing my eyes, I let out a sigh. "Half an hour exactly."

"Yes, Ma'am. I got you."

I smile and close my eyes to welcome the darkness once more and before I know it; I drift off. I don't know how long I sleep for, but when I open my eyes again, Jayden is still sitting next to me as he promised. Lifting my head, I stretch my neck and exhale. My headache has decreased, I have some of my strength back, and I don't have the shakes anymore.

"Hey, you're awake." Jayden flashes me a smile as he moves his laptop to the side so he can see my face. He has moved to the chair across from me and has his own finished project lying on the table next to him.

"What's the time?" I yawn and stretch out my arms.

"Two o'clock." Jayden responds and my arms freeze mid-air.

"What? Jay, you let me sleep for two hours?" I place my arms down and frown. "What about my project?"

"You mean this one?" He pulls out my button from the chair next to him and passes it to me, which stuns me into silence.

My project is finished. All the designs and the patterns I was stressing about are all done. I'm short of words as I take the button from him. My gaze moves from him and then back to the project. "You...you did this?"

Jayden shrugs. "I promised I'd help." He smiles and then closes his laptop.

"Thank you so much, Jay. This is so kind of you." I bring the button up to inspect his work more closely. He had been listening to all the details I had told him about earlier.

"It was my pleasure, Tee." He says and then stands up. "So Google also recommends you have a hearty breakfast if you're hungover. Since it's way past breakfast time, I figured we could get a hearty lunch instead?" He grins. "What do you say?"

My stomach growls and I wrap my arms around my torso, my cheeks warming up.

"I think your stomach has given us an answer." He laughs. "Come on."

As I follow Jayden down the stairs and out of the library, thoughts of what he has done keep poking into my mind. This was certainly not the reaction I was expecting to get from him. *Why is he so nice to me?*

Well, I'll figure that out later, but for now, I never want to come close to another bottle or glass of alcohol ever again.

A few minutes later, Jayden reappears running up the stairs and I slide his phone back—a little too hard; it almost tips off the edge. I hold my head up with my hands and massage my temples as Jayden settles in his chair again.

"Here," he places two bottles of water in front of me, a chocolate bar, and a flapjack. "They said you need to stay hydrated and get some carbs into you." He reaches into his backpack and pulls out a packet of aspirin. Placing it on the table, his hazel-brown gaze meets mine. "This should help with the headache." He pushes the packet close to me.

"I...I..." The words catch in my throat. What am I supposed to say? Why is he being so nice when I'm responsible for this mess? I sigh and take the open bottle of water from him. "Thanks, Jay."

"You're welcome." His warm smile causes heat to rise in my cheeks.

I devour the golden syrup flapjack and chocolate bar within a few minutes and then empty half the bottle of water before slipping down an aspirin tablet. "That flapjack was delicious." I smile and Jayden does too.

"I'm glad you like it. Now another recommendation is for you to get enough sleep. It doesn't look like you've had much."

I shake my head and start pulling out my project from my backpack. "Jay, I need to finish this by the end of today."

He places a firm grip on my hands to stop me. "No, half an hour will make a big difference."

"But..." I protest.

"How much do you have left to do?" He asks and I take out the project to show him.

"I need to finish these design patterns." I flip open my sketch pad which has the design for the finished button. "You know I like intricate details, so this will take a while."

"But you can't make the details perfect with shaking hands,

great! Now comes the sermon to remind me about how I'm going to hell for getting drunk.

"Tee, you okay?" He pulls a nearby chair close to me and the screeching sound worsens my headache.

"Oh, please stop." I groan and Jayden stops immediately. He lifts the chair and places it gently next to me.

"Sorry." He whispers. "You okay?" He asks again and I shake my head, saying nothing more as I brace myself for his sermon.

"How are you feeling?" He continues in a hushed voice.

I want to lie to him as much as I want to lie to myself that I'm handling this well, but who am I kidding? I don't even remember fixing my hair when I left the dorm room this morning. *I'm a mess.*

"My head hurts." Another groan escapes my lips as I bring my hand up to the top of my head where the pain lives.

"Did you speak to Ellie this morning?"

I shake my head. "She wanted to come over, but I told her I was okay. I think I've caused her enough trouble and embarrassment already."

Jayden remains silent for a few minutes and if I wasn't still staring at his sneakers, I would have thought he left. I wait for him to tell me off, or at least say the words 'I told you so,' but nothing comes. No sermon. No judgemental or sarcastic comments. Nothing.

Then Jayden speaks again. "I'll be right back." He stands up and his retreating footsteps fade in the background.

I lift my head again, catching him running down the stairs to the ground floor. *Wait, where's he going?* I scrunch up my eyebrows as my gaze drops to his unlocked phone on the table.

I know I shouldn't look, but my curiosity gets the better of me and I slide the phone towards me. I squint so my eyes can focus on the words. The page shows a list of things you can do when you have a hangover.

can you?" Jayden lets go of my hands, exposing my tremors. "Okay, how about this? If you rest for half an hour, I'll help you finish it up."

Aww, really? "Jay, you don't have to do this."

"But I want to help. Please, Tee." His pleading finally gets to me.

I need way more than half an hour, but if he's going to help me, then I won't refuse. "Okay, then." I place both arms on the table and rest my head on them. Closing my eyes, I let out a sigh. "Half an hour exactly."

"Yes, Ma'am. I got you."

I smile and close my eyes to welcome the darkness once more and before I know it; I drift off. I don't know how long I sleep for, but when I open my eyes again, Jayden is still sitting next to me as he promised. Lifting my head, I stretch my neck and exhale. My headache has decreased, I have some of my strength back, and I don't have the shakes anymore.

"Hey, you're awake." Jayden flashes me a smile as he moves his laptop to the side so he can see my face. He has moved to the chair across from me and has his own finished project lying on the table next to him.

"What's the time?" I yawn and stretch out my arms.

"Two o'clock." Jayden responds and my arms freeze mid-air.

"What? Jay, you let me sleep for two hours?" I place my arms down and frown. "What about my project?"

"You mean this one?" He pulls out my button from the chair next to him and passes it to me, which stuns me into silence.

My project is finished. All the designs and the patterns I was stressing about are all done. I'm short of words as I take the button from him. My gaze moves from him and then back to the project. "You...you did this?"

Jayden shrugs. "I promised I'd help." He smiles and then closes his laptop.

"Thank you so much, Jay. This is so kind of you." I bring the button up to inspect his work more closely. He had been listening to all the details I had told him about earlier.

"It was my pleasure, Tee." He says and then stands up. "So Google also recommends you have a hearty breakfast if you're hungover. Since it's way past breakfast time, I figured we could get a hearty lunch instead?" He grins. "What do you say?"

My stomach growls and I wrap my arms around my torso, my cheeks warming up.

"I think your stomach has given us an answer." He laughs. "Come on."

As I follow Jayden down the stairs and out of the library, thoughts of what he has done keep poking into my mind. This was certainly not the reaction I was expecting to get from him. *Why is he so nice to me?*

Well, I'll figure that out later, but for now, I never want to come close to another bottle or glass of alcohol ever again.

16

JAYDEN

After Teeyana declined my invitation to the youth group social last month, I followed Anton and Annie's advice and prayed for God to help me show His love to her. She may not be open to sharing her story now, but I believe if she spends more time with people at the youth group, it'll help her confront the questions she has.

Four years ago, I too was on the verge of giving up on God, and finding a church family made me see how God was helping me through the pain. It's a good thing we have monthly youth socials because it'll give me an opportunity to keep asking Teeyana to come.

I asked her again for the second time and honestly, I was expecting another blatant "no," but to my greatest surprise, she gave in with no hesitation. I think her heart is softening and I only have God to thank for that.

"Is that Anton—your youth pastor?" Teeyana leans in close to my ear so I can hear her above the loud music blasting in Anton's living room.

"Yup. That's the man himself. Do you want to meet him?" I place my hand on the small of her back.

"Uh...no, maybe later." She brings her cup of fruit punch to her lips and sips on it.

"Okay, then. Do you—" I open my mouth to say more, but I pause when the music stops and Anton starts speaking.

"Hello, everyone." He leads with a broad smile. "Welcome to one of our many youth socials this year. My name is Anton and this beautiful lady standing next to me is my wife—Annie." He pulls the petite woman close to him, and she wraps one arm around his waist. Annie runs her free hand over her short copper brown hair and flashes a smile at us.

"I know I usually start with a simple prayer, but today I'm encouraged to share briefly from the book of Colossians. Don't worry, kids. This is not a sermon. I promise." We all laugh as we scramble to find seats.

All twenty-four of us find a place to sit, and within a few seconds, our eyes are focusing on Anton. I take out my phone and open my Bible app, before typing in Colossians 1:9-13.

Teeyana is sitting next to me, fiddling with her fingers. After failing to get her attention, I bring my phone close to her and she shuffles close. As Anton speaks, I glance over at her a few times, studying her face to see if she's finding any of his words interesting. Each time, she glances back at me and smiles.

Oh Lord, she's so beautiful.

I shake my head and face the front as Anton says his last words. "I hope y'all have a fun evening. There'll be lots of food at the back. You can split yourselves into teams now and we'll be having our first game in the next five minutes." He glances at the clock before looking in our direction.

Anton makes his way over, and I stand up to greet him. "Hey, buddy." He hugs me before turning over to Teeyana. "And who do we have here?" She stands up and adjusts her purple headband.

"Anton, meet Teeyana—my friend from college. She also majors in Graphic Design." I grin.

"I'm happy to have you here with us today, Teeyana." Anton reaches out and shakes her hand.

"Thank you. I'm happy to be here too." She smiles back before looking at me.

"Jayden has been telling us about you." Anton adds and my eyes widen.

"Oh, has he?" Teeyana raises her eyebrows at me, before turning back to Anton. "And what has he been saying?" She asks with an inquisitive smile.

Oh, no!!!

I press my lips in a thin line as I meet Anton's gaze and shake my head at him.

Anton, this is confidential information. You can't spill.

"Oh, a lot," Anton replies with a grin. "If I remember correctly, he said you're smart and hardworking, you have a lovely smile...oh and that you're pretty, and—"

"Okay," I cut in and wrap my arm around Anton's shoulder, leading him away from Teeyana. "Oh look, it's been five minutes, and it's time for the games to begin. Aren't you coordinating?" I push him away.

Anton laughs and pats my shoulder. "I'll leave you youngsters to it, but I'll be back." He nods at us before heading towards another group of students on the other side of the room.

I let out a sigh and turn to face Teeyana. "Look, in my defence, I told him we were good friends, and I wanted to bring you to one of our socials so he could meet you." I try to explain myself in case she took Anton's words the wrong way.

She laughs at my futile attempt, and crosses her arms. "So you think I'm pretty, huh?"

Go on, Jayden, just say it. The beans have already been spilled.

"Erm...yeah?" I stutter. "Didn't I tell you that already?" I rub the back of my neck.

"Well, not to my face." She smiles.

"Okay, well. I'm telling you now. I...think you're pretty."

Her eyes light up. "Well, thank you." She tucks a piece of hair behind her ear and looks away, giving me a moment to breathe a sigh of relief.

"Anything else you want to tell me to my face?" She looks at me, her dark brown eyes staring deep into mine.

Erm...I like you? No, Jayden.

Lord, is that too soon? What if she doesn't like me back?

"Erm...no." I clear my throat. "That's pretty much it for now." I look over at Anton. "So, may I introduce you to the group then?" I ask, extending my arm to her, and hoping not to leave things awkward.

"Sure." Her eyes twinkle as she locks her arms with mine.

"Yo, Bob." I call out to my roommate, who is talking to Warryn and some other guys from the basketball team.

"Teeyana, this is Bob—my roommate, and this is Warryn—my basketball buddy I was telling you about." I point to them as we approach the other side of the room.

"How's it going, Teeyana?" Warryn waves at her and we all talk for a few minutes.

"Now, who's ready for some games?" Anton exclaims.

"Me!!!" Everyone replies and we gather around again.

As the evening progresses, we start by playing heads up, charades, and then Bible trivia. I go for a few rounds of Bible trivia and charades before encouraging Teeyana to play with me, but she declines and cheers everyone on instead.

"I don't think I know my Bible as much as everyone else in this room, Jay." She whispers in my ear when I ask her to go for the next round of Bible trivia with me.

"I think you know way more than you give yourself credit for." I wink at her before going for my last round.

Teeyana sits not too far away from me and watches. More often than not, when I turn my head, I see her smiling at me. To be honest, I'm not sure if I'm doing this for the fun of it or to impress her.

Oh, who am I kidding? Of course I'm trying to impress her.

After the games, we sit on the bean bags around the TV and start watching a movie as we devour our burgers. "Does this burger taste better than the one you had at the freshman barbecue?" I ask Teeyana. "It's okay. You can be honest."

She nods and bites into her burger. "Home-made burgers are the best." She muffles and wipes the corners of her mouth.

"I think so too." I laugh as the ketchup drips from her burger and stains her top.

"Oh, dang it. This is what you get when the food is too good." She smudges the ketchup with her fingers and makes the stain even bigger.

"Very true. We'll always blame it on the burgers." I hand her some tissues, and she chuckles.

Lord, would now be a good time to ask her out on a date? What about lunch? Or supper?

Oh, never mind. I can try again another day.

It's in times like this I wish Tyler was here. He would've known exactly what to do in this situation.

17

TEEYANA

"Yes, I got the results I wanted." I smile at Mom and Dad on my laptop screen as I wave my finished button project at them. "My professor was impressed, so I hope I get a good grade for it." I catch a glimpse of the perfect patterns and my heart swells with gratitude. I would've never done it without Jayden.

"Sweetie, that's great and we're so proud of you." Mom cheers. "You should keep that button as a souvenir—your first completed project of graphic design school." She locks arms with Dad and he nods in agreement with her.

"So...how is your new friend?" Mom changes the subject. "Did you say his name is Jayden?" She inserts a cheeky smile before looking at Dad.

Of course she remembers his name. Mom never forgets the details even if you mention something once. I place the button on my bed and wipe the dust off my laptop screen with the sleeve of my hoodie. Then I bury my face in my hands to hide the broad smile on my face.

"Oh, what does this smile mean? Please tell us, because we

have no idea." Dad grins. Of course he's in on this too. I know what they want to hear, but I won't tell them.

"Jayden is fine, Mom." I uncover my face and adjust my headphones. "I went to his youth group social last month, and it was fun."

"That's great." Mom says. "And what about church?"

"Erm...Jayden found a church and I'll be checking it out soon. It's called Faith Baptist Church, and I've met the youth pastor there. His name is Anton, he seems cool, and he reminds me of Kevin."

Even though I only accepted to go to the youth group social as a thank you for Jayden's help, I ended up having a lot of fun. I'm still not interested in going to church with him, but he keeps asking nicely, so I promised I'd think about it. After all, all I have to do is show up and *not* listen. I've been doing that well for the past four years anyway.

"I'm so happy you've found a church, honey." Mom smiles. "I'm sure Kevin will be pleased to hear that too. He always asks after you."

"What about that book Kevin gave you? Have you made a start yet?" Dad asks.

Oh, crap!!!

"Erm...yeah." I drop my gaze to my laptop keypad. "I did."

To be honest, I opened it with every intention to read, but I couldn't bring myself to do it.

"I read the first few chapters the other day, but I haven't gotten very far. I'll update you when I read more." I glance outside my window, hoping Dad won't ask more questions.

"Great!!! So are you sure you don't want to tell us more about Jayden?" Mom jumps in again, her eyes wide with excitement.

"*Ugh*, Mom. Please let it go." I whine. "If there's anything to tell, I'll fill you in when I come home for Christmas. How about that?"

"You promise?" She raises her eyebrows.

"Yes, I promise."

"Okay then, if you say so." She relaxes again in her seat.

I glance at the time at the bottom corner of my laptop screen and gasp. "Oh no, I have to go now. I'm meeting my study group in ten minutes. Please send my hugs and kisses to Danny. Tell him I love him and tell Grandma and Grandpa I miss them, and can't wait to see them at Christmas. I love you." I spew out the words all in one go.

"Oh okay, honey. We love you. Bye." Mom and Dad wave at me.

I close my laptop and put my headphones down, before rubbing the back of my neck.

"It must be nice to have a functional family." Heather says, while laying on her bed with her back facing me. "It must be nice." She repeats, with a sarcastic tone.

"I thought you were sleeping. Sorry, did I wake you?" I ask.

"Why do you care?" She replies, with her back still facing me.

I sigh and turn my face away. Every conversation with this girl is an uphill battle. *Why do I even bother?*

"I care way more than you think, Heather. If you give people a chance, you'll see that they're not what you've made them out to be." I respond. "And yes, I'm grateful for my family. I'm blessed to have them." I drag myself to the edge of my bed and jump off.

"Blessed?" Heather scoffs. "So you believe in this God stuff too? I would have thought an intelligent girl like you would know better than to put your trust in empty promises from some man-made book."

Oh, is this the part where I have to say something to defend my faith? Ugh, give me a break.

"Heather, there are many intelligent people out there who

believe in some sort of...higher power. I'm not the first and I'm sure I won't be the last." I slip my feet into my trainers and crouch down to tie my shoelaces.

"I see. So why do you believe? Because He blesses you? He loves you? He has made you smart, and pretty, and given you a functional family?" Heather turns to look at me.

"What about people like me, huh?" She continues. "Some of us who don't have anyone to call a family? Would you still believe in God if things weren't working for you? If you didn't have all you have now? Would you?" Her green eyes pierce right through me, almost as if we had a personal score to settle.

I open my mouth to say something—anything, but I can't. I don't know if Heather's burning green eyes are causing the words to elude me or if I just have nothing to say. I avert my gaze and let it slide to the tattoo on her wrist. The word drawn in black ink is now in full view, but I'm too far away to read what it says.

Bringing myself back to the conversation, I take a step towards Heather. "Look, I understand where you're coming from but—"

"Do you really?" Heather snorts and I frown.

Does she think she's the only one with problems?

"Trust me, I do." I respond, trying to suppress the annoyance now bubbling up in my chest. "I'm still trying to figure things out for myself. But everyone around me believes leaving it all to God is the best thing to do."

"That's being lazy though, don't you think?" Heather sits up and leans her back against the wall. "Don't you think you should take control of your *own* life and live it the way *you* want? Why do you have to depend on a God you can't see when you can make do with the things you have at your disposal?"

If I had had this conversation with Heather before I met Jayden, then we would have been best friends now. But I'm not sure what I believe anymore. All I've felt is resentment towards God for the past four years, but perhaps I'm missing something because Jayden is content with his faith.

I've wanted to tell him so many times how ridiculous and naïve he sounds when he talks about how good God is. But I can't do that because I can see for myself that he is happy. Something about him intrigues me. I want to know why he's so confident, and why he has no problems. But of course I won't tell Heather this. We're not even friends.

"Erm..." I rub my forehead and pretend to look around for my dorm room keys, which I know are in my bag.

Okay, Teeyana, this is the part where you have to either agree with her or disagree. Come on, say something clever.

I open my mouth to speak, but my phone starts buzzing and Jayden's name flashes on my screen.

Oh, just the right person to save the day. This is clutch!!!

"Hello?" I press the phone against my ear. "Yeah...no that's fine...yeah, I'm on my way."

I pick up my backpack and head for the door. "I would have loved to continue this conversation, Heather, but perhaps some other time." I rush out the door and try my best to avoid her gaze.

~

"Can you pass me an ornament, please?" I elbow Jayden, who is standing next to me.

"Sure, what colour do you want?" he asks, before bending over the box of ornaments sitting on the windowsill.

I shrug. "I don't mind."

He rummages through the box and hands me one. "There you go."

"Why did you go for the purple one?" I take the ornament from his hand.

"Eerm...because purple is your favourite colour? Duh!" He grins, clearly feeling pleased with himself for getting that right.

I smile and tuck loose baby hairs behind my ears.

He glances over at me and our eyes meet, making my heart flutter. I turn to face forward again, before reminding myself of the real reason I asked for the ornament—to hang it up on the Christmas tree in front of us.

We've spent the last two hours decorating it for our Christmas social, and I can already see how much Anton's apartment has been brought to life. Looking out the window, I catch a glimpse of the flashing Christmas lights and decorations all around his neighbourhood.

Anton even asked Jayden to wrap tinsel around the fire escape stairs. I don't think it can get any more Christmassy than this.

"Gather around, children. It's time to light this bad boy up and you don't want to miss this." Anton announces as everyone gathers around the tree and starts counting down.

"5...4...3...2...1"

Anton flips the switch and loud cheers erupt from us as the room beams with flashing red, green, and blue lights. Annie turns on the Christmas tunes and everyone settles down as we go straight into our first game of the night.

Unlike the first time when I refused to take part, I'm willing to join in this time because it looks fun. Plus, I don't want to have to explain to everyone why I'm not playing.

We divide ourselves into six teams of five, and each team has to create an aspect of the Christmas story in an hour—using nothing else but tin foil.

Jayden and I are on the same team, and we're going to recreate the scene of Jesus in the manger. Anton and Annie will be the judges and they patrol the room, making sure everyone is adhering to the rules. We plunge straight into our task and the room is soon filled with giggling, chattering, and rattling.

An hour later, a representative from each team uses one minute to present their work, and an applause rises every time someone walks up to the front. Our team is the last to present and Jayden takes the lead.

He presents our miniature baby Jesus in a manger, Joseph, Mary, and the three wise men with their staff. He also draws attention to the hay we made with bits of tinfoil and also our attempt to light up the scene using the torchlights from our smartphones.

Everyone in the room applauds our efforts and they turn to Anton and Annie, telling them our project is the best.

"Wow, y'all don't know much about competition, do you?" Anton gasps. "Y'all just going to make them the winners?" He points towards us and everyone nods. "Just like that? Jeremy, I thought your attempt at the donkey was quite good." He says to the tall, blonde-haired guy.

Jeremy shrugs. "Yeah, but with my height, I look more like a giraffe or a camel than a donkey." He laughs and points to the tin foil on his head which is supposed to be his donkey ears.

"Well, the final decision still lies in our hands." Anton smirks and puts his arm around Annie, drawing her close to him. "We'll be back in five minutes." They turn their backs against us, pretending to be serious about trying to choose a winner.

"Attention, little ones." Anton announces again and we all turn to him. "As you know, we're all winners in Christ and above all, we're more than conquerors." He grins.

"Yeah, but only one team gets the chocolate." Jayden shouts out, drawing laughter from the crowd.

"Yes, Jayden. I was about to say that only one team gets to

take home this perishable prize." He waves the massive box of chocolate shaped like a Christmas tree.

"The winner of this year's *Game On* is...drum rolls, please?" We stamp our feet. "Give it up for Team Jayden with their creation of Jesus in the manger." Everyone cheers as we bow and receive our prize.

I give Jayden a high five, but he catches me off-guard when he hugs me instead and lifts me off the ground. His broad frame swirls me around before putting me back down again, and I smile so much my cheeks start hurting.

A few minutes later, Annie announces it's time to exchange secret Santa gifts. After giving my gift to Laura—the girl who majors in Biology, Jayden places a wrapped gift in front of me.

"Who is it for?" I scrunch my eyebrows.

He tilts his head. "Really?"

"What? You refused to tell me who you were buying for, remember? I wonder who picked my name." I scan the room. Everyone else has received a gift, including Jayden. Then it all makes sense.

"Wait...is this for me?" I point to the gift and smile at him.

He rolls his eyes and shakes his head "It only took you ten years to figure it out, didn't it?"

"Hey," I push his arm. "In my defence, I wasn't expecting to get a gift from you."

"Well...I have a confession to make." He rubs the back of his neck.

I lean forward and rest my chin between my cupped hands. "Spill it, boy." I try to keep a serious face, even though his charming hazel-brown eyes are distracting me.

"I didn't pick your name out of the hat—Jeremy did. But I chased him down and begged him to swap with me." He flashes me a nervous smile.

"Really? Why?" I arch an eyebrow.

He shrugs. "Well, let's say I wanted to buy you something?"

Aww. Why do I feel so warm and fuzzy inside? I mean, he didn't have to do this. He could have bought me something, anyway. He's so adorable.

Jayden pushes the gift towards me. "So...are you going to open it?"

"Of course." I strip away the wrapping paper to reveal the back of a large photo frame. When I turn the frame over, there's a photo of myself smiling.

I gasp and my hand covers my mouth. "Oh my God. Jay, when did you do this?" I run my hands over the Bible verse next to my smiling face.

"I know you have a thing for quotes. You have them stuck to your notebooks and your phone. I bet you have a whole wall full of quotes in your room, so I thought I'd give you not just an empowering quote, but a Bible verse. It's my favourite Bible verse and I hope when you look at it on your wall, it'll remind you of me, how beautiful you are, and how much God loves you."

I'm not sure what warms my heart more, the fact that he took out time to do this for me, the fact that I love the photo he chose, or the fact that he called me beautiful.

"Thank you so much, Jay. This was so thoughtful of you. I love it. I know I'm not photogenic, but this photo is gorgeous."

"It's your smile." Jayden nods. "It's charming, and it lights up a room."

I shake my head. "Hmm. Hmm. If anyone has a charming smile here, boy, it's you. Your smile could light up the world." *Well, it could light up my world.* "But I'm sure you've heard that compliment many times before." I continue to run my hands along the photo frame.

"Even if I have, I think it sounds better coming from you." His dimpled smile draws a giggle from my lips.

He sure has a way with his words.

Our little moment is interrupted by Jeremy giving everyone a dance challenge. He asks us to put on the radio and dance to the first song that comes on. Anton presses the button on the radio and of course, the first song is our one and only "All I Want For Christmas" by Mariah Carey.

As I struggle to mimic Mariah's high notes, Jayden drags me to the dance floor, but I resist. "Oh gosh, no. Jay, I can't dance."

"Nuh-uh." He cuts in. "With God, everything is possible, Tee. Besides, I can't dance either and there's no way you're letting me embarrass myself on my own." He winks at me and moves my arms in accordance with the rhythm of the song.

We push the sofas and tables against the wall to create a central open space as more people join us on our pretend dance floor. Jayden pulls me in and closes the gap between us as we move from side to side. I put my arms around his broad shoulders and he holds my waist as we dance.

He is close enough that I can feel his breath against my forehead. Close enough for me to make out his strong jawline. Close enough to notice his dimpled cheeks covered in stubble. *I bet he'd look so good with a full beard.*

I let out a breath when our eyes meet and wish everything around us could fizzle away so I could get lost in his hazel brown eyes for as long as I can.

18

JAYDEN

I park my car next to the curb and take a quick glance at my watch. "Yes!!!" I pump my fists in the air. "I told you I was going to get you back before ten p.m. Who's laughing now, hmm?"

Teeyana laughs and shakes her head. "Well done. I shouldn't have doubted you." She relaxes in the passenger seat.

"Sometimes, you gotta have faith." I adjust the collar of my shirt, trying too hard to look pleased with myself.

"Yes, I think you deserve the accolades on this one." Teeyana nods. "Thanks for driving me home, Jay. I had a lot of fun tonight."

"I'm glad you had fun. Everyone loves you. You're part of the family now, so please come to church with us anytime you want." I nod.

Her smile fades, and she clears her throat.

Lord, I hope mentioning church again hasn't put her off.

"Anton reminds me of my youth pastor back in Boston." Teeyana turns to face the front. "His name is Kevin, and he's cool too. He gave me a book called *How To Stick To Your Faith At College*."

"Oh yeah? I've read that book. It has practical examples of things you could do, and I'd recommend it if you're interested." I nod at her.

"Yeah, I read the first chapter some time ago. It said to stick with like-minded people and that's why I've been trying to get involved." Her gaze drops to her phone on her lap.

"Well, if my opinion means anything to you, I think you made a good decision." I wait for her response, but she remains silent.

I wait some more, but her head is still down, and she's now tapping her phone with her fingernail.

Lord, should I wait until she's ready to talk or should I prod her a bit more?

"Tee?" She lifts her head and looks at me. "Are you okay?"

After what feels like forever, she lets out a sigh and speaks.

"Why are you so confident, Jay?" she asks. "This confidence you have in God—what is it based on? I thought I was confident, but I have so many doubts."

"Why do you have doubts, Tee?" I pause. "Did something happen? Do you want to talk about it?" I raise my eyebrows.

She nods and looks out the window. "Over four years ago, my parents and I lived in L.A. My dad was working for a big PR firm called EKC at the time and we were *very* comfortable. My mom was pregnant with Danny. I'd been praying for a little brother for so long, so I was excited for him to join our family." She pauses and takes a deep breath.

"I used to believe that God looks out for His children and saves them from any kind of harm. I believed He delivers the righteous from all afflictions and always has their backs." She sniffs.

I wait patiently and attentively for the second half of her story. She takes her time, but I don't push her or say anything. I just let her speak.

"But then," she continues. "One night my parents came back home after they'd been out all day. I spent the entire day with my Aunt Bella, shopping, painting each other's nails, and I tired her out by making her watch the *The Prince of Egypt* twice through." She laughs.

"After Aunt Bella prayed with me and returned downstairs, I sneaked out of bed and started working on a drawing so I could stay awake until my parents got back. I suspected they were all hiding something from me and I was right." Her voice strains as she palms the tears rolling down her cheeks.

"My dad got into trouble at work because his company was involved in some dubious business with one of their most committed clients. His boss asked him to be part of it and my dad—being the honest man that he is, chose not to get involved. They gave him a choice to be part of them or suffer the consequences, and when he refused to join them, his boss fired him." Teeyana shakes her head.

"My dad had been working in that company for twelve years. He'd worked his way from the bottom, all the way up to the marketing communications manager. But they didn't care about any of that. What hurts the most, is that not only did they fire him, but his boss went the extra mile to sue him for fraudulent activities."

"No way!!!" I exclaim. "That's horrible. How did he do that? What evidence did he have?"

"I don't know." She shrugs. "They knew my dad was going to fight back, so to prevent him from ratting them out, they made sure he had nothing to defend himself with. They took my dad to court, and it was their word against his. We lost all the money we had in that four-month ordeal. By the time the case was over, we had no money, no source of income, a baby on the way, and no place to lay our heads. We couldn't afford our house anymore, so we left L.A. and moved in with my grandparents in Atlanta."

I sigh and shake my head. "I'm so sorry to hear your family went through all that. How did your mom handle it with the pregnancy?"

Teeyana closes her eyes and more tears roll down. "Mom had a lot of complications during her pregnancy. The stress got to her, and she spent a lot of time in the hospital for many weeks leading up to Danny's birth. Her blood pressure went through the roof and she was diagnosed with preeclampsia. The doctors told her the only way out was to deliver Danny early. Danny was born prematurely, and he had problems with his lungs and his heart." She sniffs.

"You should have seen him, Jay. They stuck so many wires to his tiny body, and they had a machine that helped him breathe because his little lungs weren't developed enough. He also had several operations to fix the problems with his heart." She sobs.

"Every morning when I woke up, I prepared myself for the news that Danny was gone. But he kept fighting, and he stayed in hospital for fifty-four days. I still don't know how both he and my mom survived all of that." She covers her face with her palms and sobs.

Looking inside the glove box of my car, I take out a box of tissues and hand it to her. She takes one tissue out of the box and blows her nose. "When the madness was over, we had to pay all the hospital bills, but we didn't have enough insurance. My dad had to take up a job at the church where he worked with my grandpa. After two years, we were able to save enough money to move to Boston when Dad's friend helped him find a job in his PR firm."

"My dad worked there for a year, but then quit the job and took up a full-time job at our church as one of the mission leaders. He has been working there ever since and he says he is loving it." She shrugs.

"I'm glad he loves his new job." I smile at her.

"Yeah." She tries to smile, but it fades away again. She unbuckles her seatbelt and adjusts into her seat. "I've always wondered why, Jay." When she looks up at me, I can make out the desperation in her eyes. A desperation for answers.

"Why did God let all these things happen to us? They accused my dad of a crime he didn't commit, and he never got the justice he deserved. All that stress, the sleepless nights, the tears, the pain, my mom and brother almost dying? Was all of that necessary?" She shakes her head. "My dad is a good man, so why him? What did he do wrong? Does God punish people for no reason at all?"

I take a deep breath and anticipate when I should come in. *Lord, please give me the right words to say.* I wait for Teeyana's sobs to die down and when she stops wiping her eyes; I hold on to her free hand and give it a gentle squeeze before giving her a moment to calm down.

Tonight reminds me of all those nights I rolled in my bed, hoping that someone would explain to me why my world was crashing down. It reminds me of all the times I thought I would never get out of that dark tunnel of depression. I only ever saw the light again because God helped me, and now, all I want to do is point Teeyana towards that light. The same light which saved me.

"You know the story in the Bible about the man who was born blind?" I ask.

"Erm...it sounds familiar, but I don't remember the details." Teeyana says as she brushes off tissue particles stuck to her damp cheeks.

"Jesus' disciples asked if the man was suffering for his sins or the sins of his parents, and do you know what Jesus told them?"

I pause. "He told them that neither the man nor his parents had done anything wrong. He also said it had happened so that the works of God could be displayed in him. That day, Jesus restored sight to the blind man, and he went on testifying about the goodness of God. Now my question to you is, if this man hadn't been born blind, would he have ever known Jesus to be a healer?"

Teeyana shakes her head. "I guess not."

"There's a song by the late Andraé Crouch which I love." I continue. "It's called 'Through It All' and the second verse says that if we never have any problems, then we would never know that God is a problem solver and then we would never know what faith in God could do." I wipe off the remaining bits of tissue from her cheek.

"You went through a lot, Tee. But when the situation felt hopeless, and you thought your mom and Danny were going to die, they didn't. Your family lost everything, but God provided for you. He was walking beside you even though you didn't realise it. I don't believe our trials are in vain, Tee. I believe that there's no pain without a purpose."

Teeyana sighs. "That's what I wanted to believe, but I never thought God was with us or with me. I thought He'd left me a long time ago. He feels distant, and my relationship with Him has become non-existent. That's why I try to figure everything out on my own. I thought that if God isn't for me, then I won't sit around and do nothing. I'll work hard and achieve my goals and not let anything break me."

"I have no doubt that you're a strong girl, Tee. But I also have no doubt that God is the *only* source of the strength you have." I squeeze her hand again. "He is the One who empowers you to be the beautiful genius you are." I tilt my head and smile at her.

She returns my smile and sniffs. "Maybe you're right." She looks me in the eye. "I'll think about what you've said."

I nod and lean closer. "Tee, you are not alone in your battles. You need to surround yourself with a family you can draw strength from. Please come to church with me tomorrow?"

I hold my breath, waiting for her to reply as she stares at me.

She blinks many times and replies, "Okay, I guess I could come to church with you before we go back to Boston."

"Really? That would be awesome." I straighten in my seat. "Do you...want me to pray with you right now?" I ask.

"Erm, no that's alright, but thanks anyway. You have no idea how much this conversation has helped me."

"No, thank you for talking to me. It takes a lot of courage to open up the way you just did." *The courage I don't have.*

"You can talk to me anytime you want, okay?" I reassure her.

She nods. "Okay. Sorry if I look a mess—these tears weren't planned, I promise." She pulls down the sun visor mirror and fixes her hair as her curls brush her shoulder.

"A little tears never hurt anyone, Tee." I grin. "And you look fine—beautiful, if I must say." The words leave my lips, so carefree now, and they make Teeyana smile.

I take a glance at my watch again. "Whoa. It's almost ten p.m so little Missy, you need to get some rest." I touch her nose and she chuckles. "Church starts at nine a.m. tomorrow, it's way past my bedtime, and if I don't sleep soon, I'll sleep through my alarm."

"Oh, don't worry, I'll make sure you wake up even if I have to drag you there myself." She smiles.

I step out of the car and walk to the other side to open the door for her. She steps out and takes me off-guard when she wraps her arms around my torso and buries her face in my chest.

I relax into her embrace and engulf her tiny frame, supporting her head on my chest and stroking her hair. She has stopped crying, but I can still feel all her emotions through her hug. My heart grows heavy and I swallow the lump in my throat as my vision blurs with tears. *Lord, please help me be strong for her.*

"You're going to be okay, Tee." I wipe the tears from my face and rest my head on hers. "No matter what happens, please keep holding on to God. You're going to be okay." Little does Teeyana know these words are as much for me as they are for her.

19

TEEYANA

Christmas decorations at our local mall in Boston are a sight worth beholding. Pastel-coloured flashing lights hang around the doors of every shop, and a giant Christmas tree sits at the centre of the mall. The tree is surrounded by at least a hundred boxes of fake, beautifully wrapped gifts which have grabbed the children's attention.

Amara and I are wandering around the mall as we always do, our arms linked, and our thick coats clenched against our chests. This time, we're trying to find a last-minute Christmas gift for Danny while Amara tells me about her experience at Spelman.

"So all the girls in the sorority were wearing blue and white striped overalls and they stood in a straight line," Amara leans in. "Each girl wrapped her arms around the waist of the girl in front of her and then, before my eyes, they all leaned backwards until the head of the last girl touched the floor." Amara's eyes widen in awe.

"No way!!! And they were all still linked up?" I try to create the scene in my head.

"Yeah, and the girl at the front of the line got her feet off the ground and her legs were facing upwards to the sky." Amara raises her voice. "All I could think about was how I can't even bend over to touch my toes." She giggles. "Girl, I need to get some serious stretching lessons to get my back to bend like that." She clicks her fingers.

"Yeah me and you both." I nod and head towards the toy store. "Let's try that store over there." I drag Amara by the arm as we push against the crowd of children and parents going in the direction of the queue to see Santa.

"Girl, if you're going to drag me around like this, then you have to reward me by telling me what happened at the Christmas party. I can't be the only one telling you stories." Amara stops to catch her breath.

"*Ugh*, Amara, there's no time for this. The mall is closing soon." I try to take her by the arm again, but she steps back.

"Nuh-uh. The mall closes in two hours, so we've got time." She leans in and wiggles her eyebrows.

"What?" I frown, pretending not to know what she's thinking.

"Oh, come on. You know what I mean." She pushes me with her hip, upsetting my balance. "What happened between you and Jayden at the party?"

My face lights up at the mention of Jayden's name. I turn my head away to hide the broad smile creeping up on my face, but Amara sees it.

"Wow, you like him, don't you?" Amara puts her arm around my shoulder.

"Well, he's cool, genuine, and a gentleman." I avoid her question.

"That's what I like to hear but girl, give me deets, please?" Amara sits on one of the benches attached to the wall and beckons to me.

I roll my eyes and plop down next to her. "We danced

together, and when he hugged me, it felt like we were floating in the clouds. I'm not even joking." I grin.

"Oooh, did you guys kiss?" Amara grins.

"*Pfft*. Girl, no." I push her arm. "I told you we're just friends."

"No, you're not." Amara rolls her eyes. "You can't hug a friend and feel like you're floating in the clouds."

"Oh, whatever." I wave my hand dismissively, even though I know she's right.

"He likes you and soon I'll be singing, '*Teeyana and Jayden sitting in a tree. K-I-S-S-I-N-G.*'" Amara claps her hands in my face.

"Girl, be quiet." I laugh. "Don't you think if he liked me, he would have told me already?" I ask.

"Yeah, but what if he's scared to tell you?" Amara defends him.

I shake my head. "Nuh-uh. He told me I was pretty, and I *specifically* asked if he had anything else to tell me, but he said no."

"Oh, be patient, girl. I'm sure he'll tell you after the Christmas break."

"Hmm." I bite my bottom lip. "Amara, I think your ears have heard enough so let's go, please." I stand up.

"No, wait. My ears can never hear enough." She pulls me by the arm, forcing me to sit down again. "How is the red-haired girl?"

My smile disappears. "Heather? *Ugh*, I don't know what her problem is, you know?" I shake my head. "From the little I've gathered, her parents are divorced, and she lives with her dad, who she bullies with every opportunity she gets. She also finds pleasure in bullying me because she can. I've tried countless times to be nice to her, but she keeps pushing me away, so I won't bother anymore."

"Wow, sounds like the girl has got some mad problems."

Amara taps her chin with her forefinger. "I'm sorry, girl. You never get a break from people like Olivia Hastings, do you?"

"That's what I told Jayden when I was ranting to him about it." I pause and my smile returns. "But he insisted that everyone has a potential to do good things, no matter how vile they may be. Even Heather and Olivia."

"Well, I think no matter how hard the rain falls, it can never wash away a leopard's spots." Amara sneaks in a Nigerian proverb. "It's hard for people to change. I'm not saying they can't. I'm saying it's hard."

"Yeah, but even though I don't like Heather, a part of me is hoping she'll come around because I think there's more to her than that barrier she's put up." I say.

Amara touches my forehead with the back of her hand—a joke she does when I say something unexpected and she wants to "check if I'm okay."

"Wow, this Jayden boy has changed you, hasn't he?"

I push her hand away. "No, I'm just realising that the world is not only full of bad people after all. There are genuine, and kind people out there too, you know?"

"Kind people like Jayden, huh? Well if you say so, girl." Amara sighs.

"Okay, now I think your ears have heard enough, so can we go? I need to get that race car toy for Danny before it goes out of stock." I hold Amara's hand and drag her around the group of teenage girls next to the jewellery stand.

We're about to enter another toy store when my phone vibrates in my pocket. I take it out and press the answer button as we walk further into the store.

"Hello? Mom?" I strain to make out her words as I'm standing underneath the loud speakers blasting "Jingle Bells."

"Hello?" I place my forefinger in my free ear to block out the noise, but the call cuts off. We walk out of the store and move to a corner of the mall with fewer people. I dial Mom's number again and this time, I can hear her clearly.

She's sniffing. She's crying.

"Mom? What's wrong?" Before Mom can say anything, the call cuts off again.

Amara stares at me blankly. "What's going on?"

"I don't know. I...I need to go home now." I rush past Amara and we both run to the nearest exit. I dial Mom's number again, but I can't reach her.

Ugh, the service at this mall can be terrible sometimes.

When we get outside, I stop next to a curb-side recycling bin when my phone rings again. My heart thumps as I bring the phone to my ear.

"Mom?"

"Teeyana? Baby, please come home. Please come home now." Mom's shaky voice comes through.

"Okay, Mom. I'm on my way." I was right. She is crying.

Amara and I slip on our coats and put on our gloves before running down the street to my house, which is a ten-minute walk away. A million and one thoughts run through my head as I swing my hands side by side and channel my energy into my sprint.

I hope this is Mom freaking out about something irrelevant, like she always does. Please, let it be something irrelevant.

20

TEEYANA

My heels hit the ground hard and the force from the impact travels up to my knees as I run. Looking over my shoulder, I spot Amara's big curly weave a few meters away, striving to keep up with me. I slow down and power walk so I can catch my breath before picking up speed again.

As I round the corner onto our street, memories of Danny break into my thoughts. He has always been a playful child and he has kept me on my toes for the past four years.

Every time Danny and I walk down this road from the mall, he would challenge me to race him. He would start running as fast as he could, without caring about the carrier bags in my hands.

"Race you." Danny would say before taking to his heels. I always let him run farther ahead, before I start running. I'd watch him stomp his little feet as fast as he can until he gets to the lamppost, which is our official finish line.

Sometimes, I pretend to have leg cramps to get out of running, but Danny would run up to me and help me get back on my feet. I always let him win in the end, and every time he crossed the finish line, I'd cheer him on with every breath in me. "Yes, Danny!!! You go, boy. Someday, you'll be the next Usain Bolt."

Danny would let out his cute giggle and strike a pose like Usain Bolt as he leans his body to one side and points both his arms to the opposite side.

This time around, running down this same road sends a repulsive wave of anxiety through me. After everything that has happened in my family, I don't think my heart is strong enough to bear another piece of bad news.

I hope Danny is okay.

I look over my shoulder again to check if Amara is still behind me. "Don't worry girl, I'll catch up with you. You go ahead." Amara shouts between breaths.

I nod and pick up speed again, running down the street until our house comes into full view. Stopping in front of the stairs, I clutch on to the left side of my abdomen, waiting for the gripping pain to disappear.

As I climb up the stairs to the front porch, something in my peripheral vision catches my attention. It's a blue Toyota Corolla parked in our driveway.

My eyes widen when it hits me.

That's Aunt Bella's car. What is she doing here?

It's six days until Christmas and we planned to travel to Atlanta in four days to spend Christmas with my grandparents. Mom told me Aunt Bella was going to meet us there, so why is she here?

I shake myself out of my thoughts and wrap my knuckles around the doorknob, but I'm unable to move my legs. I want to go in but I'm afraid—too afraid to face what is waiting for me inside.

I close my eyes and try to expel all the negative thoughts in my head when Amara touches my shoulder and I flinch. "What's wrong, girl?"

I turn around and hug her and she squeezes me tight. "What if something has happened to Danny? I can't bear it." My heart races again.

Amara cups my face in her hands. "Girl, what if nothing has happened?"

"But my mom was crying. That's not a good sign." My chest heaves in between my words.

"I know, but girl, you are strong." Amara grabs both my arms. "You can face whatever is waiting for you in there."

I shake my head as the tears run down my face. "I can't do this—"

"Yes, you can." Amara cuts in. "I'm right here with you, but you have to face this, okay? You have no choice. You have to do this and you have to do it now."

Amara moves her hands up to my shoulders and gives me a reassuring squeeze.

After taking a few deep breaths, I let go of Amara and exhale. She laces her fingers with mine as I open the door and we enter the house together.

We walk down the corridor and into the living room and the scene we walk into looks uncomfortably familiar. Mom is sitting on the sofa across from the TV, and Aunt Bella has her arms wrapped around Mom's shoulders. Dad is sitting on the sofa next to them, his head buried in his palms.

This is a deja vu moment. I've seen this all before.

This is the same scene I walked into that fateful night, four years ago, when Dad told me our lives were about to change forever. The only difference now is that Aunt Bella is crying, and I don't think I've ever seen her cry before.

My stomach tightens, and I swallow to wet my dry mouth.

When the wave of nausea passes, I let go of Amara's hand and step forward. "Mom, what's wrong?" My bottom lip quivers.

Whilst waiting for her response, I scan the room, my eyes searching for Danny, who was sitting in his special chair watching *SpongeBob* when we left for the mall an hour ago.

"Where is Danny? Is he alright?" My voice cracks. Part of me doesn't want to know the answer, but the other part of me wishes my parents wouldn't be so good at withholding information.

"Danny is okay, Sweetie." Mom replies between her sobs. "He fell asleep while waiting for you, so I took him to his room."

I breathe out a sigh of relief. "O-kay, so what's going on? Aunt Bella, why's Mom crying? Why are *you* crying?" Her tear-filled amber eyes stare at me. She brushes her burgundy faux-locs to the side of her face and opens her mouth to speak, but the words don't come out. She looks at Mom and they both start sobbing again.

"Dad?" I give up and turn to Dad. He is my last resort. I should've known I wouldn't be getting anything out of Mom or Aunt Bella.

"Sweetie," Dad lifts his head to look at me. "We need to leave for Atlanta today."

I study his face as the words come out of his mouth. "Oh, I thought we weren't leaving until Wednesday? Do Grandma and Grandpa want us to come earlier?" I search his face again, and his muscles tighten. My eyes widen.

Does this have anything to do with my grandparents?

"Honey," Dad stands up and walks up to me. "Your grandma was involved in a car accident."

My intestines shrivel up inside me as if I've been punched in my stomach. I take a few steps back, trying to find my balance, and almost bump into Amara, who I'd forgotten was standing behind me.

"What...what happened?" I stutter and Amara holds my arm.

"Your grandpa called, and he said she was hit by a truck while crossing the road earlier this morning." Dad responds.

"A truck?" My heart thumps faster and louder. "Is...is she still alive?"

"Yes, honey." Dad nods.

"Is she going to be okay? Is it bad?" My hands tremble.

"I don't know, honey." He shakes his head. "She's currently in a coma and that's all we know." He squeezes my shoulder. "We need to leave now."

21

TEEYANA

The car journey to the hospital is long and quiet—our silence being a clear sign that everyone feels the impending doom lurking around the corner. Well, everyone except Danny—who is fast asleep in his car seat next to me.

I look out the car window and catch the grey clouds floating in the distance. *I can't believe I'm about to say this but...God, if You can hear me, I know everyone says You are good so please, if that is true, let Grandma survive this.*

Aunt Bella sighs on the other side of Danny and adjusts her seatbelt. Her eyes are closed, but I know she's not sleeping. She taps her fingers on her lap from time to time, tears occasionally leaking from her eyes.

Mom and Dad sit in silence as Dad drives, his hands fixed on the wheel and his eyes never leaving the road. Mom is leaning her head against the window and I wonder if she's praying too, or if she's bracing herself for the worst.

We've been driving for almost two hours in silence. I know Mom hates the silence, and she usually makes sure we have music playing in the car. But now, it seems the silence has engulfed her.

I lean forward to speak, but Mom moves her head away from the window and looks over her shoulder at us. "Do you mind if I play some music?" She asks, her voice gravelly from all the crying. "I know this isn't the best time, but I'll keep it down. I need something to keep me distracted so I don't go insane." She sniffs and blinks her now-puffy eyelids.

"It's okay, Mom. I don't mind." I squeeze her shoulder before leaning back in my seat.

"Bella?"

Aunt Bella nods with her eyes still closed, but she doesn't utter a word.

Mom opens the glove box and looks through some CDs. She slips one of them into the radio and a song starts playing. Mom keeps her word by turning the volume down, and I snap my head up at the familiar guitar rhythm.

Why do I know this song?

I squint and tilt my head, ransacking my brain to remember where I'd heard it before when it hits me.

It's from Jayden's car.

He mentioned it was called "Whom Shall I Fear?" and that someone he knows loves Chris Tomlin. The song came up every time he drove me in his car.

I lean back and hum the chorus. Those are the only lyrics I know because Jayden sings them out loud every time. "*God is on your side, Tee.*" That's what Jayden would say if he was here. I hope he's right.

The last time I spoke to him was yesterday before Amara and I left for the mall. He promised to call me today, but I'm glad he hasn't. I'm not ready to speak to him yet.

My phone vibrates in my pocket and when I take it out, it's a text notification—from Jayden.

. . .

Hey Tee :)

Sorry I didn't call you earlier. I was kinda caught up with family and Christmas prep.

We got our Christmas tree this morning :) How are you?

My thumbs linger over my keypad, and I type out a reply before deleting it again. I don't know if I should tell him everything or let him distract me. Leaning forward in my seat, I rest my elbows on my thighs and start typing.

Hey Jay,

I haven't had much sleep in the last 6 hours tbh. My grandma was involved in a hit and run yesterday. She's in a coma and in hospital. We had to take a flight to Atlanta yesterday evening and we're driving to the hospital now.

I fix my eyes on the screen and wait for a reply.

Oh no :(

Tee, I'm so sorry.

Are you okay?

At this point, I want to lie. I want to claim to be the strong girl I've made myself out to be. But there's no point. Jayden has seen me vulnerable before and for some reason, I trust him.

Honestly, no, I'm not okay.
All I want is for someone to tell me she'll be fine.
I'll do whatever it takes to get her out of this.

I'll be praying for her, Tee.
I'm here if you need to talk about anything.
Please keep me updated when you get to the hospital.
And please, take care of yourself.

I'll do that.
Thanks, Jay.

I place my phone on my lap, and look outside the window as the car turns left towards a large white and beige-coloured building. Dad finds a space in the parking lot, a few yards away from a sign which reads *Wellstar Kennestone Hospital.*

Uncertainty. Anxiety. Worry.

That's all I see on the faces of everyone walking past us in the hospital hallway. I guess that's what they see on our faces too —that's certainly what they see on my face.

Mom is pushing Danny in his stroller ahead of me, and Aunt Bella is walking beside her, her hands tucked inside the pockets of her warm, navy blue fleece jacket.

The freezing cold air blows through the open windows into the long hallway, forcing me to put up the hood of my jacket.

Wheelchairs line one corner of the hallway and a pregnant woman waddles towards us, clutching the arm of a tall, bearded man walking beside her.

She stops a few meters away from us and holds onto the railing on the wall, taking deep breaths as the man rubs her back.

At the end of the corridor, we turn left and follow the signs leading to the elevator. Outside the window, I catch a glimpse of a beautiful garden at the front of the hospital building. Benches line the perimeter of the garden and snow covered hedges dot around the central pond.

An elderly man wearing a blue knitted jumper is sitting in a wheelchair on the far right-hand side of the garden. He stares into the pond, with his eyes focused on the ripples on the water and he pulls his brown winter hat to cover his ears. My mind trails off and I wonder why he's sitting out there on his own.

Does he have a relative in hospital? Has he lost someone he loves? Is he a patient?

I wrap my arms around myself as the cold air sends shivers down my spine. Dad arrives at the elevator first and he stands at the door to keep it open for us. We all flood in, one by one, before he lets the door close.

Dad presses the button inside to take us to the fourth floor, where the intensive care unit is located. Grandpa mentioned that they moved Grandma there from the operating resus after they stabilised her.

After a painfully slow ascent, the elevator reaches the fourth floor and Dad steps out first, following the signs to the intensive care unit.

As we approach the ward, distressing scenes flash through my mind—scenes from the weeks before Danny was born, when I thought Mom was going to die. Scenes from the fifty-four days Danny spent in hospital, when I thought he was going to die too.

Walking down these hallways again brings back all the feelings I had—feelings that God had abandoned me. Five years have passed, but all the emotions are still the same—as if it only happened yesterday.

We follow Dad's lead as a man walks towards us, pushing an older woman in a wheelchair. The woman's left leg is red and swollen from her knee down to her foot. She's holding her leg, as if trying to protect it from harm, and her facial expression says it all.

Pain. Agony. Suffering.

Another person in anguish, hoping for some kind of relief.

Dad stops in front of us, before turning around and stretching out his arm towards double doors. The sign at the top reads *Intensive Care.*

After speaking to the nurse on the intercom, Dad opens the double doors and lets us in. As soon as we walk through the doors, I spot an older man sitting in a small room opposite the nurse's station. His greying head rests on his hand, as he leans on his walking stick, and adjusts the glasses on his face.

I would recognise that face anywhere. "Grandpa?" My voice startles him and he lifts his head to look in our direction. He gets up from his seat and opens his arms wide as I run into them, making sure not to upset his balance.

His face looks weary and worn out and the dark circles under his eyes are a sign that he hasn't slept much in the last twenty-four hours.

He forces a smile and hugs everyone tight, but his smile fades when Mom bursts into tears. "Dad, how is she?" She sniffs and fixes the collar of his grey and white plaid shirt.

"She's still in a coma. The doctors did a CT scan yesterday, and they found a bleed in her brain. She has already been to the OR and they are going to monitor her for the next forty-eight hours." He shifts his weight to his left leg and leans on his stick.

"Dad, how did this happen?" Aunt Bella holds his hand and encourages him to sit. He pauses for a moment and gulps before trying to recount the story.

"We were cleaning the house and planning to receive you all on Wednesday." He starts. "She told me she wanted to get some baking supplies at the corner shop because she wanted you girls to have fun baking together."

He looks at me and smiles. "She wanted to teach you how to make her apple pie, Teeyana. She was excited about sharing her recipe with you."

The lump in my throat grows bigger and I swallow to force down my tears.

Grandpa lowers his head again and continues. "When she arrived at the shop next to our house, she called me to say that they didn't have the pie crusts she wanted." Grandpa turns to Mom. "Knowing your mother, she refused to use what they were offering her, so she decided to walk the extra ten minutes down to the grocery shop in town to get it."

Mom squeezes Grandpa's hand. "She promised she wouldn't stay long. I told her to leave it for when we go grocery shopping later. I told her to let me drive her there, but she stood her ground."

Grandpa takes off his glasses and removes tissues from his shirt pocket, which he uses to wipe the tears sliding down his cheeks.

"About half an hour later," he continues. "I heard banging on the front door and it was our neighbours—Jamie and his wife. They told me...that she...that she was involved in a hit-and-run accident at the traffic light five minutes away. He said the truck driver was on his phone and he didn't see that the light had turned red when he rounded the corner."

Anger rises in my chest and tears escape my eyes, but I wipe them off. I don't care what the doctors are saying; I want to hear

Grandma's laugh and see her smile again. I want to believe that I'm going to bake that apple pie with her.

"Mr. Thompson?" A middle-aged man walks into the room, dressed in a white coat, a black stethoscope around his neck, and a chart in his hand. "Hello, my name is Dr. Richards." He stretches out his hand to Grandpa and shakes it. "I apologise for the long wait. My colleague told me he has already spoken to you earlier today about what the CT scan showed us?"

"Yes, he has." Grandpa nods and puts on his glasses again.

"Okay so..." Dr. Richard's voice trails off as he looks at us, scanning our faces one after the other.

"It's okay, doctor." Grandpa speaks before he asks. "We're all family. My wife would have been okay with it." He gives him a half-hearted smile.

"Right, okay then." He looks down at his chart and assumes a seat across from Grandpa. "Like my colleague explained earlier, your wife had a nasty fall, and she hit her head hard on the pavement after the impact. She obtained some fractures to her skull and her ribs, and we found bleeding and swelling in her brain as well. This has put so much pressure on her brain and it's the reason she's in a coma." He stops and looks at Grandpa.

"We've done everything possible to fix the fractures, and we're now trying to relieve the pressure in her brain to prevent any further damage. We're going to continue monitoring her closely overnight and do some more scans if we need to, but we can't do any more until tomorrow. I'll pass on all the information to the night team and I'll be back here tomorrow morning."

Grandpa nods and smiles.

"Doctor?" My voice croaks and everyone looks at me. "Do you think she'll ever wake up from the coma?"

Everyone's heads snap back to look at the doctor, and he clears his throat.

"Well, erm...unfortunately, I'm not able to say at the moment. There could be various outcomes depending on how much damage has been caused. Some people wake up from comas, some go into a vegetative state and others may unfortunately.....not survive it." He presses his lips together, sympathy written all over his face.

"Thank you, doctor." Grandpa breaks the silence. "I appreciate all you've done for my wife. God bless you." Grandpa shakes the doctor's hand again.

"Doctor, please, can we see her now?" Moms asks when he stands up to leave.

"Yes, of course. Right this way."

22

TEEYANA

Dr. Richards opens the door to Grandma's room and ushers us in. The familiar smell of medicine hits me when I step in first. The room's layout looks strikingly similar to the one Danny was in when he was born.

I walk towards the beeping sound coming from the corner of the room and everyone follows closely behind. On the other side of the half-drawn curtain, my eyes fall on those grey curls I've wanted to touch for a long time.

"Grandma?" I reach for her hand and plant a kiss on it, before holding it tight against my chest. Mom parks Danny's stroller at the end of the bed, and wraps her arms around me.

Aunt Bella settles close to Grandma's head, her eyelids still swollen from all the crying she's done over the past six hours. Dad and Grandpa take their stance on the opposite side, and then sadness takes over the room.

"Mom? If you can hear me, we're here for you. All of us. We want you to know that we love you." Mom strokes Grandma's hair.

Grandma's neck is in a brace and the doctors have inserted a tube into her mouth, securing it with thick white tape across her face. The tube runs down the side of the bed to the machine behind me—the same machine with the constant beeping sounds which are driving me crazy.

I watch Grandma's chest rise and fall and realise those breaths aren't even hers. The breaths she could take so freely before are now controlled by a machine. The bruises on her forehead and cheeks give me goosebumps, and I can only imagine the pain she's feeling right now.

I've never seen Grandma in such a state. The bubbly, joyful woman I know is not the one lying on the bed now. She still looks beautiful, but she's pale—almost as if she's not here. Almost as if she's already gone. The woman who lays here is only a shadow of the one I call my grandma.

When I close my eyes, possible scenes of the accident flash in my mind—the moment the truck ran into her, throwing her off her course. I imagine how it must have crushed her slim frame, pushing her to the ground. I imagine her head hitting the ground, her skull fracturing from the impact, and the pain that must have shot through her body. I imagine her laying there, helpless in a pool of her own blood, suffering for someone else's careless mistake.

I cast my thoughts to the driver of that truck, wondering what he was thinking. How could he have thrown caution to the wind when he knew the lives of innocent people depended on it? Another look at Grandma turns the pain in my heart into resentment.

This should never have happened. All she wanted to do was spend time with her family. What crime did she commit?

This whole situation aches my being. It's another unfair and unnecessary tragedy that has happened to my family. I can't deal with this anymore.

My gaze moves from the bruises on Grandma's face, wandering past the dozen skin tags on her cheeks, up to her kinky curly grey hair. Her hair is currently in her favourite hairstyle—the "*wash and go.*" This hairstyle makes her kinky curls pop, and she loves wearing it in an afro.

Grandma always described her hair as having its own personality, so she let it do its own thing. A few years ago, she cut it and embraced her greying short hair, which complements her beautiful bronze skin.

Unlike many who associate greying hair with ageing, Grandma embraced her greys with grace and she carried them well. Whenever she wanted to braid my hair, she counted the number of grey strands I had and told me it was a sign that God has blessed me with wisdom.

"Honey, your hair looks healthy." She complimented while using the rat tail comb to part my hair last Thanksgiving.

"Thanks, Grandma. I want my hair to be like yours. I've been looking after it the way you taught me." I smiled at her.

"You go, baby girl." Grandma gave me a high-five. *"Too bad you ain't natural. I would have taught you how to get these voluminous Bantu knots."* She teased and fluffed her own hair, flipping it dramatically in my direction.

I pouted. *"Aww, but you told me it didn't matter if I was natural or relaxed. You said the Bantu knots would work either way."* I crossed my arms against my chest.

"That's right, honey. I'm only teasing you." She hugged me. *"But if you ever want to cut your hair, let me know and I'll do the honours."* She pinched my cheeks before continuing to do the Bantu knots on my hair.

I've been thinking about doing the "big chop" like Grandma suggested and one of the reasons I was looking forward to spending time with my grandparents this Christmas was because I had decided to do it. I was hoping Grandma would do the honours like she promised. But I never imagined we would spend Christmas in a hospital.

I lean over and kiss Grandma's cheek, avoiding the bruises on her face. "Grandma? Please, wake up. Please. Breathe." I whisper in her ear. Warm tears I've been holding gush out of my eyes and fall on her skin, trickling down her face too. Mom reaches out and hugs me again.

"Mom? It's me, Bella." Aunt Bella sobs. "I'm sorry I haven't been there for you as much as I wanted to. I've been away for too long, but I'm here now. Jamilla is here too. Mom, please wake up. You were excited for both of us to spend Christmas with you this year. Now we're here. Please, wake up." The sound of our sobs is the only thing that fills the room until Grandpa speaks.

"We should pray." He sniffs and holds Dad's hand. I clear my throat before reluctantly linking hands with Mom and Dad. I don't feel like doing this now, but I'll play along.

"As we pray for her," Grandpa continues. "I want us to ask that God's will be done... and not ours."

My eyes widen as I stare at Grandpa in disbelief. "But Grandpa?" I protest and everyone turns to look at me. "Shouldn't we be praying for God to heal her? Doesn't He have the power to do that? Isn't that what we all want?" I look around at them.

"Yes, honey. We should definitely ask God to heal her and we will do that." Grandpa responds. "But I also want us to remember that God is sovereign over this situation. Let us surrender our will, knowing that He alone is good, so we need to trust Him now." He forces his eyes shut, enhancing the wrinkles on his face.

I look around the room at everyone else, their eyes closed, concentrating on the words Grandpa is saying. Then, I look at Grandma again and out of guilt; I close my eyes and allow the thousands of questions in my head to consume me.

God's will? What is God's will in this situation?

Is He going to heal her or is He going to let her die?

23

JAYDEN

G*od won't abandon you in the rough waters.*

These words have been echoing in my mind since I had my quiet time this morning. I want to tell Teeyana and I want her to believe them too.

Placing my Bible on my bed, I pick up my phone from my bedside table and open my text messages, clicking on her name and then pausing.

Lord, should I text her?

She hasn't updated me since I spoke to her yesterday, and I've been thinking about a million possible things that could have happened.

If she hasn't messaged me, then perhaps I should leave her alone?

Teeyana only ever said good things about her grandma, so I can only imagine what she's going through now. I don't want her ending up in the dark tunnel of dejection I was in. It's a hard tunnel to get out of, and I wouldn't wish that on anyone.

Pressing my phone against my ear, I tap my fingers on my thigh as it rings, biting my lower lip in anticipation.

"Hello?" Teeyana's soft voice comes through from the other end of the line.

"Hey, Tee?" I clear my throat. "I'm sorry if this is a bad time. I wanted to find out how you're doing. Is everything okay?" I ask, my voice coming out more shaky than I would have wanted.

She hesitates before replying, "Yeah, I'm alright...I guess."

"Are you at the hospital now?"

"Yeah, I came in this morning with my mom and Aunt Bella. Dad is at home with Danny, and Grandpa is on his way to the hospital."

I swing my legs from my bed so my feet touch the floor. "Okay. So what are you doing now?"

"Well, the hospital has a pond and I've been sitting next to it for the last half hour, staring into the water, and wishing I had a reset button for my life. I saw a man sitting here yesterday, and he looked rather peaceful, so I thought I'd try it out for myself."

"And...is it peaceful?" I ask.

"Well," she sighs, "it's a helpful distraction for now."

"Okay then. And your grandma? How is she doing today?" I ask.

"Grandma is still in a coma." She sighs, but I can tell that sigh is only a mask to hide her true feelings. "We're waiting for the results of the MRI scan to see if there are any signs of hope." She adds.

"Okay, but how are you feeling—really?" I emphasise, hoping she'll take off the mask and talk to me.

"Do you want me to be honest or should I sugar-coat it so I don't have to bore you with the details?" she asks.

"I'm all about honesty, Tee. Trust me, if I find you boring, you would know." I try to lighten up the mood, but when she doesn't respond, I get the cue that this is not the right time. "Please, you can talk to me if you want to. I'm here for you."

She lets out another deep sigh before replying. "I'm scared, Jay. Grandma suffered a serious head injury from that accident. I'm scared about what the scans will show. I don't want her to die. She has done nothing wrong to deserve this. It's not fair." She sniffs and my heart melts for her.

It's hard enough to hear Teeyana sound so upset, but it's even harder not being able to do anything about it. Flustered, I rub my forehead, thinking of what to say, and then the words come flooding back.

God will not abandon you in the rough waters.

"Tee, I learned something today, and I wanted to share it with you. Do you mind?"

"I would do anything to hear some encouraging words right now." Teeyana sniffs again.

"Okay, one thing God taught me today during my quiet time is that He won't abandon us in the rough waters. I know it's difficult for you right now, but I believe God wants you to know that He's right by your side. You'll get through this, by His grace. Do you want me to pray with you?" I ask, hoping she'll say yes this time.

"Yeah...please help me talk to God, because I've been trying for the last half hour and I don't know what to tell Him or how to start. I want to tell Him how I feel, but I don't know how I feel. Everything sucks." Her voice cracks.

"I'm sorry you feel that way, Tee. I can certainly pray with you." I close my eyes and start praying. I pray for healing for Teeyana's grandma. I pray for comfort for her and her family. I pray that God gives Teeyana strength to go through this, and then I pray that God's good and perfect will be done.

"Thanks, Jay. I needed this, but I have to go now. My mom just texted me. She said the doctor is back with the scan results."

"Oh, okay. Please let me know what happens—if you want to, that is." I respond.

"Yeah. I'll call you later. Thank you for doing this for me."

"It was no problem at all. Please take care of yourself." I drop my phone on my bed when she ends the call, and I lay on my back, letting out a deep sigh.

Please Lord, let her grandma survive this.

A few seconds later, the smell of bacon fills the air in my room and I find myself walking out the door and down the stairs to the kitchen.

"Morning, Mom." I walk up behind her and plant a kiss on her cheek, before taking a seat at the table.

"Hey baby, did you sleep well?" She flips the bacon over in the frying pan.

"Hmm." I shrug. "I think I have a headache or something."

"Or something?" Mom shoots a worried glance in my direction before turning back to the bacon.

"Well, it's Teeyana. I'm worried about her because her grandma was involved in a hit-and-run accident two days ago, and she's in the hospital."

"Oh, no!!! That's terrible." Mom turns away from the cooker and walks towards me.

"Good morning, peeps." Dad walks into the kitchen. "I smell bacon and I'm hungry." He rubs his palms together before kissing Mom's forehead and taking a seat next to me on the table.

"Morning, honey. You know Teeyana—the friend Jayden always talks about? Her grandma was involved in a car accident." Mom picks up a plate of bacon from the kitchen counter and places it in front of me.

"Oh, no. Is she alright?" Dad turns to me.

"I don't know." I shrug before picking up my fork. "She's in a coma and they're getting scan results today. Teeyana is very upset about it."

"Oh Lord, the poor thing. Of course she'll be upset." Mom places a plate of bacon in front of Dad. "I hope the scan results show some good news." Mom picks up a third plate of bacon and joins us at the table.

"Yeah, I hope so too." Dad responds. "There's always hope, son. Let's hold on to that and keep her in our prayers." Dad squeezes my shoulder before picking up the bag of bread lying in front of him.

"Yeah...there's always hope." I repeat and smile at him as we link hands around the food, getting ready to say grace.

There's always hope.

It's a miracle that I can still say this after Tyler's death. Only God has worked wonders to get me to this point. But the truth is, I'm scared for Teeyana. I pray her grandma survives this because if she doesn't, Teeyana might walk away from God for good.

24

TEEYANA

I shift my bodyweight to my right leg when an elderly man enters the elevator in his wheelchair. He is wearing thick round glasses and a cozy-looking blue jumper, while the nurse accompanying him is wearing teal scrubs. She has tied her black hair up in a bun, and her eye bags are sagging underneath her bloodshot eyes.

The elderly man has wrinkles around his mouth and eyes. He has silvery grey hair like Grandpa, except Grandpa's hair is short and kinky, while this man's hair is silky, and it falls forward, covering the wrinkles on his forehead.

As the doors close in front of us, I twist my messy ponytail into a low bun and wipe my face, trying to look somewhat presentable. But no amount of wiping can hide my crying-induced swollen eyelids.

Unlike the woman I saw yesterday with the swollen leg, this man looks peaceful. But when the elevator starts moving, he clutches the handles of his wheelchair and turns his head to face the nurse behind him.

"Ooh, did I forget the flowers, love?" His British accent is the first thing I notice as his eyebrows furrow in concern.

"No, Rupert," the nurse replies with a warm smile. "They're in this bag right here." She touches a white plastic bag hanging from his wheelchair before patting his shoulder.

He relaxes again and turns to me. "Sorry, dear. An old man like me gets a little anxious sometimes. I'm going to see my wife, you see. She's been in a coma since her car accident. Lilies are her favourite flowers and I bring them to her every week, hoping she will wake up." A genuine smile forms across his face as he pulls his brown winter hat to cover his ears. For a man going through something like me, he doesn't look half as miserable as I do.

How can he still be smiling so much when all I want to do is sit in a corner and cry?

And his face...his face looks strangely familiar.

"Sorry if this is a silly question, but have we met before, Sir?" I tilt my head.

He turns to me again and squints. "Well...I think if I'd seen such a beautiful face before, I would remember. But I'm getting old, love. I can't trust my memory anymore. I've been in this hospital every day since my wife's accident two months ago. Sometimes, I sit outside in the garden next to the pond."

The pond!!! The brown winter hat!!! The blue jumper!!!

"No way!!!" I exclaim. "You're the man I saw sitting in the garden yesterday. You inspired me to check it out today, and I have to admit that looking at the ripples in the pond gave me some peace of mind."

"Ah well, God always works in wonderful ways, my dear. I'm glad He used the pond to remind you of His peace. Who have you come to see? Are you going to the fourth floor too?"

"Yes, I am. I'm here for my grandma. She was involved in a hit-and-run accident a few days ago and she's in a coma too."

"Oh, I'm sorry to hear about that." He squeezes my hands. "I hope our good Lord comforts you and your family."

If Grandma ever met a miserable eighteen-year-old girl in an elevator, I'm sure she would say the same thing.

"Thank you so much, Sir." I say as tears blur my vision.

"Please call me Rupert, love. Rupert Cartwright."

After what seems like forever, the elevator dings and the nurse wheels Rupert out and turns left. I step out after them and turn right. "I love your jumper, Rupert."

His face brightens up, and he smoothes the sleeves with his hands. "Thanks, love. My dear Marjorie knitted it for me. She is very talented."

"Indeed." I flash a smile at him. "Well, I hope she wakes up so she can see how beautiful these lilies are." I nod in the direction of the flowers.

"Thank you, love. You are so kind. I'll be praying for you, and your grandma." Rupert shouts out as the nurse turns him round so he can have a last look at me.

"Thank you, Rupert." I wave as the nurse wheels him further down the hallway. When they are no longer in sight, I stand there, in the middle of the hallway, staring into nothing.

Okay, God. If you want me to believe that You are good, here's the chance to prove Yourself. Let Grandma live, and I promise I'll believe. I promise I will.

I pause in front of Grandma's door and knock softly before opening it. Mom, Aunt Bella, and Grandpa are sitting in the chairs surrounding Grandma's bed. Dr. Richards is back, like he promised.

I want him to say that Grandma is going to be fine. That even though she doesn't look good right now, she's going to wake up.

Please, God. Let him say those words.

"Hey, honey." Mom gestures for me to sit next to her. "The results are here."

Dr. Richards looks fatigued, but his expression is blank. He exhales, and opens his mouth to speak. "So, Mr. Thompson, as you know," he starts, looking at Grandpa. "We did some scans, and some further tests to find out how much damage has been done, and if the treatment is working." He pauses. "Based on the results, I'm afraid to tell you that...it's not good news." His eyes move to Mom, then to Aunt Bella, and finally to me.

"What do you mean, doctor?" Aunt Bella asks, leaning forward in her seat.

"Unfortunately, the damage to her brain is more significant than we thought." He maintains eye contact with Grandpa. "Mr. Thompson, I'm sorry to say that...we don't think your wife will wake up from this coma."

My throat clogs up, and a wave of nausea engulfs me.

No. It can't be. It can't be.

"But doctor," Mom's voice shakes. "Yesterday, you said there was a chance she could get better." Tears stream down her face.

Dr. Richards looks at her, nothing but sympathy written all over his face. "Ma'am, we've been treating her since she got here, but her brain is not responding to any of the treatment. The scans have shown that there is no activity in her brain. I'm afraid Mrs. Thompson is brain dead."

My chest heaves and tears escape my eyes. I squeeze Mom's hands, a million thoughts running through my head. Grandpa lowers his head and buries his face in his palms.

"We don't think she'll recover from this. I'm sorry." Dr. Richards throws in again.

"No!!!" Aunt Bella objects. "Surely there's something you can do. Surely you can try something else." She shuffles forward to the edge of her seat, glaring at Dr. Richards.

"Bella? Please, calm down, honey." Grandpa calls out softly, but she ignores him.

"Are you going to take her off her life support and let her die?" Aunt Bella raises her voice.

"Bella?" Grandpa calls out again.

Dr. Richards sighs but remains calm. "Ma'am, the damage caused by the accident cannot be reversed. Without the life support, she won't be able to breathe on her own so...we think it'll be in her best interests to stop the treatment and make her as comfortable as she can be."

"That's ridiculous!!!" Aunt Bella springs to her feet. "Would you stop if it was your mother lying in that bed?"

"Bella!!!" Grandpa's voice comes out much firmer and louder this time. "Please sit down, honey." His soft tone returns.

Walking up to her, Grandpa touches her face with his trembling hand while leaning on his walking stick. "Bella, honey? We need to let her go." Tears fall from his eyes.

Aunt Bella's gaze moves from Grandpa to the doctor, and then back to Grandpa. The anger in her eyes washes away as her tears gush out. "Dad, please, don't let them give up on her like this. Please." Her lips quiver and she buries her face in Grandpa's shoulder. He wraps his arm around her and she sobs.

No. No. No. This can't be happening.

I shut the next few words Dr Richards says out of my memory. The last thing I hear is Mom asking if they can leave Grandma on life support until after Christmas so we can spend her last Christmas with her.

I walk over to Grandma's bed, and put my head on her chest, my arm resting on her abdomen. My head rises and falls, matching the rhythm of her chest, and Grandma's hospital gown becomes wet with my tears. The door opens and closes in the distance, and I assume it's Dr. Richards leaving. Mom wraps her arms around me, and Aunt Bella's loud sobs fill the room.

I asked God to prove to me He is good...but He didn't.

Everything I feared has happened. All the hope I had is gone.

25

TEEYANA

Everything has been hazy since Dr. Richards broke the news to us. We've spent almost every moment in hospital since then, and I think I'm justified in saying this is the worst Christmas ever.

The most wonderful time of the year? No, not really.

A time to remind me of a hope I have in Jesus? Absolutely not.

From now on, Christmas will always remind me of the pain and resentment I feel in my heart right now. It'll always remind me about the second time I dared to trust God, and He let me down—again.

Everyone around me seems to have accepted the reality of the situation. Soon I'll be expected to accept it too. But my heart aches. I can't believe in a few days, Grandma will be gone.

After Dr. Richards left, Grandpa sat next to Grandma's bed, holding her hands, and weeping without uttering a word. He paced back and forth in the hospital room, shaking his head several times, as tears slid down his cheeks.

My grandparents were inseparable, and I can't believe I'll never see them together again. During my water baptism, they were both present, cheering me on and encouraging me. Even though we were struggling financially, my grandparents organised a party for me and invited my friends from church, making sure I had a good time.

At the lowest point in our lives, my grandparents supported us in every way they could. Grandpa helped Dad get a job at the church and Grandma looked after Danny at home, while Mom tried to find a job.

And now, I can't believe such a brilliant—or should I say *God-ordained partnership*—has been dissolved by the foolishness of another. I'm glad the driver was caught. I hope that when he goes to court; he receives the sentence deserving of this kind of destruction.

Mom hasn't stopped crying since we got back from the hospital. She has now found comfort in Dad's arms. I watch them from a distance as Dad strokes her hair—her head buried in his shoulder, and her sobs muffled.

Not wanting to disturb Mom and Dad, I walk away from them and towards Aunt Bella—who is sitting on the other side of the living room all by herself. Her eyes are closed, but I know she's not sleeping.

"Aunt Bella?" I call out to her and she opens her eyes. "Can I sit with you?"

She doesn't respond, but instead, she presses her lips together and extends her arms to me, wrapping them around my shoulders as I rest my head on her chest.

After kissing my forehead, she speaks for the first time since we left the hospital. "I should have come to see her more often," she whispers in my ear. "I was always so busy with work and didn't make time for my own parents." She sniffs. "Now I'll never get the chance to tell her I'm sorry." She presses her head against mine. "I can't tell her how much I love her."

"It's okay, Aunt Bella." I move her faux locs away from her tear-stained face and wipe her tears with my thumb. "Grandma always told me how much she loved you and Mom. I'm sure she knew you loved her too." I smile, succeeding in drawing a half-hearted smile from her too.

My phone vibrates in my pocket and I hold down the home button, a text notification popping up on my screen. It's from Jayden.

After we got the news yesterday, I turned off my phone because I didn't want to tell anyone about what happened. I told Amara earlier today, but I haven't told Jayden yet. I'm sure he'll keep trying to find out how I'm doing, but I don't want to talk to him. Bringing my phone close to my face, I type a quick reply.

Hey,

The results from the scan came back and they're not good.

She's not gonna wake up from the coma and they'll take her off her life support after Christmas. I know you're trying to help, but I need some space right now. Thanks.

I hit send, turn off my phone, and slip it back into my pocket.

"Everything alright, honey?" Aunt Bella lowers her head to meet my gaze.

I sigh. "Yeah, everything will be fine."

The three days before Christmas, we camp out in Grandma's room. I sit in a chair in the corner, numb, staring at the Christmas hat perched on Grandma's head while a blur of well-wishers, carolers, and plates of food come and go. My phone chimes from time to time as new messages from Jayden come through, but I don't reply.

At eight a.m. on December 27th, I jolt out of my sleep at the sound of commotion. Dr. Richards and three nurses are back and everyone is awake—eyes fixed on Grandma as they prepare to turn off her life-support machine.

I push myself up from my chair and walk closer to the group until I'm standing next to Mom, Aunt Bella, and Dad. Grandpa sits closest to Grandma and holds her hand as they turn off the machine and remove the tube out of her mouth.

Soft sobs escape my lips as we all watch Grandma's shallow breaths with occasional deep breaths in between. A strong pulse appears on her neck and I hold on to the last hope that perhaps the doctors were wrong. Perhaps she doesn't need life support.

But fifteen minutes pass, and her breathing becomes shallower by the second. The pulse in her neck slowly disappears, her face becomes paler, and before our very eyes, the machine flat lines—beeping continuously to let us know that she's no longer with us.

~

This pain is excruciating, and the agony is unbearable. My heart aches as I stand in the front row of the crowd of fifty people gathered around Grandma's soon-to-be grave.

I lift my glasses and wipe the tears spilling out from my eyes as the pastor speaks. These glasses hide the dark circles around my eyes, and also my red, swollen eyelids which I don't want the world to see.

I look around the graveyard, focusing on the trees, the birds, and the clouds, so I won't have to listen to what the pastor is saying. In his all black suit and white bow tie, the pastor stands there, talking about this poem he likes called "The Weaver."

After reading it out to us, he invites us to sing a hymn and Deaconess Taylor from the choir leads us into it. Within a few seconds, melodious harmonies and melodies replace the once quiet atmosphere. I look around as everyone sings and concentrates on the words in their hymn book—everyone except me.

I remember Grandma saying she preferred hymns over contemporary worship songs. She said hymns have a deeper meaning which you will get if you listen intently. So I listen intently to the words of the song, hoping one last time, that they'll explain why I have to live through this day.

Tempted and tried, we're oft made to wonder
Why it should be thus all the day long
While there are others living about us
Never molested though in the wrong

Of course, I could never have said it better. People who put their trust in God are the ones getting knocked down—the ones getting attacked. It seems like a punishment and the crime is serving God.

When death has come and taken our loved ones
It leaves our home so lonely and drear
Then do we wonder why others prosper
Living so wicked year after year

This is the reason why I'm so angry. If God has the upper hand and the full authority, then why doesn't He stop all the unfairness? All the suffering. All the pain. All the agony.

Often I wonder why I must journey
Over a road so rugged and steep;
While there are others living in comfort,
While with the lost I labour and weep.

I don't think I'll ever be able to understand how allowing suffering is needed. It's unnecessary in this case, and I don't think this is helping me.

Farther along we'll know all about it
Farther along we'll understand why
Cheer up my brother live in the sunshine
We'll understand it all by and by

Well, I'd very much appreciate it if He explains it to me now. I want to know now.

I turn my head away when the crowd ends the song with an "Amen." The pastor puts away his book of hymns and steps forward again to speak. Mom and Dad stand still on my right while Aunt Bella stands on my left, not saying a word as the pastor continues.

"In sure and certain hope of the resurrection to eternal life through our Lord Jesus Christ, we commend to the Almighty God, Hannah-Grace Elizabeth Thompson, and we commit her body to the ground," the pastor bends over and picks up a handful of the earth that had been dug up, ready to cover up Grandma's coffin.

"Earth to earth, and dust to dust." He lets the earth slip

through his fingers and onto the coffin. Then, four men dressed in black suits lower Grandma's coffin into the ground as everyone starts singing again.

Grandpa nods in agreement to the words of the song, as if those same words I detest are the ones giving him hope right now. He steps forward, eyes thick with tears and his lips quivering from all the pain in his heart. He picks up a handful of the earth and also lets it slip through his fingers onto the coffin in the ground. "Goodbye, my love. Till we meet again someday."

One by one, everyone picks up a handful of the earth and does the same.

Everyone—except me.

I watch from a distance, my hands tucked in the pockets of my jacket and my throat aching from the tears I'm trying to push down. In about half an hour, Grandma's coffin is covered up with the earth and one by one, the crowd disperses. Time passes and soon, I'm the only one left standing there, all alone, staring into the emptiness.

I don't remember how long I've been standing there when gentle arms wrap around my shoulder and a kiss is planted on my temple. I turn around and stare into his dark brown eyes—just like mine.

"Dad." My shaking voice surfaces as the tears I've been suppressing break free. "Please tell me this is all a dream." My lungs gasp for air.

Dad hushes me and draws me in, giving me the warmest hug. "It's going to be okay, honey," he whispers in my ear. "You're going to be okay."

26

TEEYANA

It's been a week since Grandma's funeral, and walking through college campus doesn't feel the same. I'm not the same.

When I started college, my plan was to take control of my life and work hard to achieve my goals. The plan was to discover my own path, make my own choices, and find my own answers.

But I'm ashamed because I let myself get carried away. I believed Jayden when he said God will always have my back. How far did that get me? What gain did that bring me? I thought God would make me happy like He's done with Jayden. I thought things would be different this time, but I was wrong. I have failed myself.

Whatever it is I've done, God hasn't forgiven me for it. I trusted Him, but He chewed up my hope and spit it back in my face.

That's okay though, because I don't need His help. I don't need anyone's help. I can do this on my own like I originally planned.

Jayden has messaged and called several times in the last two weeks. Sometimes I ignore him and other times, I send him a one-word reply to let him know I'm still alive. I hope he takes the hint and stops trying. I don't want to talk to him.

I've been intentionally going to class later, so I don't get to sit next to Jayden. If I bump into him, I come up with my favourite excuse—I'm hanging out with Ellie.

It's not a lie though. I've done nothing else but work on my Google internship application since I got back. It's my only priority right now.

Getting this internship will be the consolation I need to convince myself that I'm taking the reins back, sitting in the driver's seat, and writing my story on my own terms.

I hope someday things will feel right again. But Grandma is still gone, and she's never coming back. Things will never be the same.

I rub the back of my neck and stretch as I take out my dorm room keys out of my backpack. Tonight's study session in the library was a killer, and I can't wait to sleep.

Stepping into my dorm room, the strong smell of alcohol and cigarette smoke hits my nostrils. I cover my nose and fiddle on the wall to find the light switch. When the light comes on, I find Heather and her new boyfriend making out on her bed.

Whenever this happened before, I would leave them to it and find something to do to distract me. But not this time—not today. If there are things I'm not okay with, I'll speak up about them. I'm not keeping quiet any longer.

Take the reins, Teeyana.

I clench both my fists at my sides and straighten my back. Then I clear my throat and they both look up at me. "You know you can take this somewhere else, right?" I cross my arms against my chest, bracing myself for the turbulence I'm about to cause.

Heather sits up and stares, her eyes wide with shock. "You

haven't had a problem with this before. What's up with you now?" She frowns.

"Heather, you're not the only one living in this room. You know we're not allowed to bring alcohol in here, so why would you do it? You can't do whatever you want whenever you feel like it. There are consequences for your actions, and I could be implicated." I shoot a daring glare at her boyfriend. He whips his blonde hair to the side and averts my gaze.

"Heather?" He speaks up. "It's cool. We can go to Ryan's place across the block." He pulls his t-shirt over his head and climbs down from the bed.

"Yeah, thank you. And make it Ryan's place from now on." I order, placing both hands on my hips.

"Excuse me?" Heather replies, sending a glare in my direction.

"I said what I said." I stare back and Heather laughs before turning to her boyfriend.

"Babe, give me two minutes. I'll meet you downstairs." She plants a kiss on his lips and nudges him out the door before slamming it shut behind her.

"And who the *hell* do you think you are?" Heather walks towards me, her nostrils flaring and her hair looking redder than I've ever seen it before.

Sit in the driver's seat, Teeyana.

The only other time I've seen Heather this angry was when she was screaming at her dad in the parking lot on move-in day. The good thing is, I'm not her dad. She can't walk all over me. I won't let her.

"I'm Teeyana Joy Sparks. That's who I am." I smirk. "Do you want to know my date of birth as well?" I maintain my gaze, looking her straight in the eyes.

Do not back down, Teeyana.

"You have got some nerve." Heather squints. "How *dare* you

think you can talk to me or my boyfriend like that?" She raises her voice.

"And how *dare* you think you can treat me like a child?" I snap. "I did nothing wrong, Heather."

"You were rude." Heather points a finger in my face.

"No, I wasn't." I push her finger down. "*You* were rude. You know the rules you signed when you moved in here. Heather, your attitude towards me has been nothing but unacceptable from the very second I met you. The fact that I've been tolerating you gives you no right to walk all over me. I've tried to be civil with you, but that doesn't mean I have nothing to say about your repulsive behaviour."

I stare into her watery green eyes, which tell me my words have cut through her. But I don't care. I know I'm right and she can't tell me otherwise.

"So I'm the bad guy now, huh? Are you being serious right now? Oh, I'm sorry, Miss *Perfect*, Miss *I'm-Always-Right*, Miss *Goody-Two-Shoes!*" Heather inches closer. "I hate people like you, Teeyana. You always act like the whole world revolves around you. You are one selfish, spoilt brat and you have no idea what it feels like to have things going bad for you in this life."

"What are you talking about? I just lost my grandma." I resist the urge to shove her.

"Oh, shut the hell up!!!" Heather screams in my face. "Are you the only one who has lost someone? There are children dying all around the world and families being torn apart as we speak—even babies who have done nothing wrong and you have the nerve to stand here and sulk over some old woman?"

Heather's words make my nostrils flare up, and my heart pounds faster. I grit my teeth and make tight fists to stop myself from going out of control. Images of the accident flicker in my mind—the truck slamming into Grandma, her head hitting the pavement, and the man driving off and leaving her to die.

Don't back down, Teeyana, Heather cannot see you cry. Be strong.

"Heather, how can you be so vile?" My strength betrays me and tears leak from my eyes. "Why are you so bitter? Well done! You've now made the top of my list for the most despicable person I've ever met."

"Oh, please, whatever." Heather rolls her eyes. "You think you can walk in here like a perfect little princess and order people around? Try to ruin things for others because you're having a bad day? Grow up and stay the hell out of my business!!!" And with that, she turns around and heads for the door.

Surely I have something to say. Surely she's the one in the wrong. A million words flood in my head, but nothing coherent comes out of my mouth as the door slams shut in my face.

Am I really a selfish person?

Am I truly overreacting about Grandma's death?

Do I have no right to be angry?

Is Heather right about everything she said about me?

I wrap my arms around myself, shivering as the tears continue falling down. Then, I bury my head in my pillow and in a few minutes; it soaks up all the tears I don't want the world to see.

27

JAYDEN

It's been three weeks since Teeyana returned to college, and my longest conversation with her lasted five minutes. I understand she needs space. I needed space too when I was dealing with Tyler's death. But my healing process only began when I started talking. I want to help Teeyana understand that it's okay to talk.

She hasn't come to church or Bible study since she got back. I'm convinced something is wrong, but I don't know how to help her.

Lord, am I overthinking this?

Is this just her way of dealing with grief?

I won't know unless I speak to her. "I need to speak to her." I mutter to myself as I approach the stairs on the first floor of the library.

It's 5:45p.m on a Friday evening and basketball practice starts in fifteen minutes. I've spent the last ten minutes scanning the floor, but just like it's been every day for the last two weeks, I can't find Teeyana.

With shoulders slumped, I turn around to leave when I spot

Ellie climbing up the stairs from the ground floor, two other girls chattering by her side.

"Hey, Jayden." She smiles when they brush past me.

"Hey." I smile back. "Oh, quick question, Ellie."

She stops in her tracks and turns toward me. "Yeah?" She nudges her friends to go on without her before approaching me.

"Sorry to bother you, but I've been trying to find Teeyana all day. She usually studies on the first floor, but I haven't seen her here today. Do you have any idea where she might be?" I ask, a tinge of hope lingering in my voice.

"Yeah. She's in the social area downstairs." Ellie points to the bottom of the stairs.

My eyes widen. "She is?"

"Yeah. I spoke to her ten minutes ago. Hurry though, because she was about to leave."

"Thank you so much. I owe you one." I give Ellie a brief hug before dashing down the stairs.

Lord, please let her still be there.

At the bottom of the stairs, I turn left, my eyes searching across the whole area, but there's no one sitting at the tables. Then I turn right and my eyes fall on her.

She's leaning back in her chair, her head lowered, and three single braids falling on the side of her face, with the rest held up in a giant pony tail. She has her fingers wrapped around her phone and her eyes glued to it. The books on the table in front of her are closed, so without any hesitation, I walk toward her, my breath catching in my throat.

Lord, please give me the right words to say.

Coming up to her table, I sit in the chair across from her and place both arms on the table. "You've been avoiding me." I look straight into her dark brown eyes.

She looks around, as if to make sure no one else is watching, before replying. "No, I haven't. What are you talking about?" She places her phone face down on the table.

"Tee, you said I could meet you outside your dorm after class yesterday and you stood me up. Didn't Heather tell you I came by looking for you?" Teeyana sends me a glare as I mention Heather's name.

Clearing my throat, I continue. "Okay, if I did something wrong, please let's talk about it. For the past month, I've been trying to figure out what I've done to you and it's driving me crazy."

Instead of answering, Teeyana turns her head away from me and focuses on the group of students climbing down the stairs and heading out of the library.

Lord, please help me.

"Hello?" I wave my hand in front of her face and she turns to look at me.

"Look, Jay. I've been busy, okay? I came in two weeks later than everyone else because of the funeral, so Ellie has been helping me get back on track," she responds.

"Okay—but I thought we were study buddies. I could've helped you get back on track." I say, nudging her a bit more.

She shrugs. "Yeah, but the application deadline for the Google internship is in two weeks and I haven't finished sorting out my portfolio and my resumé. Ellie is helping me with that too," she adds.

"Okay—I understand that. But why do I have a feeling your internship application is not the problem on trial here?" I raise a brow.

Teeyana frowns. "What are you trying to say?" She demands.

I lean forward. "Tee, you can't even look me in the eye when you talk to me. I tried reaching out to you so many times after you told me what happened to your grandma. I called and sent you messages, but you didn't reply to any of them. And then after returning to college and avoiding me for three weeks, you're just going to sit there and tell me nothing is wrong?"

"Okay, fine." She snaps. "You want the truth? I'll tell you the truth. Yes, I have been avoiding you." She folds her arms across her chest but says nothing more.

I breathe a sigh of relief. Finally, this conversation is going somewhere. But I need to choose my words carefully. I need to give her the assurance that she can talk to me.

"Okay—so what did I do again?" I ask in a low voice.

She shrugs. "Nothing. You didn't do anything, Jay. But I'm avoiding you for what you're going to do."

I bury my face in my palms and groan. "Tee, you're not helping me here. What are you talking about? What don't you want me to do?"

"I don't want you to tell me that God cares about me because He clearly doesn't, okay? He never did and He never will. All of that stuff you told me the day I opened up to you in the car? Yeah, I don't want to hear any of it. It's all lies." Her voice is stern, but tears are forming in her eyes.

"My grandma did nothing wrong to deserve that." Teeyana continues. "And Heather had the guts to tell me I have no right to be sad or angry because other people have it worse? That makes no sense to me."

I open my mouth to speak, but Teeyana carries on.

"Jay, this woman was fit. She was healthy. I loved her." Her voice cracks. "But God didn't care about any of that when He let her die, did He? He watched her slip away and He *chose* not to intervene, didn't He?" She sniffs. "Go ahead. Tell me it's all part of the plan. What plan?" She raises her voice.

"What plan, Jayden? God's plan? Sitting up there, dictating who gets to be president and who gets to be run over by a truck? He must think this is some sort of joke, right? Well, I don't find this joke funny and it hurts." She sobs. "It hurts so much."

I sit there and stare at her as she buries her face in her hands. Her sobs make my heart ache—as if I'm the one in pain.

Lord, what do I do?

What can I say or do to take away the pain Teeyana is feeling right now? My legs take the lead and I walk around the table, settling in the chair next to her. At first, I'm not sure if she'll let me, but when I reach for her arm, she brings her head in and rests it on my chest.

I let her cry on my chest, and I stroke her braids. When she quiets down, she raises her head up and looks at me. "I work hard every day, but it seems like all my plans are getting thwarted by some supposedly all-knowing, all-powerful God. Didn't you say He has my best interests at heart? Why does it feel like He's playing with me? I don't like this game, Jay. It frustrates me." She sniffs.

"You understand Him so please, tell Him to make it stop because I'm tired. Why did He allow what happened to my dad? My mom? Danny? My grandma? You told me there's no pain without a purpose, so I want to know how this senseless and unfair death brings glory to God. I want to understand, Jay. Make me understand." She bangs her fists on the table.

"And you," Teeyana pushes me away, looking at me for the first time, with what seems like anger in her eyes—anger towards me. "You can't sit here and tell me you understand what I'm going through. You're God's favourite, right? No problems? No struggles? So it's easy for you to smile and tell me everything is going to plan?"

Her words cut through me like a knife and I shake my head in disagreement. "Tee, that's not fair."

"Not fair?" She interrupts. "You can't talk to me about things not being fair. What about the unfairness I have to deal with every day, huh? Did you have to deal with people like Olivia Hastings who made mine and Amara's lives a living hell in high school? Do you have a roommate like Heather who finds pleasure in hating you without a justifiable reason? Do you have to deal with trying to find hope when grief is the only thing that strikes your face every morning? I guess not. So don't you *dare* talk to me about life not being fair. If God had the power to part the Red Sea, then I know He has the power to stop bad things from happening." She wipes her eyes.

"Tee, please, give me a chance to—"

"No!!!" She shakes her head. "You are wrong. You've been wrong all along. There's no such thing as a good God. I had a plan to work hard, get top grades, get that internship, work at Google, and show everyone around me that I don't need God to get what I want out of *my* life. It's *my* life. Mine—and I was doing fine until you came along. You convinced me to believe that God has all the answers."

"Tee, I'm on your side. I'm only trying to help you."

"Well, you've done enough. There's nothing you can do to help me now. God is punishing me, can't you see? I want nothing to do with Him or with you, so please, leave." She turns her face away.

Please, Lord, don't let this friendship end like this. Please, Lord.

"Tee, please listen to me." I cup her face in my hands, but she shakes her head free and shuffles away from me.

"Don't worry about me, Jay. This is not your cross to carry. I know I'm broken and I need fixing, but you can't fix me—and neither can your God. I'll find answers. I'll find some meaning to all of this, but I'll find them on my own." She starts packing up her things.

"Teeyana—"

"Please, Jayden." She cuts me short. "Please, let me be. Let me figure this out on my own. I need some space. Please."

I nod and push my chair away from her and she puts all her books in her backpack, before standing up and walking away.

A few yards away from me, she turns around again. "You know, the problem isn't that I didn't believe in God. The problem is that He let me down every single time I put my trust in Him. It doesn't make sense, does it?"

I know she can see the look in my eyes. The look that says, "I wish I had answers for you." Or "I wish I could say something helpful right now, but I've got nothing."

"Does it?" She repeats, her lips quivering and tears gushing out of her eyes.

I want to say something—anything that will make her stay, but when I open my mouth, nothing comes out. So she turns around and leaves, without once looking at me again.

Back in my dorm room, I lower myself on my bed and let my backpack slide down my arm onto the floor. Then, letting out a heavy sigh, I throw myself on my bed and shut my eyes.

You're God's favourite, right? No problems? No struggles?

Teeyana's words echo in my mind and I shake my head, emotions welling up in my chest.

She couldn't be more wrong. She's being ridiculous and I don't know if I'm mad at her for believing in a pain-free life, or if I'm mad at myself for not telling her about Tyler, or any of my current struggles.

This is all my fault. If she trusted me enough to tell me everything she'd been through, I should have done the same. We wouldn't have gotten to this point, and I wouldn't have lost my best friend.

Images of Tyler flicker in my mind as I cover my face with my hands. I still remember the sympathy written all over the faces of the well-wishers from church who dropped by our house when the news of Tyler's death became public. I remember the walls of darkness that closed in on me every time I tried to wake up in the morning. Those same walls have returned and it all feels real again—like it only happened yesterday.

How did I get back here, Lord? I had come so far and made so much progress. Why do I still feel this way? I know You're good, but nothing about this feels good. Nothing at all.

I swallow a lump in my throat as warm tears run down my face. Then, continuous vibrations from my phone zap away the silence in my room. I wipe my eyes and sit up before bringing my phone up to my ear.

"Hello?" I clear my throat.

"Yo, Jayden. Where you at, bro?" Warryn's worried voice comes through from the phone. "We've been waiting for you and Coach is not happy you're late."

Oh, no. Basketball practice.

Taking a quick glance at my clock, I rub my forehead and sigh. "I'm sorry, man. I should have called you earlier."

"That's okay. When will you be here, though?" Warryn asks.

"I...uh. I'm not coming today." I press my lips together, anticipating his reaction.

"What? Why? Jayden, the tournament starts next month. We need everyone's commitment right now."

"Yeah, I know that, bro. But there's been a family emergency and I have to drive back to Boston to see my parents tonight."

"For real? Is everything okay?"

"Yeah, man. Please tell Coach I'll call him later tonight."

I drop the call and scroll through my contact list. Bringing the phone up to my ear again, I open my mouth to speak when I hear Mom's voice. "Hello? Jayden, honey? Are you okay?"

The sound of her voice melts my heart, and the tears start falling again. "No, Mom." My voice breaks. "I'm not okay. Please, can I come home?"

28

JAYDEN

When Tyler and I were kids, Mom's special hot cocoa with cinnamon and homemade cream was the only antidote to sad times. Sipping on the rich hot drink while watching our favourite TV show always took the pain away, no matter what caused it. But as I grew older, I discovered the painful truth that life is way more complicated than that.

Mom and Dad are sitting on either side of me on the sofa as I sip on the hot drink. Dad's hand is on my shoulder while Mom is squeezing my free hand, encouraging me to talk some more.

"Things have been good since I stopped seeing Mary last year." I lower my head and watch the steam rise from my cup. "I found the counselling sessions with her very useful, and I followed all her suggestions. I've been consistent with my personal Bible study and spending time with other Christians. Mary also suggested listening to more Christian songs, so I've been listening a lot to Tyler's CDs." I sniff.

"I have good days where I sail through no matter how much it hurts. But some days, like today, I find myself in the same dark hole I thought God saved me from. And it's days like this when I don't know what to do." I look up at Mom, who takes a quick glance at Dad before turning to me again.

She sighs softly and says, "Baby, there's something we want to show you."

"Honey," Dad places his hand on Mom's shoulder. "Are you sure this is the right time?"

"There's never going to be a right time, Trevor. He needs some closure." Mom pleads.

I place my cup on the table and lean forward. "What's going on?" I ask Dad. He doesn't reply, but instead, he stands up from his seat and walks towards the TV.

Picking up a laptop lying in front of it, he resumes his seat beside me and places the laptop on the table. He opens his folders and clicks on a video. Giving Mom one final look, he presses play.

A song starts playing, and it's not just any song. It's "Blessed Be Your Name." The screen is black, but it sounds like someone is playing the song on a guitar.

Then, before I get the chance to make sense of this, I hear his voice—that same voice I never thought I'd hear again. So deep, so crisp, so beautiful. "Tyler?" I almost choke on my own words.

The video comes on, and Tyler is sitting in his room, on his bed, the same spot I sit in every time I go in there, and he's playing the same song I play every time.

My eyes start watering and the clip changes to a video of Tyler sitting in his college dorm room.

"Hey, little bro. An interesting thought occurred to me right now. How cool will it be if I kept small video diaries of myself throughout college so you can see the life lessons I have for you when you start college, hmm?"

He brings his face close to the camera like he used to do to me whenever he asked me a question, his hazelnut brown eyes sparkling.

"Well, I'm going to assume you think it's a cool idea, so here are a few clips from me called 'Life lessons with Tyler' and they'll be my college send-off gift to you."

Tears stream down my face as I laugh my way through all the hilarious clips in the video. Tyler documented his first basketball try out, his first heartbreak, and when he failed one of his tests for the first time, then the second...and then the third.

I always thought of Tyler as the smart, good-looking charmer he was, and he knew I thought of him that way. This video has shown me a different side I never imagined I'd see. He recorded all his failures, all his mistakes, and all the things he didn't do right.

The date on the last video entry was two days before my fourteenth birthday. That was the day after he told me he'd be coming home for Thanksgiving and how he was working on a surprise for me. It was on that same day Mom received the phone call that they had found him dead in his dorm room.

Tyler smiles at the camera, but for the first time, I see pain in his eyes.

"Lesson number 20. Jay, no matter how tough life gets, when you feel inadequate, when you feel there's no reason to keep going, always remember that...it's all going to plan. A good plan. I love you, Jay, and hey, I know you always loved my guitar. You can have it. I'll see you soon."

He smiles again; the dimples forming on the sides of his face before the screen goes black. I lean forward and hold on to my knees, trying to stop the tears from flowing out.

"He could've taken his own advice. He could've—" I bite my lip to fight back more tears. "He thought he was a failure? He thought it was going to matter that he had made all those mistakes? I would have never stopped loving him as my brother.

Why didn't he say something?" My voice croaks and I push myself up from my seat.

Mom stands up and walks towards me, tears leaking from her eyes. "He was going through a tough time, baby."

"I know that, Mom." I snap. "But he still shouldn't have done what he did. Wasn't he thinking about you, or Dad, or even me?" I pace back and forth. "How long have you guys known about this video?"

"Since the day we went to get his things from his dorm room." Mom lowers her head. "Your dad and I watched it then, but we weren't sure if it was a good idea to show you."

I stop pacing, and my heart rate slows down. "Is there...is there anything else he left that I don't know about?"

Mom looks at Dad, and he nods at her.

"There's one more thing he left behind, honey." Mom sniffs and removes her old phone from her back pocket. "He left a voice note when he tried to call me that day." She fiddles with her phone. "I was at work and didn't find it until days later."

"Can I listen to it?" I stretch my hand towards her.

"Are you sure you want to listen to it, son?" Dad asks.

"Please, let me listen to it."

Mom hesitates, but then hands the phone over to me. My thumb hovers over the play button for a few seconds before pressing it, Tyler's trembling voice coming through.

"Hello? Hello? Mom? Mom, I'm so sorry. I didn't mean to do it. Please, forgive me. I've called...I've called the ambulance, but I don't know when they'll get here. Please forgive me. Please ask God to forgive me. Please tell Jay I'm sorry. Tell him I love him. Tell Dad I love him. I love you too, Mom. I'm sorry. Mom...I'm sorry."

The phone beeps and I drop it on the sofa. "So...he regretted his actions?" I ask between shaky breaths. "He regretted his actions, and he still died?" I turn to face Mom, her face soaked with tears.

"It was too late when the ambulance got there, honey." Her lips quiver. "They tried all they could, but they couldn't save him. He was already dead when they got to the hospital."

"He loved you, Jayden." Dad walks up to me and squeezes my shoulder. "I know he made a mistake—a huge one. But he loved you, son. Please, find a place in your heart to forgive him. Please."

Dad's words cut right through me, finally dawning on me that I've been holding grudges all this time. Not just against myself, but also against Tyler.

I give in to my emotions and bury my face in Dad's shoulder. His strong arms wrap around me as I sob. Then Mom hugs me from behind and presses her head on my back—her own tears soaking into my t-shirt.

~

My feet ache as I drag them across the floors of Faith Baptist Church—every step feeling like I'm carrying a heavy weight on my shoulders. I sit at the end of one of the pews and stare at the big wooden cross hanging on the wall behind the pulpit.

Leaning back, I listen to the music playing from the large speakers as Anton's voice echoes into the main auditorium from one of the rooms inside. Only Anton would sing hymns in church on a Saturday morning. It's good to know that at least someone is happy today. I knew he'd be around because there's a church leaders meeting in a few hours and he always comes in early to set up and do admin work.

Resting my head on the pew in front of me, my eyes beg for the sleep I couldn't get last night. After trying all night, I gave up and rolled out of bed at 8 a.m. this morning to come here, hoping to find some peace.

"It Is Well" is one of Anton's favourite hymns. I've never met a man who loves hymns as much as he does. He says the lyrics are poetry and have deep revelations behind them, so I Iisten and pray some hope sparks up in me right now.

When peace like a river, attendeth my way
When sorrows like sea billows roll;
Whatever my lot, Thou has taught me to say,
It is well, it is well with my soul

Towards the end of the chorus, a heavy hand rests on my shoulder, startling me and forcing me to sit up.

"Sorry, buddy. Didn't mean to scare you there." Anton says and I relax again in my seat. "Everything okay?" He asks, tilting his head.

"Yeah...I guess." I lie.

"You sure?" Anton raises an eyebrow.

"Actually, no, I'm not." I rub my temples to ease off the headache I've gained because of my lack of sleep.

"Mind if I sit next to you?"

I shake my head and shuffle down the pew.

"What's up, buddy?" He asks.

"Well, first of all, I'm worried about Teeyana." I start. "She was avoiding me, so I confronted her about it."

"Okay...and what did she say?"

"She said she didn't want me to convince her that God cares about her." I shake my head. "She's hurt, Anton. Losing her grandma has taken a huge toll on her faith. She had doubts and questions before, but I think she wants to quit now—if she hasn't done so already."

"Hmm. Grief." Anton sighs, pressing his elbows into his

thighs and clasping his hands. "It has a way of making you believe that you're all alone in this world, doesn't it?"

"Yes, it does."

"Well, like you said, she's hurt. She's grieving, and that's okay. Let her grieve, Jayden. If she wants space, let her have space. Perhaps she said all those things because she's hurt and not because she wants to quit." Anton places a hand on my shoulder.

"I know you care about her, buddy. And trust me, I know what it feels like to see someone you care about suffer without being able to help. That was me last year when Annie and I lost our baby. Being in that position makes you feel useless, doesn't it?"

I nod.

"Moments like this show us how limited we are in our abilities as humans. Sometimes, we want to press in to show our loved ones how much we care when all they need is space to figure things out and spend time alone with God." Anton nods.

"I know, but the other thing is, after I spoke to her on Friday, those old feelings of guilt came back. It feels like I've been taken back in time to all those horrible months when I blamed myself for Tyler's death."

I lean forward. "I know God wants me to be strong and be of good courage. I know He is with me through this suffering and that's *exactly* the problem. I know all this and I believe it with all my heart. So why do I still feel this way?" I straighten my back and face Anton, my vision blurring with tears.

"No amount of encouragement can bring Tyler back. I've been living a lie, Anton. I thought I'd moved past this, but I can't even bring myself to talk about Tyler's death because I know how much it breaks me when I do."

I wipe my eyes. "I'm not qualified to encourage anyone. Tyler needed me, Anton. I could have helped him. I could have done something to make him stay, but I didn't. Teeyana opened up to me and I failed her like I failed my only brother." Tears break free from my eyes and I try to bury my face in my hands, but Anton stops me.

"Hey, hey, hey." Anton pushes my hands down and grabs my shoulders, which forces me to look at him. "Jayden, listen to me. What happened to Tyler was not your fault, alright? There's nothing you could have done to change the situation. And neither is what's happening to Teeyana your fault. You can't comfort her and as sad as that sounds, it is the truth. God is the only one who can give her true comfort, so please, don't blame yourself for this."

"I'm trying, Anton. I'm trying hard, but I can't help it. Teeyana hates me now when all I've tried to do is help her see how much God loves her. I don't know what to do anymore."

"Jayden, you can't make everything right. You don't have the power to fix everything. Only God does. When we can't do things, we seek help from the One who is able to do exceedingly abundantly above all that we can ever ask or think. We look up to God for help because He is the One who knows and understands us. Now is not the time to blame yourself. It's time to fight in prayer. We need to pray that God gives Teeyana the comfort she needs right now, and that He draws her closer to Him."

Anton squeezes my shoulder. "We also need to pray that God comforts you too. You can't run on empty, Jayden. Go back to the place of intimacy with Jesus and let Him fight for you. Let Him fill you up with His hope again. He did it before and I have no doubt in my heart that He will do it again."

29

TEEYANA

"Girl, you can't be serious!!!" Amara's angry voice comes through from the phone after I tell her about my confrontation with Heather. "You know none of what she said is true, right?"

"I'm not sure about anything anymore, Amara." I slump my shoulders. "All I'm asking is that you be honest with me as my best friend. Am I really overreacting to this? Am I selfish?"

"Teeyana Joy Sparks. Listen to me and listen carefully." Amara lets her "*Nigerian Mom*" side out. Whenever this side of her comes out, it means she's serious and wants to make a point I have to listen to.

"That Heather girl had no right to say all those things she said to you." Amara continues. "Only an insensitive person would expect you to brush off the loss of a loved one. She's trying to break you because she feels threatened by your strength and confidence. You can't let her have her way. You cannot, and you will not. Do you hear me?"

"I hear you, girl." I sigh and lay down on my bed, staring at the ceiling. "But there's something I need to tell you, Amara. I'm not strong. I know you say I am, but that's only because I've been pretending all these years. I act like situations don't bother me, yet I live in constant fear of losing everything and everyone I know. Grandma's death was a big blow and I don't know who I am anymore." I pause and think about the next few words I'm about to say. I have to tell Amara the truth.

"Amara, I don't think this God thing is working for me anymore. I've tried, and I feel betrayed. I'm tired and I don't see the point of putting my heart out there only to get it crushed over and over again." I bite my bottom lip, anticipating Amara's response.

There's silence on her end for a few seconds before she speaks again. "Girl, I'm sorry you feel this way. I can only imagine what you're going through right now. I'm sorry because I don't know if I have anything to say to make you feel better."

"It's okay. I wasn't expecting you to come up with magic words to make everything better. I'm not okay, but I'm trying to work things out, so I'll be fine."

"Yeah, but girl, that's what you've always said; that you'll work things out yourself. I've been trying to tell you that won't work because—"

"Things take time, okay?" I cut Amara short. "I was doing fine until..." I stop myself from mentioning Jayden's name.

"Until what?" Amara asks, but I don't reply. "Look, girl, you may not like the sound of what I'm about to say, but have you considered talking this out with someone else other than me? You have so many people around you who would do anything to help you. Why don't you want to open up to them? What about your parents? Kevin? Anton?" she pauses. "Or even Jayden?"

I cover my face with my palm and groan. "Amara, I don't think I'll be speaking to Jayden anymore."

"Erm, why not? What happened between you two?"

I let out a deep sigh. "It's a long story, but let's just say we had a fight."

"A fight? About what? What did he do to you?" Amara raises her voice.

I sit up in my bed. "Nothing. He did nothing wrong. It's me. I was angry, okay? I was raging mad at the world, at God, and at Jayden for luring me back into believing all the lies about what God can do. I poured out my anger on him and told him I needed space to sort my life out. I understand he's trying to help me. I understand everyone is trying to help me, but there are too many things going through my head right now and I need space."

"Right, I understand that." Amara's voice softens. "But girl, do you *really* need space, or are you just running away from the things that make you uncomfortable and scared?"

"I'm not sure I understand." I frown.

Amara sighs and continues, "Remember you told me you were angry because the events in your life didn't reflect your idea of God? So do you think the "God thing" is not working for you because He doesn't fit into the box you've been trying to put Him into?"

I think about Amara's question—long and hard. I don't know what surprises me more, the fact that her question sounds about right or the fact that this is the first time I'm hearing her speak so passionately about God.

"Last week at my youth group Bible study," Amara continues, "I learnt that sometimes we face trials that will make us question God's goodness. But when we are open to talking about our questions, we allow God to reveal His good nature through these trials. God doesn't fit into boxes, girl. There's so much we don't know about Him, but guess what, He knows everything about us. The closer we get to Him, the more He'll reveal His love for us. You can't keep running away and shutting everyone out. You need to face your fears, girl."

Amara's words leave me stunned. There's this new excitement and confidence in her voice. She sounds like she believes what she's saying. "Wow, Amara. I've never heard you talk about God like this before," I say.

Amara chuckles. "Well, let's say attending Bible studies here at college was the best decision I ever made. I have a spiritual mentor at church and I've been speaking to her about the questions I have from my personal Bible study. You wanted me to be honest with you, so as your best friend in the whole wide world, can you promise me you'll speak to someone? Pretty please?" she begs.

I lean forward and rub my temple. "Okay. I'll consider it. Thanks, Amara. I love you."

"I love you too, girl."

I end the call and spread my arms wide on my bed.

So this God thing has worked out for Amara, Jayden, my parents, and everyone else.

Everyone except me.

Just great!

I scan the aisle of sweets and chocolate, unable to decide what my next study snack will be. My mind is all over the place, so I'm hoping these snacks will help me stay focused. I use them as rewards for studying and for making progress on my Google internship application.

I have to admit that it's been hard not talking to Jayden—especially when I see him everywhere I go. He sat in front of me in our hand lettering class today and at first, he didn't look my way. But at the end of the class, when he got up to leave, he smiled at me.

It was the same charming smile he sent my way when he handed me that burger the first time I met him. It wasn't a fake smile. It wasn't half-hearted either. It was pure and genuine, but it made me feel ashamed for destroying our friendship.

Sometimes, I get the urge to walk up to him and apologise so he can make me laugh again. I want things to go back to the way they were, but it's too late now. I said too many things and I can never forget the hurt I saw in his eyes that Friday night. My views about God will never change, so I don't want either of us to get hurt any further.

As the days fly by, I'm starting to realise how indecisive I am —so indecisive I can't even pick which snack I want. After walking up and down the aisle at least ten times, I grab a pack of jelly beans and head to the cash register. I arrive there as the man in front of me finishes paying for his drink. When he turns around to leave, our eyes meet, sending ringing bells around in my brain.

"Teeyana? Oh wow, it's been a long time." Bright white teeth flash at me, and his light skin and curly hair glisten under the light.

"Hey, Anton." I adjust to an awkward stance, not knowing what to do with myself. Normally, when I see him, we would hug each other. But after missing Bible study for so many weeks, I think a hug would be pushing it.

To my greatest surprise, his attitude is still as warm as ever and he invites me in for a hug. "How are you, kiddo? Jayden told me about your grandma. I'm sorry about your loss." He tilts his head and purses his lips.

Of course. That explains it. He's been speaking to Jayden. I wonder what else Jayden has told him.

"Thanks, Anton. How is Annie doing?" I ask, forcing a smile out of my tired-looking face.

"She's doing great, and she keeps asking after you. Everyone misses you at church. It's not the same without you. We hope you can join us again soon." He adds with hope in his voice.

I send him a smile and for a moment; I don't know what to say.

Should I give him hope and say I'll come soon? Or should I say I may never come again?

"I miss you guys too." I respond. "I'm still trying to sort a few things out for myself. Mainly my application for that internship I told you about?" I try to divert the conversation.

"Oh, yeah. I remember that. When is the deadline for that again?" He asks.

"Monday. So only three days left to go. It's taking up a lot of my free time, but my friend—Ellie, is helping me out."

"That's amazing. I'm glad you're getting the support you need. Well, we're all praying for you and your family. I hope God crowns all your hard work with success." He smiles at me again.

"Thanks, Anton. I hope to see you all soon." I give him false hope.

"It'll be great to see you. I know it'll make Annie very happy. Have a blessed week." He waves at me before heading out the door and towards the car park.

Strangely enough, talking to Anton makes me miss all our Bible study sessions. I miss the family and the love I felt. I miss the conversations Jayden and I had after every session. I miss how we would talk on the phone until one of us fell asleep. I miss Jayden.

No, stay focused, Teeyana.

I shake my head and walk up to the cashier to pay for my sweets.

Back at the library, I sit across the table from Ellie as she scrolls through my portfolio on my iPad. I wrap my hands around my cup of coffee before bringing it to my lips and sipping the black, non-sugary liquid.

Ugh, I don't even like coffee, but I'll do anything to stay awake so I can get this application finished this weekend.

"Teeyana?"

I lift my head to find Ellie staring at me. "Huh? Sorry, did you say something?" I set my cup down on the table before leaning forward.

"I asked if you are okay. You seem a bit distracted today." She says, her gaze moving from me to my cup of coffee, and then back to me.

"Oh, sorry." I pull my jumper sleeves over my hands to warm them. "I just have a lot on my mind."

"Oh? Are you sure you're okay? You know you can talk to me about anything, right?"

I nod. "Yes, I know that. I'm okay, Ellie. Thank you." I smile warmly.

"Well, then. I think we're done here." She returns my smile and hands my iPad back to me. "I love how you laid out the book cover designs from your church. The t-shirt designs from your summer experience look great too. The brochure designs from your youth group look amazing. My favourites are the website designs and your patterns from your classes. You're very talented, Teeyana. I think you have a good chance at getting this internship."

"Really?" A broad smile appears on my face.

"Yes. Really. All you need to do now is add in your resume and your five hundred word essay. I already looked at those and emailed them back to you with only a few minor corrections. Once you're done with that, you can send it off whenever you like."

"Thank you so much, Ellie. You have no idea how much this means to me."

"No problem at all. Let me know when you get the internship so we can get drinks to celebrate." She winks at me before standing up from her seat.

Memories of that frat party pierce into my thoughts and

leave a sour taste in my mouth. I'm never going to let her convince me to taste another glass of alcohol again.

"Okay, I have to leave for class now. Call me later." Ellie hugs me and then rushes down the stairs to the ground floor. When she's out of my sight, I look down at my application again. Ellie is right. I can do this. I've got what it takes to get this internship. I can make this work out in my favour.

On Sunday evening, I proof-read my whole application again and after spending half an hour staring at my laptop screen, my fingers hovering over the keypad, I take a deep breath and hit send.

30

TEEYANA

My phone buzzes next to me and I jump on it, pressing the home button with the speed of lightning. But yet again, it's not from Google.

Slumping back in my chair, I stare out my dorm room window, watching students pass by, their umbrellas shielding them from the rain, and broad smiles plastered on their faces like they have no cares in this world.

It must be nice to feel that way.

Ever since I sent my application a month ago, I've tired myself out by refreshing my emails a million times a day. They promised to send out interview invites a week after the deadline, but spring break is almost here, and I've still heard nothing.

Now my heart skips every time my phone vibrates, my edges are thinning out, and several spots have broken out on my face.

Could this get any worse?

If I could, then I would call Jayden so he can tell me something positive and make me feel better. But a month has passed since the argument and he has backed off.

I know I should be grateful because that's what I asked for, but I miss him. I miss our long phone calls where we reflected on our day. I miss how he encouraged me to look forward to the next day. I miss the daily devotions he sent me; I only read them because I knew he would ask me questions about them later in the day.

I miss Jayden.

Pushing my books to the side, I sigh and lean forward on my desk. I should be studying for finals but instead, I've been sitting here all day, wrapped up in my blanket, and watching the rain trickle down my window.

My eyes fall on the framed photo Jayden gave me for Christmas, and I read out his favourite Bible verse on it.

"But He knows the way that I take; when He has tested me, I will come forth as gold." -Job 23:10

Jayden put so much effort into this gift and it's special to me. Who would have a friend like Jayden and push him away? Only an idiot—like me.

I groan and pick up my phone, unlocking it with an intention to scroll through my previous text messages with Jayden, but a new email notification pings through—from Google. My stomach churns, bile rises to my throat, and a wave of nausea engulfs me. But after a few breathing exercises, I open the email and scroll.

Dear Miss Sparks,

. . .

We apologise for the delay in getting back to you regarding your recent application to work for us this summer. This year, we have received over a thousand applications and we have been reviewing each of them. Based on your submission, it is my pleasure to inform you that you have been shortlisted for an interview. We would like to meet with you on Friday the 8th of April at 9 a.m. Please confirm with us if you will be able to make this date as soon as possible. We look forward to hearing from you.

Kind Regards,
Michael Tall
Google Internship Team

I squeal for a good minute while checking my calendar to make sure I'm free on that day. After sending a quick reply to the email, I open up my contact list and type in "Mom" but I change my mind and type in "Jayden" instead. I scroll through our previous messages, trying to decide if I should tell him or not.

After going back and forth for another minute, I make a decision and start typing.

Hey,
Guess what. I got invited for an interview at Google.
I'm so close to getting this internship. Can you believe it?

I place my phone down and stare at the screen, waiting for a reply. Two blue ticks appear next to the text, letting me know my message has been seen, and then my phone starts ringing. I pick up the call and bring the phone close to my ear. "Hello?"

"Eeek!!!" Amara squeals. "Girl, I just saw your text. Congratulations. When is the interview?"

In the end, I chose not to bother Jayden with the news. I don't think he'll want to talk to me. I haven't seen him much around campus, so I'm sure he's busy with basketball training.

"Thanks, girl. It's next week, Friday." I sigh. "Amara, what if I mess this up? What if I throw it all down the drain?" I rub my forehead.

"And what if you don't?" Amara jumps in. "Come on, girl. You've worked hard for this. You'll be fine. Remember, the power is not in your hands. If God wants you to get it, you will get it. You have to believe that." Amara reassures me.

That's exactly what Jayden would have said. Everything and everyone now reminds me of him.

Ellie's useful interview tips boosted my confidence when I left for Atlanta yesterday. I settled into the accommodation the Google team provided for us and called my parents to tell them I had arrived.

Mom mentioned that Danny wasn't feeling well, so I video called him and read him his favourite Bible story. Not long after Danny fell asleep, I went to bed so I could wake up early for my interview this morning.

In the waiting room, I spoke to the other candidates who seemed nice, but also well qualified. Of course that shook my confidence and now I'm unsure of how well I did in my interview. Some questions were hard, and not what I had prepared for, but I'm glad it's all over now and I'm back at college.

Letting out a heavy sigh, I trudge back to my dorm room, my feet aching with each stride. After having a nice long shower, I lay on my bed, grateful it's the weekend and I don't have any classes. I close my eyes to rest and drift off to sleep within a few minutes.

Then I'm running and laughing. I'm running down the same road leading from the mall to our house in Boston. The same road I ran down when I got the call from Mom about Grandma. This time, it's not a nervous run. I'm happy because I'm running after Danny. I run as fast as I can and his little legs take him farther and farther down the road.

Then like a flash of lightning, Danny disappears from my sight. I can still hear him giggling in the distance, but I can't see him anywhere.

"Danny? Where are you?" I look around, but I can't find him. My heart thumps as his laugh fades away. I look around me and realise I'm alone. All alone.

"Danny?" I call out, but there's no response. "Boy, I ain't playing with you. Please come out from where you're hiding." I keep looking around me, but I can't find him anywhere. "Danny? Danny? Please come back. Danny?"

"Danny? Danny?" I jerk out of my sleep. My top is drenched in sweat, as if someone poured a bucket of water on me. My face is wet too, but not with sweat—it's wet with my tears.

I look around my dorm room and I'm still alone. My head turns swiftly to the clock and it's 5p.m. "Oh, shoot!!!" I jump down from my bed and slip my feet into my trainers. I planned to meet with Ellie at the café opposite the library half an hour ago.

I have to get out of these clothes. I can't leave looking like this.

I head for my closet but freeze in my tracks.

My dream!!! Oh God!!! Danny!!!

I search everywhere for my phone before finding it under my duvet cover. I have three missed calls—one from Ellie, and two from Mom. I also have a text notification from Mom, which I click on.

. . .

Hey baby,

I tried calling you, but I think you're probably knocked out from your long trip. Your Dad and I are in hospital. Danny collapsed at school this morning and the doctor says he has meningitis.

"Oh, no. Oh, no." I drop my phone on my bed, pressing my hands against my temples. "God, no. Please, not Danny. No." A sharp pain shoots through my chest as my heart thumps. The room spins, and I lean against the wall to stop myself from falling.

"Danny. I need to see Danny." My shaky voice comes between wheezes.

After catching my breath, I grab my phone and pick up my backpack, before running out of my dorm room without looking at my phone a second time.

31

JAYDEN

God taught me many lessons through my friendship with Teeyana. I wish He had taught me these lessons differently, but I've learnt there are some things I can't change—because I'm not God.

I took Anton's advice and gave Teeyana the space she asked for. Being away from her has given me time to deal with the baggage I've been carrying around all these years. Inside this baggage was a mixture of guilt, resentment, and unforgiveness, which I thought I'd moved past, but apparently not.

I've started seeing my Christian counsellor—Mary Perkins, again and I've been driving back home to Boston every other weekend to attend our scheduled face-to-face sessions. Out of the kindness of her heart, Mary has also included weekly telephone catch up sessions. My parents and Anton have also been supportive. They've given me the space I asked for, but they've also been there to encourage me when I needed it.

I stopped attending basketball practice, which means I couldn't take part in the games this year. Coach Simpson wasn't pleased at first, but he was very understanding when I explained my situation to him. It's been two months since I went back on my journey to recovery, and I'm in a much better place now.

As much as I care about Teeyana, I can't do God's job for Him. Anton was right. I've first come to terms with the fact that I'm limited in what I can do. So I've been praying that God works everything out according to His good purpose in her life.

I still think about her though—all the time. And I miss her —very much.

Perhaps someday, she'll decide to speak to me again, but for now, I'm choosing to let God do whatever He wants. He's in control, after all.

Pressing my phone against my ear, I climb up the staircase leading up to Donovan Hall. It's where Teeyana lives, but I'm not here to see her. The boys won their basketball match today, and they're having a party tonight. It would be great to see Teeyana, but I don't think she'll want to talk to me.

"Hey, man. Yeah, I'm on my way. Just walking up now." I end the call with Warryn and open the double doors leading into the hallway.

The smell of feet and sweat is the first thing that hits me, but as I walk further down the hallway, loud victory chants steal my attention.

On the left-hand side of the hallway, next to the elevator, the boys are jumping around, waving their shirts, and bumping their chests as they celebrate their victory. I smile and head towards the group, greeting everyone before joining in with their chants and cheers.

"Congrats, man. You guys killed it." I say to Warryn, who breaks off from the group to greet me.

"Did you see that last basket Jason made? That was sick, right?" He exclaims.

"I know!!! I watched the game live. Bro, it was wicked!!!" I grin.

Warryn's smile fades, and he rests his arm on my shoulder. "It wasn't the same playing without you, though, man. How you holding up?" He jerks his head towards me.

"I'm good, man. Thanks for asking. There's always next time and I'll be back on that court soon. God willing." I reassure him.

"Ayyy, that's my man." Warryn squeezes my shoulder. "Party is upstairs in Jason's common room." He points towards the group of chanting boys, who are now heading to the elevator.

I follow close behind him, but stop in my tracks when my eyes fall on her. Teeyana is running down the hallway towards us, looking distressed and frazzled. She bumps into one of the boys, which slows her down. "Sorry. I'm so sorry." She says before quickening her strides again.

Then she trips on one of the sneakers lying on the floor, and lands on her knees. One boy helps her up, and there's some laughter going around, but she doesn't stop.

I stand back and wait for her to come through, and as she's about to run past me, I grab her arms, stopping her from moving any further.

"Whoa, Tee, slow down." She resists my hold and when she snaps her head up, our eyes meet and she resists even more.

"What's wrong?" I ask. "Why are you crying?" My grip loosens.

She opens her mouth to speak, but no words come out. Instead, her whole body sinks to the floor, and my hold on her becomes firm again. Kneeling in front of her, I take her shaking hands into mine. She breaks down into uncontrollable sobs and muffles a few words.

"Danny. It's Danny." She forces the words out, and my heart sinks.

"Okay. Breathe. Tee, look at me. Breathe." I put her hands down and hold her head steady, forcing her to look me in the eye. "Okay, slowly now, tell me. What happened to Danny?"

"I-I-I need to go home." She says, her lips quivering.

"Is everything alright? What happened to Danny?" Her dark brown eyes glisten with tears.

"I slept off when I got back from my Google interview this morning and I had a terrible nightmare. Danny went missing in my dream, and I couldn't find him anywhere. Then I woke up to see a message from my mom saying Danny is in hospital. Mom says he has meningitis—that's the stuff that kills children, right? My brother's going to die. Danny's going to die." She runs her hands through her curls.

I squeeze her shoulder. "What else did your mom say?"

"That's all she said. I want to go home. I want to see Danny." She tries to stand up, but I hold on to her again.

"Tee, wait. I'll drive you home."

"No. Please, Jayden, you don't have to do this." She shakes her head. "I'll be fine. I—"

"I know I don't have to do this, but I want to. Please, let me drive you home. I wouldn't want you traveling on your own for two hours like this. Please." I plead.

After what seems like forever, she finally nods. When her hands stop shaking, I help her stand up. The crowd of onlookers has dispersed but there are still a few people standing around, staring.

"Do you have your phone with you?" I ask Teeyana.

"Erm yeah, I think I threw it in here." She rummages through her backpack and pulls her phone out. "*Ugh*, it's turned off. I forgot to charge it when I got back."

"That's okay, you can charge it in my car. I wanted to make sure your parents can reach you." I brush off some dust from her cheek.

"Jayden." Warryn walks towards us. "Is everything alright here?"

"Hey, man. Listen, Teeyana's younger brother is in the hospital."

"Oh, no." Warryn brings his hand up to cover his mouth.

"Yeah, man. I need to drive her to Boston now. Please tell Jason I'll call him tonight."

"Sure, man. You go on, and I'll catch you later. Hope your brother is okay, Teeyana." Warryn waves at us as he retreats back to the elevator.

"And congrats again on your win." I give Warryn a thumbs up before turning to Teeyana again. "You ready?" She looks at me and nods.

"Come on then, let's go." I extend my hand to her and after much hesitation, she slips her hand into mine.

My hands grip the steering wheel as I resist the urge to turn my head and look at Teeyana. She is sleeping in the passenger's seat next to me and I don't blame her. I can only imagine what an exhausting weekend she's had. I'm grateful I came to her when I did and that I got this chance to be there for her.

There are so many things I want to tell her now that she's here—so many things I could have told her earlier, but I don't know what she's thinking. I don't want to say something that will jeopardise any hope of us being friends again.

I try to focus on the road, but I can't help stealing quick glances at her as she snores softly by my side. The poor girl has been through so much in such a short space of time and if I were in her shoes, I would be overwhelmed too.

Teeyana's charging phone lights up and starts pinging away with hundreds of notifications, and a few minutes later, her phone starts vibrating.

"Tee? Tee?" I call out to her and she moves her head a few times. "Tee, I think someone's calling you."

She rubs her closed eyelids before reaching for her phone. Bringing it up to her ear, she straightens in her seat.

"Hello? Mom? Yeah, I saw your message. Is he okay? I'm on my way home now. Jayden offered to drive me." She turns her head and looks at me.

My heart pounds as I try to focus on the road, but all I want to do is listen to what Teeyana's mom is saying. I want to stay positive but my thoughts are running wild.

Lord, please. Let Danny be fine.

"Wait, what?" Teeyana takes the phone away from her ear, and my heart sinks into my stomach. She opens up her messages and scrolls through. Then she covers her mouth with her hand, looking at me with eyes I can't read into.

"Oh, my God." She whispers, tears forming in her eyes.

"Tee? What's wrong? Is everything alright?" I ask, barely resisting the urge to pull over.

Teeyana doesn't answer, but starts sobbing while still covering her mouth. At this point, I give in and pull the car over.

Parked safely on the side of the road, I take off my seatbelt and turn towards her. "Tee? Is...Is Danny alright?" The words make my mouth heavy.

Teeyana exhales and nods. Placing the phone on her chest, she says, "He's okay." She looks at me, her eyes wet with tears. "He's going to be okay. It's a mild form of meningitis. The viral form. It's not life threatening."

"Oh, thank you, Jesus." I rest my head on the steering wheel, my heart rate slowing down again.

"Hello? Mom?" Teeyana presses the phone again against her ear. "I didn't see the full message, and I panicked when I saw the first bit you sent me, so I thought I'd come home." She continues.

"Okay, Mom...that's okay. I'll see you when I get there. I love you." She ends the call and leans back in her seat.

"He's going to be okay." Teeyana repeats. "The doctors have discharged him from the hospital and he's at home now. They said he should recover over the next week. All he needs is rest and some pain relief."

"Wow, that's something to be grateful for. I'm so relieved." I rub my forehead.

Looking down at her phone, she says, "I was so scared, Jay. I thought I was going to end up alone. After everything that has happened, I expect bad things to happen to me all the time." She leans her head back and closes her eyes, tears trickling down her cheeks.

"But you're not alone, Tee." I lean closer, almost reaching for her hand, but I restrain myself. "You've got your family, Amara,...and you've got me." I swallow as she opens her eyes and looks at me. "You've still got me."

I turn my head away and look out the window when she doesn't respond. Shaking my head, I muster the courage to tell her everything I should have told her in the library that day.

"God doesn't enjoy hurting you, Tee. He's not some malicious being who sits up there and enjoys watching you suffer. He cares about you. Heck, He loves you so much He gave up His own Son for you. He knows you're hurting, and He's reaching out to you because He wants to comfort you."

"Of course He wants to comfort me." She scoffs. "He allowed this mess to happen in the first place. Does He feel guilty? Is He using these things to get my attention? He already has my attention, so what else does He want from me?"

"He wants you to trust Him." I look at her. "Totally and completely. He wants you to understand that He knows what He is doing. He wants you to see that He is sovereign over all things and that His infinite wisdom is always working for the greater good of everyone who trusts Him even when they don't see it. He wants you to stop trying to work out everything on your own because you're only going to get disappointed and hurt."

"It's hard, okay? It's hard because sometimes I don't feel Him. How can I let Him take control when I'm not even sure if He's there or not? I'm not like you, Jay. You feel His presence all the time, don't you?" She looks at me.

The look on my face gives away my response before I shake my head slowly. It's time to be vulnerable.

Teeyana's eyes widen. "You mean sometimes...you feel God is distant too?"

I nod. "Yes, many times, I've felt like God is far away from me."

"Wow...and I thought I couldn't feel Him because He was punishing me."

"Why do you always think God is punishing you?" I ask.

She pouts and looks down at her phone. "I don't know...for doubting Him? For trying to run away from Him?" She shrugs. "Punishing me for not being the perfect Christian?"

"Nobody is a perfect anything, Tee. God is not like that at all. Moses doubted God. Sarah—Abraham's wife, doubted God and even Thomas—one of Jesus' own disciples doubted Him. The doubts will always come, so that's not the problem. The problem is how we respond."

Teeyana sighs and leans forward. "So, how do you respond?"

I pause. "This might sound ridiculous to you, but I walk up to the mirror and tell myself that God is good, and that He loves me until my doubtful heart believes it." I send her a nervous smile.

Teeyana chuckles. "You do that? You talk to yourself in the mirror?"

"Every day—if I have to." I grin, feeling pleased that I've pulled a smile out of her. "Whatever happens, and whatever you decide to do," I sigh. "I hope you can remember that God is good, and that He loves you."

Her smile fades away, and she lowers her head. "I'm sorry for making you go through all this trouble for me, Jay." She changes the subject. "Especially now that you didn't really need to drive me all the way back to Boston, after all. You could've been having fun at your basketball party tonight."

"It's my absolute pleasure doing this for you." I put on my seatbelt again and she does the same. I start the car and begin driving on the road. "And congrats on your interview. I hope it was everything you wanted it to be." I smile to hide my disappointment that she didn't tell me.

"Thanks." She responds and averts my gaze. "How about we put some music on? Do you mind?"

"Erm...well, I have a few CDs over there." I use my chin to point to the glove box. "But they're all Matt Redman and Chris Tomlin CDs. You can also use my phone and find a Spotify playlist if you want."

"No, it's okay. The CDs will do just fine." She smiles at me and slips one of the CDs in the car radio and of course, "Blessed Be Your Name" starts playing—Tyler's favourite song. They're all Tyler's CDs and I held onto them because I couldn't bring myself to throw them away. They are another piece that reminds me of him.

I sigh and take a quick glance at the green and yellow ribbon on Teeyana's backpack before turning back to face the road. I'm glad Teeyana feels better, and that Danny is fine too. Perhaps, someday, I'll get the chance to tell her about Tyler.

32

TEEYANA

Jayden parks in front of our house as it strikes eight p.m. We spent the rest of the car ride listening to all the Chris Tomlin and Matt Redman CDs he had in his car.

The last thing I remember was shutting my eyes for a minute, and before I knew it, we were in front of my house, with Jayden's voice waking me up from my slumber.

"Thanks again for doing this, Jay." I rub my eyelids and yawn. "Would you like to come in and have something to drink?" I ask. "My mom makes good hot chocolate."

"No, that's fine, Tee." He shakes his head, the tiredness in his eyes pleading his case. "You need some time alone with your family and I already told my parents I'm on my way." He smiles.

"Okay then. Well, promise me you'll drive safe?"

"I promise I'll try my best." He places his hand on his chest—a sign of his oath of honour. "My house is only half an hour away, so I'll let you know when I get home."

"Okay. Please tell your parents I'm sorry for dragging you away from college." I clasp my hands together in front of my face.

He tilts his head and raises his brows. "Tee, for the

umpteenth time, I'm a grown man and I decided to drive you down here. I'm sure my parents will understand." He brings my hands down. "There's nothing wrong with going the extra mile for the people you care about." His hazel brown eyes twinkle at me.

He still cares about me after everything I said to him? Should I apologise now? Will he forgive me?

"Thank you, Jay." I unbuckle my seatbelt and get out of his car, resisting the urge to slap myself for my own cowardice.

Standing on the stairs leading up to our front porch, I watch Jayden drive off and wait for his car to disappear from my sight before entering the house. After giving Mom and Dad long hugs, I rush up to Danny's room and lie next to him in his bed.

Mom gave him some pain relief an hour ago, so he's able to sleep now, but I wish he didn't have to go through this pain at all. Brushing my lips against his forehead, I whisper, "I love you, Daniel Sparks. Please don't scare me like that again. I can't bear the thought of losing you."

After dinner, Mom and Dad rope me in to watch *Facing The Giants* with them. Ignoring my fatigued muscles begging for rest, I squeeze between Mom and Dad on the sofa and we cover ourselves with a large fleece blanket, each one of us clutching a bowl of popcorn.

When I was younger, before Danny was born, Friday night was always movie night. We used to order pizza and watch movies for hours. *The Lion King* and *The Prince of Egypt* were our favourites. We watched them over a thousand times, singing along to all the songs until we were exhausted.

Today feels like one of those old days, when I still had hopes that life would be perfect for me. I had no idea then that my life would be the roller coaster ride it is today.

Jayden and Amara were right about the support I have around me. My parents have always tried to help and look out for me. Yet, they were the first people I shut out when I started struggling.

Perhaps if I'd spoken to them at the beginning, I wouldn't be in the mess I'm in right now. Perhaps this is the second chance I'm getting to right my wrongs and to work on the relationships I have with the people around me.

I link up my hand with Dad's and I lay my head on Mom's shoulder when the movie starts. At the end, we take turns talking about our favourite parts.

"I love how loyal his wife was to him." Mom speaks first. "He went through a lot, but I'm sure it was a great help for him to have such a supportive wife. She had her own struggles, but she never left his side. It's the complete opposite of what Job's wife did, isn't it, honey?" She brushes my chin.

"Yeah, it is." I nod and give her a weak smile.

"Hmm, do you know what my favourite scene was?" Dad asks rhetorically, but I shake my head anyway. "It's the part where he told God he was going to praise Him even if He didn't give him a child. It meant he had come to a place where he was satisfied in God and that even if he didn't get everything he wanted, he had Jesus, and that was enough for him."

"Hmm." I nod.

Satisfied in God? What does that even mean?

"Honey, what about you?" Mom's voice breaks into my thoughts. "Have you learnt anything?" She strokes my unmoisturised single-stranded-knotted hair.

I nod. "I...uh..learnt that running away makes us cowards and God wants us to face the giants in our lives. You know, like Jonah?" I look at Mom and then Dad.

"That's right, baby. Just like Jonah." Mom squeezes my hand.

Amara was right. I've been running away from my giants for too long. Everybody says God has all the answers so I'm ready.

I'm ready to face the uncomfortable truths and seek answers from God.

~

I wipe my sweaty palms on my jeans as I walk to the front of the room where we usually have our youth Bible study. Finding a seat at the front, I lower myself onto it, and lock eyes with Kevin, who is talking to a group of teenagers at the front. He smiles at me before dismissing the group and occupying a seat in front of all of us.

I straighten in my seat and clear my throat. I'm determined to give this my one-hundred percent attention as Kevin opens his Bible. *Please God, let him talk about something that will push me to ask questions. Please.*

Kevin says an opening prayer before placing his Bible on his lap. He spends a few minutes recapping what they learnt in their last book study on Galatians. Then, flipping through his Bible pages, he announces the next book. "Today, we'll be starting on the book of Job."

A tall, slim, bearded guy sitting behind me reads the first chapter, then Kevin starts talking. He goes in-depth about how Job was righteous and how he found favour in God's eyes. He then goes through the whole chapter talking about how Job lost his servants, his cattle, his sons and daughters. The further into the story Kevin goes, the more unsettled I become, and the more my thoughts overwhelm me.

Job did nothing wrong.

Kevin reads the last sentence of the first chapter and says, "Despite this, Job did not sin by charging God with wrongdoing."

I bow my head and tuck my hands underneath my thighs to stop myself from fidgeting. At the end of the teaching, Kevin leads everyone in a closing prayer and the meeting comes to a close. People hang around for a while, talking to each other, and a few of them walk up to me to say hello. I smile briefly at them, but remain seated as they come and go.

The crowd slowly disperses until it's just me and Kevin left in the room. He drags a chair and places it across from me before lowering himself on it.

"Teeyana? Is everything okay?" he asks and I lift my head to look at him.

I shake my head and swallow a lump in my throat, thinking about where to start. "You said if I had any questions, I could ask you, right?" My voice shakes.

"Yes, of course. Ask away." Kevin encourages.

"You believe that God is good...all the time, right?"

"Yes, I do with all my heart." He replies without hesitation.

I nod. "Yeah, I thought so." I adjust in my seat. "But why Job?" I ask. "I mean, the Bible talks about him being a righteous and upright man and even God himself bragged about how faithful he was to Him." I rub my palms on my knees.

"So why Job? Does God bring suffering upon those who serve Him faithfully? Job did nothing wrong, yet he had to go through all of that injustice and it wasn't considered as wrongdoing?" My lips quiver and my eyes water. "All my life, I've watched my dad serve God faithfully, and he has been so dedicated to his calling. But when my dad was falsely accused, God didn't spare him suffering even though my dad was honouring His name?"

I exhale again, and at this point, even though the tears are gushing out, I don't stop. I've already put one foot in, so I'm going to go all out and ask all my questions today.

"My grandma had a heart for God and all she ever did was talk about Him. She talked about Him at the dinner table, when she told us bedtime stories, and even when she was sad or angry.

She never left Him out of anything she did. Did God forget about her when He allowed her to be unfairly killed by an irresponsible driver? Could He not have spared His faithful servant that pain too?"

I shake my head as more tears fall. "I don't understand. If He can deliver us, why doesn't He just do it?"

Ugh, I wish these tears would stop.

This is why I never ask questions—why I always pretend to have everything together. I don't want to look weak. I always try to keep everything under control, because that's where my confidence comes from.

"Stop it, Teeyana." I turn away from Kevin and cover my face with my palms. "You are not weak."

"And what is wrong with being weak?" Kevin asks, and I snap my head up to look at him.

"What's wrong with being weak?" He repeats, looking at me straight in the eye.

Is this a trick question? What does he mean? Everything is wrong with being weak.

"Erm, it...it shows that you have lost control?" I stutter.

"Ah, but is losing control such a bad thing, Teeyana?" He pauses and I turn around to face him again.

"Who knows you more than you know yourself?" He asks when I fail to provide an answer to his previous question.

"Erm, God?" I reply, even though I'm not sure if I believe that or if I'm telling him what he wants to hear.

"And who has laid the path out for you from the beginning of time?"

"God." I reply, because that's what they taught me in Sunday school.

"And who knows your future and where you will end up tomorrow?"

I sigh. "God." I remember how I used to take comfort in this when I was younger, and when I used to ask Grandma if everything would get back to normal again for us.

"*Only God knows the answer, baby.*" She replied. "*He alone knows where we are all going.*"

"Do you know what's going to happen tomorrow? Do you even know what could happen in the next second or minute as we sit here?" Kevin asks again.

I open my mouth to give another quick response when it hits me. After spending the last four years planning my life out and having it still turn into a jumbled mess, I think I can give an honest answer to this question. "No...no I don't."

"So please, permit me to ask again, why are you afraid of God being in control? If you believe He knows it all, past, present and future, why doesn't it sound like a good idea to follow His lead?"

I remain silent. I'm speechless. I can't even defend my own life mantra. You get out of life what you put into it? Yeah, right!

Many people work hard and put in so much into life, yet they don't get half as much in return. And some others don't even have to bat an eyelid, yet they enjoy the luxuries and pleasures one can only dream about.

They say life gives you lemons so you can make a lemonade, but they don't tell you that sometimes, life throws bricks at you —not to build a house, but to break you into pieces.

I shake my head as Grandma's voice echoes in my head, reminding me of what she used to say about her favourite Bible verse.

He who dwells in the secret place of the Most High shall abide under the shadow of the Almighty, Our Refuge and Our Fortress— Jesus Christ.

"God is not looking for people who are strong, Teeyana." Kevin's words break into my thoughts. "Whether we want to admit it or not, the truth is that we are weak and God knows it.

But it's okay to be weak and vulnerable before Him. Do you know why?"

I lift my head and sniff. "Because He's our strength?" The words leave my mouth with no hesitation, like I'd always heard Grandma say.

"Exactly. Because when we are weak, He is strong." Kevin clenches his fists. "Teeyana, I'm so sorry about your grandma. It's sad that we couldn't do anything to spare her all the pain. The number of times I met her, she made me smile, and her love for God radiated from her personality. Of course it would have been nice to still have her here with us but it might help if you remember that physical death doesn't always mean defeat." He shakes his head.

"Nobody is going to be spared suffering in this life, Teeyana. Jesus' disciples died horrible deaths because of the gospel, and Jesus Himself suffered and died on the cross for a crime that you and I committed. Now don't you think it was unfair that they murdered Him in cold blood when all He wanted to do was save us from destruction?

"Do you ever stop to think about the fact that Jesus *actually* died? I mean, the Son of God, in all His glory, became obedient to death because of you? He did nothing wrong, Teeyana. Absolutely nothing wrong, yet He did it because He loves you. The reason we have hope and we can still rejoice in suffering is because we are confident in the fact that Jesus did not stay dead. He rose from the grave, and He kicked death in the backside." Kevin nods.

"Yeah, that's right. He crushed Satan's head and sent him running back to the pit of hell with his tail between his legs." His tone softens again. "And because Jesus defeated death, some day, we will too, when He comes back for us."

Kevin squeezes my shoulder gently. "I believe your grandma

is in a good place, Teeyana. I believe you will see her again someday...if you believe."

Wow!!! Something about the way Kevin presented this gospel message makes it more encouraging than I remember. It feels like my ears were blocked all this time and they just popped.

I need to speak to my parents. I need to tell them how I've been feeling for the past four years. If I don't rip the band aid off now and let them see how deep my wounds are, I'll never heal.

33

TEEYANA

I knock on the door of my parents' room, and Mom's voice ushers me in. She's sitting on the bed, reading a book. Her wig is off, revealing her neatly plaited cornrows which always remind me I need to learn how to cornrow my own hair.

Mom takes off her reading glasses and places her book on the bed when I approach her. "Hey, baby. How was Bible study?" She extends her arms towards me, inviting me in for a hug, and I go in for one without hesitation.

"It was good." I wrap my arms around her waist and rest my head on her chest, her heartbeat making sweet music in my ears. "Where's Dad?" I ask her.

"He's in the study, going over his sermon for tomorrow. Are you okay? Your eyes look puffy." She brushes my cheek. "Have you been crying?"

I shake my head and sit up. "There's something I need to tell you, Mom. Do you mind?" I lean my back against the headboard of the bed.

"Of course I don't mind, honey. You know you can tell me anything, right?" Her eyebrows furrow.

I fidget with the hem of my dark purple striped pyjamas,

trying to figure out a starting point. "Mom, for four years now, I've been struggling with my faith." I pause. "It all started after Dad lost his job at EKC...." I pause and look at Mom, anticipating her reaction.

"Okay?" She nudges.

"I always thought that following God meant He would spare us pain and suffering as long as we served Him faithfully. So I didn't understand why we had to go through all that. It left me with many unanswered questions, and I found myself drifting away. The main reason I was excited about college was because I was going away from you guys.

"I thought if I went away from all the God-filled ideas of this house, I would find a fresh perspective and a new way of living my life. I wanted to say something, but you and Dad were dealing with our loss pretty well. I thought I was the only one struggling, and I felt a lot of pressure to act as if I was okay, even though I wasn't.

"The only reason I wanted that Google internship was because I wanted to prove to God that my life can be what I want it to be." My voice cracks and Mom reaches for my hands. "But everything changed when I met Jayden. His love for God and ever positive attitude made me crave a relationship with God." I pause.

"But then Grandma died and that was my breaking point. I thought I'd feel better after the driver went to jail, but I didn't. I'm sorry Mom, but I tried. I couldn't help how I felt. The whole experience took me back to where I'd started—back to four years ago when nothing made sense. This time, it was worse because I lost someone I love and it felt like God had betrayed me again. It felt like I'd been stabbed in the back with a thousand knives." I blink and Mom catches a tear as it falls.

"When I saw your text about Danny being in hospital, I thought God was going to take him away too. I thought I was going to end up alone, and I thought God was punishing me for something I did or that He didn't love me at all."

"Oh, baby." Mom draws me closer and wraps her arms around me, letting me cry on her chest. "I didn't know you felt this way. You should have told me about all this. We could have talked about it." Mom cups my face in her hands and leans her forehead against mine, her own tears running down her cheeks.

"I was so worried about you." Mom continues. "I knew something was wrong, and I told your father I was worried when you didn't want to speak to me about it. I've been praying for you every single day since you went off to college. I've been praying that you come to experience the love of God."

Mom lets go of my head and holds my hands again. "Every day, as I laid down in that hospital bed, uncertain about whether I was going to come out of there alive, I felt alone and scared. I wasn't sure if I could ever live with myself if I had lost Danny. I would've blamed myself for not being strong enough to take what life threw at me, and not being able to hang on for my own child.

"When the doctors told me they had no choice but to deliver the baby, I broke down and held your father's arms as I tried to pray. Then I felt I was in an enclosed space, choking and gasping for air. I felt I was caught up in a commotion, and the voices of the people I loved were swirling all around me. But there was one voice which stood out to me—the voice which saved me."

"Whose voice, Mom?" I ask.

"God's voice," she replies. "God's voice was so still and so comforting." Mom places her hands across her chest. "He said to me, 'I am with you, Jamilla. Don't be afraid. I'm right here with you.' The next thing I knew was me waking up after the c-section and the nurses telling me they had taken Danny away for his surgeries. God's Word was the only thing I held on to. I held on to it when I was sitting next to your grandma's bedside, waiting for her to breathe her last. I held on to that truth—that He was right there by my side.

"Baby, I won't be doing my job as a mother if I told you that this life will be pain free. But just as it breaks my heart to see you hurt, it breaks God's heart too. That's why He didn't leave us to deal with these sufferings by ourselves. We have the Holy Spirit, our comforter, who will keep us going until the end."

Mom kisses my hands. "I don't know how big your storms will be, but remember that God is bigger and He will give you the strength to overcome. Just like He gave me strength, just like He gave your father strength. And God doesn't hate you, baby. All He's ever had for you is pure, unconditional love, even before you were conceived in my womb."

Mom wipes my eyes and wraps her arms around me again, and I hug her back so tight she laughs out loud. "Your hugs haven't changed at all. You've always been a tight hugger, right from when you learnt how to give me hugs." She touches my nose, and it makes me smile.

"Jayden touches my nose like that sometimes." I blurt out without even thinking.

"Jayden, huh?" Mom raises her eyebrows and plasters a sly smile on her face.

I roll my eyes and look away. "Mom, please don't even go there."

"Erm...excuse me for wanting to know more about this boy who touches my daughter's nose and makes her feel all warm and fuzzy inside." She tries to tickle my tummy.

"*Pfft!!!* What?" I scoff, guarding my abdomen from her fingers. "I don't feel all warm and fuzzy inside. How would you know?" I tuck a piece of hair behind my ear. The look on Mom's face says she will not stop until I say something she's satisfied with.

"But I've already told you he's my friend." I whine.

"Yeah, but you forgot the part where he touches your nose."

"There's nothing wrong with a friend touching my nose. It's not a big deal." I cover my face with my palms to hide my smile.

"Yeah—clearly not a big deal, alright. If not for your dark skin, I bet your face would be as red as a tomato now. You really like him, don't you?"

"All you need to know for now is that he's nice, and he loves God. Who knows, you might meet him soon." I go back to hugging her.

"Well, as long as he has a genuine love for God, baby. I'll take that for now."

"Yes, Ma'am."

It's Sunday afternoon and Dad is driving me back home from church. The last time we rode in his car together was when he picked me up from my internship a week before I started college. Today, it's the two of us again because Mom had to stay home with Danny.

Last time, all I wanted was for Dad not to bring up God in our conversation. But today, it's different. I want to talk about God with him.

We drive in silence for a little while, with Dad concentrating on the road, and me shooting occasional glances in his direction, hoping to get his attention.

After many subtle antics, Dad finally looks at me and smiles. "Everything okay, honey?"

I nod and flash him a smile. "I loved your sermon today, Dad. It was encouraging."

Dad's eyebrows shoot up. "You did?" He replies. "You've never told me what you thought of my sermons before."

"Yeah. I guess today was the first time I let the words sink in."

I'm pretty sure today was the first time I listened.

"That's great, honey. I'm glad God used it to encourage you." Dad's smile broadens. "By God's grace, there'll be many more from where that came from."

I fix the button on the hem of my black jacket before adjusting my collar. Then I look at him again. "Dad?"

"Yes, honey." He signals left as we approach our house.

"We need to talk."

"Yes, Ma'am." Dad pulls into our driveway and we get out of the car. He sits on the stairs leading up to our front porch and invites me to sit next to him.

"Do you remember the last time we sat here like this?" he asks.

I nod. "Yes, I do."

"And do you remember what I told you?"

I nod again. "You said I have no strength on my own so I should always hold on to God."

"So you were listening to me?!" Dad jokes.

My eyebrows furrow. "Of course I was listening to you, Dad. I just wasn't ready to take those words to heart yet."

"And why was that?" He lifts my chin up so I can look at him.

"Because..." I shuffle close to him, trying to find the right words. "Well, because I couldn't understand why your faith in God was still so strong after everything you'd been through. Those people wronged you, Dad. The whole situation was unfair, and I thought that if God cared, He would have vindicated you. Why aren't you angry at God? Why do you still continue to serve Him faithfully after everything He has allowed?"

Dad takes my hand in his, and our fingers intertwine. "Honey, I know this may sound crazy, but I'm glad I lost that job at EKC."

"What?" My eyes widen, almost bulging out of my head.

"Why? You worked hard to get to that position. You were only a month into your promotion when they got rid of you."

"That's true." He nods. "It was a well-paid job, and I know many people would do anything to have it. But it didn't bring me any satisfaction." Dad shakes his head. "Honey, I love working for God and teaching at the church. These years of hardship have taught me that the only thing I need in this life is God, and not some fancy job title. I've learnt that if I seek God first, He'll provide me with everything I need. I'm exactly where I need to be, fulfilling the purpose God has given me, and that is the most satisfying life I can ever live. So I have no reason to be angry because this whole time, God was up to something good."

"So you had to go through the fire to come out as pure gold?" I ask, Jayden's favourite Bible verse flickering in my memory.

Dad nods. "That's right. The Refiner's fire always makes us come out as pure gold. We often say there are two sides to a coin, but we forget that the edges make up the third side which keeps the two sides together through thick and thin."

Dad looks at me. "You see, God is like that third side. He's always involved, always keeping everything together." The expression on his face softens. "Your mom told me about everything, honey. I can only imagine how hard it must have been for you, keeping these things in and feeling like you couldn't talk to us about it. Please, don't let these doubts push you away from God. The trials you face are shaping you and building your muscles." He pokes at my lean biceps, causing me to chuckle.

"Thanks, Dad." I place my head on his shoulder. "I'm sorry. I should have told you guys from the beginning."

"It's okay, honey. This is *your* journey at the end of the day. Remember that God is constantly working on you, and He never gives up on the ones He loves." Dad kisses my forehead and we sit in silence for a few seconds until Dad speaks again.

"So—I hear there's a Jayden guy who touches your nose?"

I snap my head up to see the sly smile plastered on his face. "*Ugh*, Dad. Not you too." I roll my eyes and stand up.

"Wait, what did I do? I just want to know when I'll be meeting the young man, that's all." Dad says, before I rush into the house.

"I can't hear you, Dad. I'm too hungry." I hurry inside to hide the smile on my face.

We both knew where he was going with that. He has obviously been speaking to Mom. Those two keep nothing away from each other.

34

TEEYANA

In two days, I'll be back at college, and I'll have to face everything and everyone I've been pushing away—including Jayden. Although speaking to my parents has helped, there's one more person I'd like to speak to and that's Grandpa.

I didn't spend much time with him during the funeral because I was so consumed with my own feelings. I don't even remember the last time I spoke to him. I know how much he loved Grandma, so I need to find out how he's doing and how he's taking all this.

Oh God, I've been so selfish.

The doorbell rings downstairs and interrupts my thoughts. I sit up in my bed, trying to remember if Mom said anything about visitors today. Walking out of my room, I stand at the top of the staircase, staring down into the corridor as Mom opens the door. Dad emerges into view and drops his car keys on the table.

"Sorry, honey. I forgot my keys." Dad apologises and plants a kiss on Mom's lips.

"Hey, Dad." I wave at him.

"Hey, honey." Dad responds. "There's someone here you might like to see."

I gasp when my gaze falls on *him*. "Grandpa!!!" I dash down the stairs and throw my arms around his neck, making sure not to knock him to the ground. "I didn't know you were coming today." I plant a kiss on his cheek before letting go of him.

"Ah, well. Your dad and I are working on a project for the church." Grandpa smiles and pushes his glasses close to his face. "Now, what are you doing here, young lady? Don't you have finals to study for?" He tilts his head and pinches my cheek, his greying eyebrows furrowing at me.

Thinking about all the work I have to catch up on, my smile fades away. "Yes, Grandpa." I lower my head. "I should be studying for finals, but I panicked when Mom told me Danny wasn't feeling well and decided to come home. I'll be going back on Tuesday evening, though. My Professor cancelled my classes on Monday and Tuesday because we've covered all the material." I flash him a pleasant smile.

"Well, thank God for that, because I'm so happy to see you." Grandpa leans on his walking stick.

"I'm happy to see you too. I was just thinking about you seconds before you guys walked in." I nod.

"Ah, how nice of you to think about this old man. Believe it or not, I've been thinking about you too. We have a lot of time to catch up before you leave on Tuesday."

"Yes, we do." I hug him again.

After dinner, Mom and Dad retire for the night while I make my way to Dad's study. Every time Grandpa comes to visit us, he uses Dad's study to journal. I knock on the door and open it, poking my head through. "Grandpa? Can I come in?"

Grandpa turns his head to look at me. "Yes, of course. Come in."

I sit on the spin chair at the corner of the room and wheel

myself towards Grandpa the same way Danny does every time he comes in here. "So, what are you journaling about this time?" I stare at his perfectly cursive handwriting scribbled all over the plain journal pages.

"Oh, nothing much." He shrugs. "Just something important God has been teaching me recently." He wiggles his greying eyebrows at me, succeeding to make me chuckle.

But soon, my serious face returns. "How have you been, Grandpa? Really?"

He stops writing and looks at me. "Well, to be honest with you, it hasn't been easy. But by the grace of God, I'm still here, aren't I?"

"Yes, you are. You look well." I fix the collar of his shirt, and he smiles at me.

"You know, if she was here, that would've been the first thing she would've noticed as soon as she walked into this room. She had a particular eye for detail and she was good at showing me the error of my ways." He grins.

"Yes, and she was always right too."

"All the time." He nods. "She was an incredible woman, and God knows I would have never survived the last forty years without her. She was an angel who blessed me in ways only God can understand." He sighs. "But, her work here on earth is done and all we have left now are memories of her, which we need to hold close to our hearts. That's something that can't be taken away from us."

I nod and ask the last question I have, which has been bugging me. "Grandpa? If God causes both the good and bad to work for our good, then does that mean He can just hurt us and call it good?" I frown, eagerly awaiting his response.

Okay, here we go. This is going to make it or break it. God, please make me believe in Your goodness again. Please.

"Hmm." Grandpa leans back in his chair. "Honey, I don't

think that's how I would put it because that totally disregards all other aspects of God's character, such as Him being gracious, merciful, loving, kind, and forgiving. God *does* allow these things to happen, but you also have to think about the incredible wisdom in which He does things. It's a kind of wisdom we can never understand."

Grandpa straightens in his seat and picks up his walking stick. "You remember when I had the accident at work that injured my knee?" He rubs his left knee and I nod.

"The doctors told me the operation had a high success rate and that the possibility of failure was rare." He turned to look at me. "But it just so happened that my operation failed. Now I have to deal with this limp and this walking stick for the rest of my life."

Grandpa shakes his head and takes off his glasses, placing them on the table. "I don't know why my operation failed, Teeyana. When your grandma died, I spent days in prayer, asking God why He allowed her to be taken so suddenly." His voice breaks.

"And did you ever get an answer?" I ask, tears forming in my eyes.

Grandpa shakes his head and sniffs. "No, honey. I never got an answer and that's okay."

"But...but why is that okay?" My voice cracks.

"Because God owes us nothing, honey." Grandpa wheels his chair closer and holds my hands. "We are not entitled to anything in this life. Instead, we owe Him everything. The only thing we rightly deserve from God is His wrath for our sins, but He has so lovingly wiped them away.

"As much as I believe all things work together for the good of those who love God, I also know that we won't always know what that good purpose is in this life. Sometimes, God shows us the purpose for our pain, but sometimes, no matter how hard we try, we just won't see it. But just because we don't see it, doesn't mean the pain is meaningless. God is a God of intentionality and He never makes mistakes." He squeezes my hands.

"It's okay to grieve, Teeyana. God understands we are hurt, and it's fine to sorrow in peace." Grandpa's brown eyes start watering. "But honey, sorrow in hope that someday, when you get to the other side, God will wipe away all these tears from your eyes." He thumbs away a sliding tear on my cheek.

"Someday, on that glorious side of eternity, the One who knows all things will let us see the bigger picture and we'll finally understand why this all happened. Yes, we all loved your grandma, but God loved her first. She belongs to Him, and she was never ours to keep. The Lord gave her to us and now He has taken her away. Blessed be His name because we know she's at home with her good Father." Grandpa nods and wipes his eyes before speaking again. "Do you remember her favourite song?"

That was an easy question. "'Be Thou My Vision.'" I smile through my tears. "And I even remember her favourite verse." We stare at each other for a moment without saying a word, but we both know what we want to do. In such perfect harmony, we sing the fourth verse together.

Riches I need not, nor man's empty praise,
Thou mine inheritance, now and always;
Thou and Thou only first in my heart,
High King of Heaven, my treasure Thou art.

"Oh, I can't believe you still remember the words." Grandpa exclaims when we finish singing.

"Of course I do. She used to sing me to sleep every night even though I told her not to, remember?"

"Yes, she did, indeed." Grandpa smiles.

"Will she be singing all her hymns in heaven now?"

"She sure will, honey." He turns back to his journal. "I couldn't get her to stop when she was here, so she won't be stopping now that she has eternal access to her Father's presence." We both laugh.

I watch him write for a few more seconds and then ask. "Grandpa, I've been thinking about starting journaling." I pause. "Sometimes, I struggle to put all my feelings into words, especially when I want to pray. Do you think journaling will help me?"

Grandpa stops writing and a pleasant smile creeps across his face. "Well, I'm going to be biased here since I've been journaling for years. You'll never know if it'll help you unless you try." He raises his shoulders up and tilts his head.

"Great." I fiddle with my pyjama buttons. "So any tips for me?" I bite my lower lip.

Grandpa reaches for his satchel on the table and pulls it closer. After rummaging inside it, he pulls out a black Nu notebook. "Here you go." He hands the brand new notebook to me.

"For me?" I raise my eyebrows. I didn't expect him to have a blank notebook in his bag, ready to get me going.

He nods.

"Just like that?"

"Yeah. I always carry a spare one with me, so you can have it. I have plenty more at home." He grins.

"Aww, thank you so much, Grandpa." I flip through the plain blank pages of the book. "Now, how do I do this?"

"There's no right or wrong way to do it, honey. Write whatever is in your heart. It doesn't have to be pretty. It doesn't have to be structured. Write what God teaches you, and what you learn from others. Write your prayers, and the Bible verses you want to memorise. You can even draw in it if you want. It's all up to you. But always remember to go back and read it."

I take one of his pens from the table. "Can I start now?"

He moves his chair to the side. "Of course. Come write with me." He smiles.

I wiggle my chair close to him, take a deep breath, and stare at the blank pages.

"Don't think about it, honey. Write whatever comes to your mind. Tell Jesus all about it. He is always listening to you." Grandpa reassures me.

I give him a confident nod and then start scribbling.

As I walk up the stairs to my room, I hear the thunder claps coming from outside, the lightning bolts intermittently lighting the corridor.

Halfway across the corridor, I change direction and walk towards Danny's room to check on him. But before I get the chance to open his door, it opens up by itself and Danny's little hands emerge from the side.

"Hey, big boy. What's wrong?" I kneel next to him.

"I'm scared." He rubs his eyes before throwing his arms around me and clinging tight. The thundering noises must have woken him up again.

I carry him in my arms and take him to my room where I let him lay down on my bed. "There you go, big boy. I'm right here, okay?" I brush my finger across his cheek. "God is also here with you, Danny, so when you're scared, remember He is right here and He'll never leave you, okay?"

He nods and holds my hands close to his chest. "Will you pray with me?"

Hearing this question again melts my heart. The last time he asked, I felt uncomfortable, but now I'm grateful that God has given me another opportunity to set a good example for Danny and teach him about His love.

"I'll pray after you pray." I kiss his little hands. "Remember, God is here with us, so you can tell Him whatever is in your heart, okay?"

Danny nods and closes his eyes. "Dear Jesus, thank you for bringing Teeyana home." he starts. "Thank you for Mommy. Thank you for Daddy. Thank you for Aunt Bella and Grandpa. I'm scared of the dark and...the thunder and lightning. Please help me not to be scared. In Jesus' name."

"Amen." I say.

"And Jesus," Danny continues. "Please say hi to Grandma for me. Tell her I miss her and Teeyana misses her and we all miss her. Amen." He says before drifting off to sleep.

I can't help but envy Danny's pure and genuine words. I envy his confidence in God and his child-like faith. This is exactly what I need. Child-like faith. It's what I need to approach God right now.

After covering Danny with my duvet, I stretch my arm and open the top drawer of my bedside table, revealing my old Bible, which I haven't touched in years. As I wipe the dust off its purple cover, the embroidered words *Holy Bible* pop even more. I open the Bible to read the words written on the front page.

Dedicated to my precious granddaughter,
Teeyana Joy Sparks.

I give thanks to God for your life, and I'm so blessed to know you.

Even as you've publicly declared your decision to follow God, I pray He continues to work on your heart and strengthen you. I can't wait to see how He uses you to manifest His glory.

I love you so much.
Grandma.

I hold the Bible close to my chest and shut my eyes. The tears escape and roll down my cheeks as Danny snores softly beside me. The rain continues to fall, and the thunder continues to roar, but I keep holding the Bible, my hands shaking and the tears pouring out more than ever before.

Putting my Bible down and flipping through the pages, I find the verses I loved back in Sunday school. The verses I used to hold on to when I craved God's comfort. Those same words from Philippians 4:6-7 are the same ones I'm staring at right now, my heart now craving something different—not for my own control, but God's.

God is in control.

God is in control.

God is in control.

The words echo in my mind, over and over again, and for the first time, I have words in my head that are not my usual questions. *God is in control.*

Of course He is. Of course He has always been in control. This whole time. Why do things never go my way? Because I am *not* God.

"I give up." My words come out in a whisper. "I give up trying to fight You, Lord. I can't do this anymore. Please forgive me. I still have a lot of questions and I still don't understand why You've let so many things happen to me, but I give up trying to figure this out. Everyone expects me to be okay—but Lord, You know me. You know I'm not okay. You're the only one who knows how much I'm hurting right now. I miss Grandma and I wish she was still here with us. My heart is broken and I need You, Lord. Please help me.

"I was angry at You for so long, but all You've ever done is love me. My doubts and questions blinded me and I couldn't see how good You've been to me. I know You used Jayden to help me see what it's like to have true joy in You. But it's not Jayden's joy I want. I want Your joy. Lord, please help me. I surrender. I can't do this without You. I'm weak. I have no strength. Please help me, Lord." I sniff.

"I accept that You are God and I am not. My mere human mind will never fully understand what You do. It doesn't feel good right now, but I'm willing to stick with You. I want to know You, Lord. Please help me know You."

I bury my head in my pillow, trying hard to quiet my sobs so I don't wake Danny. My tears soak into my pillowcase and then seep through it, drenching my pillow. And then, as I continue sniffing, my tears of despair turn into tears of joy. Then I hear His gentle whisper for the first time.

My beloved, Teeyana. I know you.

Seek Me with all your heart.

You will know Me too.

A soothing presence washes over me. I can't explain it. It strengthens my heart and gives me confidence that God has heard me. He is right here with me and reassuring me again that He's got my back—like Amara has always told me. And for the first time in a long time, I believe it with all my heart.

35

TEEYANA

"Could you please pass me the whisk, honey?" Mom points to the utensil lying over the bag of carrots next to me. I pick it up and hand it to her before sinking back into my seat.

Amara is home from college too, and she has come over to make dinner with us. She's sitting across the table, peeling potatoes for the potato salad, and Mom is working on the chocolate cake.

And me? Well, I should be chopping carrots, but the only thing I've done so far is stare at the empty bowl in front of me. I let out a deep sigh and pick up a carrot from the bag.

"You know, it always surprises me how much we are alike." Mom glances at me as she whisks the cake mix.

I stare at her blankly. "Erm...well, I look like you, don't I? You clearly didn't do Dad any favours with this one." My mouth curves into a cheeky smile.

Mom rolls her eyes. "Oh, please. Danny looks like him so we're even." She shrugs. "But that's not the point I'm trying to make, honey."

I bite on the carrot in my hand and start chewing. "Oh? In what other ways are we alike, then?"

Mom stops whisking and narrows her eyes at me. "If I didn't sigh so much whenever something was on my mind, then I would've brushed off all the sighing you've been doing for the last half hour. But I'm your mother and I know better." She tilts her head and places a hand on her hip. "Start talking, young lady."

"I bet she's thinking about Jayden." Amara jumps in and I shoot a glare in her direction. Sometimes I wish she didn't know me so well, but I can only wish.

"Oh, really?" Mom smiles at Amara, and they wiggle their eyebrows at each other.

Oh, great! So this is how it feels to be cornered by your own mother and best friend, huh?

"Oh, come on, girl. You know it's true." Amara pleads. "We all know you like him and I'm sure he likes you too. I don't know why you won't admit it and text him."

"Do you like him, honey?" Mom takes a step towards me.

Oh gosh, how can they put me on the spot like this? I don't...I...oh, who am I kidding?

My gaze drops to the carrot in my hand. "Yes, I do."

"Aha!!! Told ya!!!" Amara exclaims before breaking into her victory dance.

"Shush, girl." I shoot her another glare. She puts her hands up in mock surrender and goes back to peeling the potatoes.

"I already knew that, honey. I just wanted to hear you say it." Mom grins. "Now tell me. What's the problem?"

I shrug. "I don't know if he feels the same way, and I don't want to get myself in a mess. Sometimes, he says things that suggest he likes me, but I don't want parables. If he likes me, I want him to say it, you know." I cross my arms and pout.

"Well, if you ask me, I don't think you have anything to worry about." Mom's voice remains reassuring. "If he wants something more, he'll pursue you. Don't force anything. Let him pursue you." Mom brushes my cheek.

"I want to believe that too, Mom, but I need to apologise to him first. Jayden has always been there for me, but he was the first person I pushed away when I was hurt. Even if he liked me before, he might have no interest in me now, and I don't blame him. I was angry and I think I hurt him with some things I said."

"If you ask me," Amara jumps in again. "I don't think he's still mad at you. If he was, he wouldn't have driven you all the way down here when he didn't need to. I think we're all good here." She nods and gives me a thumbs up, still managing to be so light-hearted about this mess I'm in—well, I think it's a mess, anyway.

"Honey." Mom pulls me close to her and props my chin up. "Pain and hurt can make us do things we don't mean—like building a wall and pushing others away. Jayden seems like a nice boy, from all the things you've said about him. I think your friendship is one worth fighting for, so whatever it is you need to do to fix things, you go ahead. Even if he has forgiven you, there's no harm in clearing the air so you both can get some closure. Does that sound like something you would want to do?"

Face your giants, Teeyana. You can do all things through Christ who strengthens you.

I nod and straighten my back. "Yes, Mom. I'll call him tonight."

"Or you could go see him?" Amara cuts in. "He only lives half an hour away." She squares her shoulders and grins.

"Yeah that's true." Mom returns to her mixing bowl. "Your father can drive you there tomorrow, and then perhaps Jayden can drive you back to college. Just make sure his parents are home and ask Jayden if it's a good time. You don't want to be impeding on their plans." Mom shakes her head.

"Sounds like a good idea. Thanks, Mom." I walk up to her and kiss her cheek before dipping my finger into the bowl to taste the cake mix.

Mom swats my hand away and shouts, "Teeyana Joy Sparks. You *definitely* did not learn this one from me. Now go over there and keep cutting those carrots, young lady."

"I guess Dad passed something down to me after all." I laugh and carry my bag of carrots over to Amara, who is trying hard not to burst out laughing.

Standing in front of Jayden's front door, I open my phone camera to check there's nothing stuck between my teeth, because, you know, that would be *so* embarrassing.

I'm wearing my hair down today because Mom bought me a new curling iron and I thought I'd change from the messy bun I've had for the last two weeks. Giving my soft bouncy curls one last fluff, I slip my phone in my jacket pocket and press the doorbell.

"I'll get it." My heart flutters and my stomach rumbles at the sound of Jayden's faint voice coming from the other side of the door.

Lord, please help me. I don't want to mess this up.

I took Mom and Amara's advice and messaged Jayden last night. He seemed happy when I suggested coming to see him, so I hope we can talk it out today. I'm tired of denying the fact that I've missed him.

The door opens to reveal a smiling Jayden, as always. He is wearing a dark blue shirt, with the top few buttons left undone, revealing his white t-shirt underneath.

"Hey." I wave when he opens the door wider.

He doesn't reply but instead, opens up his arms, inviting me in for a hug, which I was hoping he would. It's only when I let go of him that I realise how tight his hug was.

Yeah, I've definitely missed him.

"Was the drive here okay?" he asks, still holding my hand.

"Yeah, my dad didn't find it too bad." I nod across the road at Dad, who is waiting in the car to make sure I'm okay before he drives back home.

The door opens up even wider to reveal an older man who has the same stature and build as Jayden—except he is an inch shorter and has broader shoulders. "And who do we have here?" he asks with a cheery voice, but doesn't wait for me to reply. "You must be the one and only Teeyana. We've heard so much about you." He extends his hand, but changes his mind and hugs me instead.

"Erm...yes, I'm Teeyana." I say before he engulfs me in his massive frame—just like Jayden does.

"Honey, Teeyana is here." Mr. Williams yells over his shoulder and in less than a minute, an older woman appears with the most adorable dimpled smile I've ever seen.

No wonder Jayden's smile is so perfect.

"Well, hello there. I'm Jayden's mom." She hugs me too.

Is this how they hug everyone they meet for the first time?

"Now, what are we all doing out here? Can we go inside now? The food will not eat itself." Mrs. Williams gestures for us to go inside.

I turn around and wave at Dad as he drives off before turning back to face Jayden.

"Ladies first." Jayden moves to the side and points towards the door. I send him a nervous smile as I walk past him, but he stops me mid-way, his hands on my shoulder giving me a reassuring squeeze. "Don't worry, Tee. My parents love you."

After dinner, Jayden takes me upstairs to their balcony, which has a lovely view of their courtyard and the rest of their neighbourhood. For a few minutes, we sit in silence, watching people walking up and down the neighborhood.

An elderly couple is strolling down the street, holding hands and smiling at each other. A little boy and girl ride past the elderly couple on their bikes, screaming and giggling, while their parents yell at them to slow down.

I turn my attention away from the two little boys playing basketball in the neighbour's garden and fiddle with the hem of my pink striped shirt.

Speak now, Teeyana. Now!!!

"Your parents are nice." My words come out slow and uncertain.

When Jayden looks at me with his charming hazel brown eyes staring into mine, my heart thumps faster. "I'm glad you like them." He replies. "But most importantly, I'm glad they love you." He touches my nose and the brush of his finger slows my heart rate down.

I relax and return his smile. "I think my parents will love you too."

"You sure about that?" He raises an eyebrow.

"Positive." I smile again and then clear my throat. "Jay...about what happened that day in the library." I begin. "I'm sorry about everything I said. Nothing I've been through is your fault and I shouldn't have ignored you so—"

"Tee?" he cuts me off. "I'm not mad at you."

My eyebrows furrow. "You're not?"

"No. I'm not. You felt how you felt, and I won't blame you for that. We all have a right to rant, to ask questions, and to be left alone if we choose to. I think it's only fair." He fixes my hair on the side of my face. "You were hurt, and you needed to take time out to think, which I understand." He shrugs.

"I know you understand." I come in again before he says anything else. "But I still think you deserve an apology. I shouldn't have pushed you away. I was angry and frustrated, and I poured it out on you. I wasn't fair, and for that, I am sorry. Knowing you has been a huge blessing and I don't want to take what we have for granted."

He smiles. "Well, I'm glad you feel that way, because I feel the same. I told you our friendship is blessed, and I'd be crazy to throw away a blessing like this. And since you insist on apologising, I guess I have to say that I forgive you." He chuckles.

"Thanks, Jay." I weave my arm around his and rest my head on his shoulder. "I'm so glad we're back to being friends again. I missed you."

"I missed you too." He plants a kiss on my forehead. "And now that you're here," he reaches into his pocket, "there's a song I'd like you to listen to—that's if you want to, of course."

"Sure." I nod.

He pulls out his phone and plugs in his headphones before putting one piece into his ear and the other into mine. When he presses play, the soft piano intro of a song fills my ear, and I anticipate the lyrics. Jayden never makes me listen to a song unless he thinks the lyrics mean something.

As soon as the artist starts singing the first line of the first verse, I recognise the song. It's the hymn we sang at Grandma's funeral—well, the hymn everyone else was singing. The same one I refused to sing because I was too angry. I felt, then, that God was using the lyrics to attack me, but it's here again and I'm sure God wants me to listen this time.

I close my eyes and take deep breaths in and out, letting the lyrics sink in. When we get to the second verse, the lyrics hit me hard and before I know it, tears start rolling down my cheeks. For the first time in forever, I don't force them back in or accuse myself of being weak. For the first time, I let myself cry.

And then, we come to the last couple of verses—the ones I ignored the first time I heard the song.

When we see Jesus coming in glory
When He comes down from His home in the sky
Then we shall meet Him in that bright mansion
We'll understand it all by and by

Soon with the Lord our wonderful Saviour
We'll be at home beyond the blue sky.
There we shall meet the dear ones awaiting
We'll understand it all by and by.

Farther along we'll know all about it
Farther along we'll understand why
Cheer up my brother live in the sunshine
We'll understand it all by and by

As the piano fades towards the end, Jayden props my chin up and wipes the tears on my face. "Tee, I don't know how you feel, but I know what it feels like to lose someone you love."

For the first time, I see hurt and pain in Jayden's eyes—something I never imagined I'd see. "Who did you lose, Jay?" I ask.

"My brother." He clears his throat. "My older brother. His name was Tyler."

36

JAYDEN

It's time to be vulnerable, Jayden. You have to do this.

Perhaps this will make Teeyana realise that we're all in the same rocky boat called life, but sitting in different compartments, and looking at the same tide from different angles.

"Were you guys close?" Teeyana asks and I nod.

"Very close." I respond, turning to face her. "He used to be the only person who called me *Jay,* and I used to call him *T.*"

"Oh, I see." Teeyana's gaze softens. "Do you want me to stop calling you *Jay*? Does that upset you?"

"No, not at all." I shake my head. "Please, keep calling me Jay if you want. It makes me think of him, but that's not a bad thing. I don't want to forget him." I lean forward and clasp my hands over my knees.

"We were so alike—except he was the better-looking one and of course, the ladies loved him." I laugh. "He was in his sophomore year at college, majoring in business management, and his dream was to be the C.E.O. of his own company. He always said that when I was old enough, we would run his company together." I smile through the tears waiting to burst out of my eyes.

Then I reach into the back pocket of my jeans and bring out the green and yellow ribbon, twirling it in my palm as more memories of Tyler press in to my thoughts. "God knows I loved him." My voice breaks. "I loved him so much."

Teeyana's gaze drops to the ribbon in my hand and then back up to me. "What happened to him, Jay?"

I pause for a second and close my eyes, preparing myself to open my can of worms, and let Teeyana see my scars. Preparing myself to visit the same memories which sent me into a downward spiral of depression before. It's time to be vulnerable, and God will help me. "He killed himself," I say, wiping the tear sliding down my cheek. "A few days before my fourteenth birthday."

Teeyana's jaw drops and to be honest, that was my initial reaction when I first heard the news. I don't think I can ever get over the shock.

I straighten my back and clear my throat. "It'll be six years this November. Six years since I lost my brother to suicide."

Teeyana reaches for my hand, which has the ribbon in it, and she squeezes it.

"I always thought he had it all together and I looked up to him because he never got tired of listening to me complain or rant about my life. He was always there for me, making sure I was okay, always trying to encourage me with schoolwork and helping me out with some bullying issues I had."

Teeyana's eyes widen. "You were bullied in school too?"

I nod. "Yes, I was. Tyler was the only one who knew about it. I thought we were close enough to tell each other everything. I didn't know he was struggling in college and getting poor grades. I didn't know he'd been feeling so low and unmotivated, he'd started skipping classes. I thought whenever life knocked him down, he would always get back up again, but I was wrong." I look at Teeyana, who is now tearing up.

"I was wrong about everything, Tee. He wasn't as strong as he tried to make me believe." Teeyana wipes the tears trickling down her cheeks.

"For a long time, I blamed myself. I thought it was my fault. I thought it was my parents' fault. I thought we didn't do enough to keep him around. That we didn't do enough to make him want to stay with us. Then I went through a phase where I blamed him. How dare he think that was the only way out? How dare he think in a world like this, with endless possibilities, that was the only solution to the problems he had? I wish he had spoken to someone about it. We could have helped him." I clench my fists together and exhale.

"Then, I found out last month that after overdosing on the antidepressants he had been stockpiling, he had time to regret his decision. He called the ambulance and called my mom too, but no one could save him. It was too late." I bury my face in my hands as the sobs escape my mouth.

"Oh, Jay. I'm so sorry." Teeyana wraps her arms around my shoulders. "It must have been so hard for you and your family. I had no idea you went through all this."

I lift my head to look at her. "You didn't know because I didn't tell you, Tee. I was afraid of being vulnerable, but every time I prayed for you, I asked God to help you see that life was worth living, no matter what your trials were. When you started pushing me away, I couldn't help but think that one day, I was going to wake up and find out that you had decided it wasn't worth staying too. I didn't want to lose you, Tee. It's the reason I kept checking up on you. It's the reason I keep checking on everyone around me. Since I lost Tyler, I've constantly had to battle with the guilt that I could have done more for him and that I could do more for my family and friends."

"But you can't do everything, Jay." Teeyana shakes her head. "God knows it wasn't you or your parents' fault."

"I know. But it still didn't stop me from wondering why. For many months, I questioned God. I spoke to my parents, who were grieving too, but everything they told me didn't make sense. Nothing made sense, and I ended up going down a dark tunnel of depression. For three months, I couldn't sleep, I couldn't eat, and I couldn't concentrate on schoolwork. My search for a meaningful answer was hopeless, and I came real close to giving up on life.

"But one day, at church, I heard the song 'Farther Along.' The words cut through me like a knife as I sat in the backseat. The song brought back all my sorrows and my pain and all my unanswered questions. But it also gave me hope at the same time. It gave me hope that someday, God will fix things and make everything right. When I got home that afternoon, I searched for other songs that would help me. Then I stumbled on Tyler's CDs in his car and the more I listened to the songs, the more God comforted me with the truth of His love. In the end, I opened up to my parents about it and that's how I started seeing my Christian counsellor."

I wipe another tear before continuing, "Tee, it would be pathetic if this was all there was to life. If all this pain, agony, and injustice were the end. But God promised us it's not the end and this confidence I have isn't because I have it all together. My life has never been perfect. I have doubts, fears, and insecurities like everyone else. But since Jesus changed my heart three years ago, I've come to believe that His grace is sufficient—no matter what the thorn in my flesh is."

I exhale. "And as for Tyler, the Lord gave him to us, and the Lord took him away. Blessed be His name."

I wave Mom and Dad goodbye and watch them return into the house before turning to face Teeyana sitting in the passenger seat.

"You ready?" I ask while reaching for my seatbelt.

She nods and lowers her head, fidgeting with the ribbon on her backpack. "Yeah, I guess."

"You okay?"

She shakes her head this time, and lifts it up, high enough for me to notice her watery eyes.

"Hey." I reach for her hands. "What's wrong?"

She sniffs. "Jay, I've been thinking a lot about everything I've learnt this weekend and I've realised I owe you another apology."

"Oh, yeah?" I raise an eyebrow. "What for?"

"I haven't been a good friend to you. I've been so selfish. All this time I thought you were living the perfect life, and I resented you because I thought you weren't qualified to encourage me. I became frustrated with you because I thought you didn't understand what it meant to have struggles. I was wrong about all that and I want you to know that I'm very sorry." She purses her lips and tucks a strand of her wavy hair behind her ear.

"I spoke to my parents and my Grandpa about how I was feeling. On Sunday night, I prayed for the first time in years, and God touched me. I know He did because something about me has changed. I know God wants me to be a better friend, so I promise I'll be a better friend to you."

I separate her clasped hands, and in one swift motion, our fingers intertwine. "Tee, you have no idea how happy this makes me. Your story inspires me so much and it's proof that God is always working. We're gonna be okay." I nod and wipe the tears running down her cheeks.

"And if you ever consider talking to a professional, I recommend my Christian counsellor. Her name is Mary Perkins, and she was extremely helpful when I was dealing with Tyler's death."

"Thanks, Jay. I'll think about it." She responds.

"No problem at all." I pull her close to me and kiss her forehead. She puts her arms around me before resting her head on my shoulder.

Then we are forced apart by the vibrations coming from her pocket, and when she pulls it out, a new email notification pops up. "Oh, my God." She gasps and looks at me.

"What's wrong?" My heart skips a beat.

"The Google internship. I just got an email." She shrieks.

"What did they say?" I ask.

"I don't know." She places the phone in my hands. "Please open it, Jay."

"Tee, are you sure about this?"

She nods and I click on the email. "Here we go." I start reading it to myself.

Teeyana squeals and covers her face with her hands. She stays in that position for almost thirty seconds, waiting for me to say something, but I don't. She peeks and then puts her hands down. "So—what did they say?" She bites her bottom lip.

"That you are one beautiful, talented individual, and they'll be darned not to have you on their team!!!"

"What? Are you serious?" Her eyes widen.

"Yes. You got the internship." I turn the phone around so she can read the email herself.

"No way!!! Are you sure?" She takes the phone from my hand. "Oh my God, I thought the interview went wrong. I couldn't answer any of the questions right and I was so nervous."

"Well, seems like none of that mattered to God. It was in the books that you were going to get it and you did." I say.

"Yes!!!" She pumps her clenched fists in the air. "I can't wait to tell Mom and Dad. They'll be so happy."

I sit back and watch her send a message to her parents. It's so good to see her happy again. I thought I would never get the privilege to see her beautiful smile again, but God had other plans. "So it looks like this internship was part of the plan after all?" I turn the car key and start driving off.

"Yeah." Teeyana smiles, her eyes twinkling with excitement. "It was part of God's plan after all."

37

TEEYANA

My dorm room door shrieks open as I tiptoe into the room. It's nine p.m and Heather's lamp is on, illuminating half of the room. She's not at her desk, but there are muffled sobs coming from the direction of her bed.

"Heather?" I take a few steps towards her bed and the sobbing continues. "Heather, are you okay?" I repeat, but there's no reply.

I fiddle in the darkness, running my fingers along the wall to find the light switch. The light comes on and reveals Heather stretched out on her bed with her head buried in her pillow. She has her headphones on and I assume she's listening to music.

Or she could be ignoring me.

"Heather?" I move closer and touch her shoulder gently, but she flinches and rears her head up. She scowls and takes off her headphones, leaving her hair in a messier state than it was in before.

Her watery green eyes stare at me, tears leaking out of them and forming dark streaks of washed out mascara on her cheeks. Her red lipstick is also smudged onto her pillow case and almost all her foundation too.

Yikes, you could say this is the definition of a hot mess.

"What do you want?" Heather snaps, prompting me to stop staring.

I clear my throat. "I was...just checking to make sure you're okay."

Heather narrows her eyes at me. "Why are you acting as if you care?"

I open my mouth to speak, but no words come out.

Lord, please help me.

"Well," I tilt my head, "you're my roommate and I don't think there's any harm in us checking on each other."

"*Ugh*, leave me alone." She rolls her eyes and turns her head to face the wall.

You heard her say it, Lord. At least You know I tried.

"Okay." I shrug and head back to my bed. Holding on to my bed rails, I climb on my bed and lay flat on my back. But as I'm about to plug in my own headphones, a soft voice speaks to me.

Don't give up, Teeyana.

I take off my headphones and sit up in bed, before turning to look at Heather, whose head is buried in her pillow again.

She didn't say that, did she?

I lay down again and put my headphones on, but the voice pierces through my moment of solitude a second time.

Don't give up, Teeyana.

This time, it hits me.

Lord, is that You? Please, I don't want to do this. She doesn't want to speak to me. She won't listen. She never listens.

I am right here with you. Trust Me.

I grab my pillow and cover my face before letting out a brief, frustrated sigh. *Okay, Lord. I don't see the point, but I'll try because You want me to.*

Jumping down from my bed, I walk towards Heather's bed, my pulse pounding in my ears. I climb up the stairs and settle next to her; the bed creaking and the mattress sinking under my weight.

"What are you doing?" Heather sits up and shuffles away from me, her green eyes fuming.

Hmm, that's a good question. Lord, You didn't tell me what to say.

"I told you to leave me alone." Heather's face reddens.

"Erm...so here's the thing." I wait for the words to come to me. "Finals are around the corner and everyone is studying hard. If you don't want to study, that's fine. But I won't let you stop me from studying." I shrug.

"What the heck are you talking about?" Heather raises her voice.

"Erm.." I scratch my head. "What I'm trying to say is that if I leave you here to keep crying, I won't be able to study because of all the noise you're making. And if I leave you and go to the library, I'll keep wondering why you're crying, so I won't be able to study there either. Either way, I think it'll do us both some good if you start sharing so we can get this over and done with and I can leave you alone."

Lord, were all those words from You or from me? If they were from me, I'm sorry and if she pushes me off this bed, please catch me.

I bite my lip and brace myself for some reaction from Heather; some screaming, some shouting, or even some shoving. But to my surprise, Heather does nothing. Instead, she rolls her eyes and buries her head in her pillow again. "I don't want to talk to you."

Okay, I guess that was You then, Lord. It's working. What do I say next?

"Erm...that's okay. You don't have to talk. I will." I lean my back against the wall, my erratic heartbeat slowing down as I make myself comfortable and continue talking.

"Heather, five years ago, my dad was falsely accused of a crime he didn't commit. He lost his job when his boss and colleagues framed him for standing up for what was right." I shake my head.

"And last night, I found out that one of my best friends lost his brother to suicide and had to deal with all the anxiety and depression that came with it." I turn to look at Heather, who is now looking at me.

"Sometimes, life sucks and I've learnt that it's okay to feel that way." I nod. "You may have your justifiable reasons for not liking me, but I want to let you know that we're all in the same rocky boat called life. I believe we need each other and no matter how we choose to look at it, we're on the same side and we always have been."

To my greatest surprise, Heather sits up and rests her back against the wall next to me. She fiddles with her white crop top, giving me a close-up look at the tattoo on the palmar side of her wrist. "Connor dumped me." She croaks.

"Connor?" I frown, and my gaze returns to her puffy eyes. "Is that the blonde guy who was here with you the day we—"

"Yeah," Heather responds. "Yeah, that's him." She lowers her head.

"Oh, I'm sorry to hear that. Do you want to talk about what happened?"

She shrugs. "Nothing happened. Nothing ever happens. I wasn't good enough for him. I never was and I never will be good enough for anybody." Her eyes water again. "I wasn't even good enough for my own mother. She hated me so much, she had to run off with some dude to China because she didn't care about me or my dad. I wasn't good enough to get a decent family in this life. My dad is either always finding faults in me, trying to change me, or telling me what to do. 'Oh Heather you can't have red hair, oh Heather that's too much eyeliner, oh Heather can't you wear another coloured lipstick?'" She shakes her head.

"And with boys, I've never been good enough for any of them. They all want the same thing." She looks at me.

"The *cookie*?" I raise an eyebrow.

Heather chuckles—a sound I never thought I'd hear coming from her and a sight I never thought I'd behold. "Yup. The *cookie*." She replies. "And they dump me straight after that. Every single one of them. After trying my darndest to please them and make them stay, they still never find me good enough. I'm sick of it. I'm sick of everything."

"Hmm." I sigh.

Heather scoffs. "Yeah, I'd be speechless too if I hear how pathetic I sound right now."

"I don't think you're pathetic." I bring my knees up to my chest. "Heather, my life is a mess too, but there's someone I know who loves me despite all my flaws and imperfections."

"Well, good for you. It must be nice to find a guy who treats you right." Heather looks away. "Is this person your guy best friend? The one who plays basketball?" she asks.

"Oh no, no." I shake my head. "I'm not talking about an ordinary guy."

"Okay, so who is this *extraordinary* guy?" She scrunches her eyebrows.

I suck in a long breath and exhale. "His name is Jesus." The words roll out like lip balm from my mouth. "Heather, do you believe in God?"

I brace myself for a look of disgust. I expect her to roll her eyes, laugh out loud, or finally decide she's had enough of this roomie talk and push me off her bed.

But again, Heather does none of the above. Instead, her facial expression softens—as if she has something she wants to share. It's not a look of disgust or indifference. It suggests she's had some experience in the past.

"Heather?" I prod.

She shrugs. "I don't know what to believe anymore. I mean, if ordinary humans don't find me interesting, then why would God take any interest in me? He's too busy loving people like you, anyway." She lowers her head.

Hearing her say those words breaks my heart, because that's how I felt towards Jayden. "Heather." I place my hand on her shoulder. "God doesn't care about what people have done to you or how *Mr. Blondie* treated you."

Heather shakes her head and sniffs. "But I have too many imperfections."

"He knows that, but He loves you anyway—with your red hair and thick eyeliner and *really* bright red lipstick." We both giggle and Heather takes out a pack of face wipes from her backpack.

"Yeah, I think I went a little crazy with the red lipstick. I don't even like the colour red, you know."

"You don't?" My eyes widen. "I thought it was your favourite colour. Why do you always wear it then?" I lean forward and rest my chin on my hands.

Heather starts wiping off the make-up on her face. "When I was younger, my parents used to take me to church every Sunday. But when my mom and dad split, I was only eight years old," she explains. "I prayed to God every night that they would get back together. Every. Single. Night." She sighs. "And every morning, I woke up and ran to my parents' room, only to find that my dad was still there—alone.

"When I turned thirteen, I gave up and stopped believing. I became the stereotypical rebellious teenager, and the boys took an interest in me. I loved the attention I got and the pleasure it brought me, so I poured my heart and soul into toxic, and reckless relationships—each one of them leaving me more empty than the last. I even got this stupid tattoo to remind myself that if no one else loved me, then I would love myself and that would be enough." She flashes her wrist at me so I can read the word *beloved* inked with a bold cursive font, and a small cross on the top right of it.

"I've never been able to fill that void." Heather palms her tears away. "I believe there's *someone* out there who has the upper hand because if I had control, there are so many things I would have changed about my life. Clearly someone's plan is working."

I adjust next to her. "I can't give you all the answers, Heather. I can't tell you why you've been through all you have. I don't even fully understand why I've been through all I have. But could it be that all this happened for this very moment?"

Heather gives me a blank look. "What do you mean?"

"Could it be that you haven't found validation in anyone else because God wants you to see that He is the only One who can validate you?" I pause, then continue. "I'm so sorry to hear that your parents split, but could it be that God brought you to this place to show you that you need His help to forgive your parents? Could it be that God wants to show you He is the only One who can provide the love you've been searching for all these years?"

I take her hand and turn her palm up, bringing her attention back to her tattoo. "Your tattoo is true. It's not stupid. *Beloved* means someone who is cherished and treasured. Yes, you have your imperfections, but you are deeply loved by a perfect God. Heather, you can't love yourself or anyone else the right way until you first understand the depth of God's love for you."

Heather's green eyes mist and when she drops her gaze to the tattoo again, more tears slide down her cheeks. She stares at the word, and rubs her thumb over it, before bringing her wrist closer, as if there are hidden words in it she is trying to uncover.

For at least a minute, Heather's sniffs and sharp exhales are the only sounds in the room. She doesn't say anything but to be honest; I wasn't expecting her to give in so easily. Jayden once told me that God uses our words, actions, and prayers to plant seeds in the hearts of others and that no matter how long it takes for the seed to grow, the assurance we have is that one day it will grow and bear beautiful fruit.

Lord, please work on her heart.

"I want to believe." Heather breaks the silence and looks at me. "Trust me, I do. But so much has happened and I need an open mind. I'll definitely think about everything you've said." She smiles at me and for the first time, her green eyes light up.

I nod. "Of course. Whatever you decide, at least for now, remember that *Mr. Blondie* has no idea what he's lost. I'll be praying for you, Heather. Let me know if you need anything." I jump down from her bed and head towards mine.

"Oh, and by the way," I turn to her. "I know this is none of my business, but...I think your dad cares about you. I know he has made mistakes, but we all have. I know you're hurt, but please give him a chance to make things right. Our time on earth is short and we don't know how long we have left with our loved ones."

Heather sits up. "You...you think we can work things out?" She stares at me, hope radiating from her voice.

"I think it's worth a try." I smile.

Heather nods and picks up her phone. "Oh, and Teeyana? I'm sorry about every mean thing I said or did to you before. I misjudged you."

"I misjudged you too. I'm sorry for being a whiny and selfish roommate."

Heather presses a few buttons on her phone before bringing it up to her ear. "Hello?" She speaks, her voice shaking. "Dad? Can you talk?" She climbs down from her bed and heads out the door.

I climb up on my bed and lay on my back, looking up at the ceiling. Then, the dorm room door opens again. "Teeyana?"

When I perk my head up, Heather is standing in the doorway, pressing her phone against her chest. "Thank you." She smiles through her tears and shuts the door again.

I let out shuddered breaths, baffled by what just happened. The old Teeyana would have never done that.

Lord, You worked through me. Out of everyone else, You chose me to do this.

Tears of joy fill my eyes as I think about how far God has brought me and how much He has changed me. *Thank You, Lord. Thank You.*

38

JAYDEN

Our gruelling finals are over and that means it's barbecue time. We've been setting up the church backyard for our end-of-year youth barbecue and some boys are setting up the grill while others prep the meat and buns.

And me? Well, I should be helping too, but I've been pacing back and forth, waiting for the moment Teeyana walks through the door. I mean, I've always looked forward to spending time with her but today, I don't think I can explain this feeling.

Butterflies? Nah. Today's the day I tell her. I have to tell her.

I walk over to meet Anton, who is setting up the music playlist for the day. "You're not going to make us dance to hymns all day, are you?" I place my arm around his shoulder and grin.

"Nuh-uh. You kids need to send in your recommendations or else we will be dancing to hymns all day," he shoots back.

"No, suh." I feign a gasp. "That'll be a pathetic sight. I'll tell the guys to come in straight away." I laugh and turn around to leave, but Anton stops me.

"Oh, by the way, do you know when Teeyana will be here?" he asks.

And just like that, at the mention of her name, the butterfly feeling comes back. "Uh...yeah, I just texted her. She's on her way and she's bringing her roommate, Heather."

"Oh, really?" Anton's eyes widen. "The same Heather she doesn't get along with?"

"Yup, that's right." I nod. "It's the same Heather. They're good friends now." I inch closer and lower my voice. "Tee told me that Heather had a rough past, and God instructed her to be there for Heather when she needed a shoulder to cry on. Tee even had the chance to tell Heather about Jesus."

"Is that so?" Anton replies, placing a hand on his hip. "Man, that's so encouraging. We can't wait to meet her. I promise we won't scare her away and we'll welcome her with love." Anton puts a hand up to signify his pledge.

"With love." I copy him.

"Okay, I don't mean to pry." Annie squeezes her head between us. "But I heard the word *love* and decided to join in. Are we talking about Teeyana?" She wiggles her eyebrows at me before pressing her lips on Anton's cheek.

"Uh...yeah? Kinda. But I'm not sure where you're going with this." I give her a nervous smile.

"Okay, so you're *still* going to tell me you don't like her? Hmm?" Annie holds my arms and leans closer.

Gosh, this woman never gives up, does she?

"Okay, fine. You win." I let out a sigh.

I can't keep denying this. I mean, who am I kidding?

"You're right. I like her, but I don't know how to tell her and...I don't know how she feels." I ramble.

Anton laughs and squeezes my shoulder. "Have you prayed about it? Have you pursued her? Has she given you any vibes that she doesn't like you back?"

"Well, I've been praying about it and I've given her some

clues, but our friendship is more important to me. I don't want my feelings to ruin that."

"Aww, aren't you adorable?" Annie says before squeezing my cheeks. "Honey, let me give you another chicken nugget of wisdom." She pulls me closer. "You'll never know if she likes you back unless you tell the girl how you feel. You have to say *something*."

"Yeah." Anton agrees. "And if you've prayed about it and God is still leading your heart towards that, then do it. Pursue the girl. What are you going to lose?"

"Err, my friendship?" I reply.

"*Pfft*, nah, I don't think so." Anton wraps his arm around Annie's waist and pulls her close to him. "Tell her you like her and if she likes you back, then praise the Lord. If she doesn't, I'm sure you guys will pull through anyway. Your friendship is strong enough to survive that." Anton glances at me briefly before planting a kiss on Annie's lips.

I open my mouth to speak, but then bite back my words when I hear Teeyana's voice coming from across the garden.

Oh, Lord, she's here. Please help me.

Wiping my hands on my jeans, I turn around and there she is, walking towards me with Heather beside her. I don't know what I'm more stunned by; Heather's hair, which is now dark auburn, or how beautiful Teeyana looks in her floral knee length dress.

As they approach me, Teeyana's curls from her Bantu knots bounce every time she moves her head. The only reason I know they are Bantu knots is because Teeyana told me earlier she'll be trying them out today.

Oh, Lord, she's so beautiful.

I hug Teeyana and brush my lips against her cheek. "You look beautiful." I whisper in her ear before setting her free from my hug. Her smooth brown skin glistens in the sun, and her beautiful smile makes it even more noticeable.

She giggles and replies, "And you don't look too bad yourself."

Smoke goes up in the air and the music comes on as the cooked burgers get off the grill. Teeyana and I spend time with Heather and try to get to know her more. Apart from our revision sessions for finals, Heather and I haven't spoken much throughout the year. In fact, I would have never spoken to her if it weren't for Teeyana.

"It's crazy to think that I used to be the one Anton was trying to make feel welcome." Teeyana nods towards Anton, who is now speaking to Heather.

I slurp what is left of my drink. "Yeah, this year has been crazy, to say the least. What are you most grateful for?" I ask.

She sips her drink and puts her cup on the table. "That's an interesting question." She taps her chin with her index finger. "I'd have to say God changing my heart and restoring my relationship with my family. Also, for giving me the boldness to speak to someone about God. That's something I want to do more of." She looks in Heather's direction again.

I nod.

Teeyana looks at me again, her warm smile returning. "And for you too, Jay." She continues. "I'm very grateful for meeting you."

I have to admit that I wanted to hear those words.

"But I'm sure you already knew that because I tell you all the time." She adds. "You're my best friend and I love you." She squeezes my hand.

"Oh, so I'm your best friend now, huh? Let's pray Amara doesn't hear that." I tease.

"I'm pretty sure both of you are civilised adults who can share a space in my heart." She places her hand on her chest.

"Well, I don't think there's any need for that." I respond. "Because sooner or later, I might have a new space of my own in that big heart of yours." I blurt out.

Teeyana stares at me for a few seconds, as if she's trying to decipher what I said. "A whole new space, huh? Well, ain't you brave, Jayden Williams? That's a big deal, so you'd have to ask *really* nicely." She winks at me, and before I can get my head around what she just said, she pulls me towards the centre of the garden, which is now known as *the dance floor.*

We slide into the conga line as everyone dances and meanders around the tables and chairs in the garden. Every time my eyes meet Teeyana's, my stomach churns.

Tell her.

But Lord, what if she doesn't like me back?

Just tell her.

Okay, Lord. I'll do it only because You said so.

Without any more hesitation, I pull Teeyana away from the line and whisper into her ears, before leading her away from the crowd and into the church.

"Where are we going?" She leaps behind me.

"Just away from the noise." I reply and scan the empty church. Bringing her to the front pew, I gesture for her to sit before plopping down beside her.

I take deep breaths and lean forward, a million words swirling around in my head.

"Jay, is everything alright?" Her soft hands brush against mine, riling up all sorts of emotions inside of me.

Taking her hands into mine, I start talking. "Tee, I need to tell you something now before it drives me crazy."

"O—kay?" She tilts her head and frowns.

I take a deep breath in and exhale before saying, "I like you, Tee." I pause and look at her. "I *like* like you. I love how hard-working you are because it inspires me to work harder and aim higher. I love how your eyes light up every time you get a new idea. I love your face of determination when you power through your drawings. I love how you tuck your baby hairs behind your ears when you're nervous and you think no one else notices." Teeyana laughs, and it puts me at ease.

"I love the way you look at me, Tee." I stare into her dark brown eyes. "Just like you're doing now—giving me your one hundred percent attention. You always make me feel like I'm important.

"And your smile, oh, Lord, please don't get me started on your smile. I know you'll say this sounds corny, but your smile was the only thing I thought about after we met. The only reason I approached you in class that day was because I couldn't get you out of my head all weekend." I shuffle closer.

"Tee, you know I've always been serious about intentionality, so I wanted to be honest with you about how I feel. I hope that by now, I've been able to show you I care about you. What makes you happy, makes me happy, and what makes you cry, totally rips my heart out. I've been praying about this because I wanted to be sure that it's what God wants and that I'm ready for it, so here it goes."

I squeeze her hands. "Teeyana Joy Sparks...I would love to take you out on a date with me, not just as my best friend, but as my girlfriend. What do you say?" I hold my breath and anticipate her reply.

"Actually, before you say anything," I continue. "I want you to know that you don't have to agree to this. I want this to be what you want and what you feel God is leading you to do. I know there's a possibility that you might not feel the same way and I'm very open to that possibility. I just thought I'd get this off my chest because I couldn't hold it in anymore. You can take as much time as you want to pray about it, and whatever it is you decide to do, I promise I'll respect your decision."

She chuckles and then brushes my cheek with her thumb. "Are you done with your speech now?" she asks, smiling at me.

"Uh, well yeah, I guess so. So what do you say?" I remind her she hasn't answered my question.

"Well, isn't it about time?" She raises her hands above her head before wrapping them around my shoulders. "I like *like* you too, Jay. I like you a lot." She cups my face in her hands.

"Really?" I gasp.

"Yeah. I'm surprised you hadn't noticed. I thought it was quite obvious."

"Well, now that I think about it, any girl who would spend four hours on the phone talking to me about random things surely must have an interest in me." I smirk and she pushes my arm.

"Oh, please. Don't get too puffed up with pride now, lest the Lord humble you."

I laugh at her sly attempt to use scripture to make me feel guilty. The sparkle in her eyes grows wider. "I would love to be your girlfriend, Jay." She finally answers my question.

"Yes!!!" I pump my fists in the air before pulling her closer and kissing her forehead. "Now be honest, what did you think of my speech?" I grin.

"I think Tyler taught you well." She smiles and I kiss her nose. Moving my lips lower down, I let them hover over hers, getting closer and closer and—

"Jayden!!!" Annie's voice jerks us apart. I lift my head to see her copper brown hair in the distance, her feathery rainbow-coloured earrings bouncing as she runs down the aisle towards us.

"So? What did she say?" Annie asks, looking like she's about to burst with excitement, as Anton jogs behind her.

"She said yes!!!" I shout out and Annie shrieks before wrapping her arms around Teeyana. "See? I told you she liked you." Annie turns to me and we all laugh.

Anton squeezes my shoulder. "It wasn't as hard as you thought it would be, was it?"

"Oh, yes, it was." I laugh out loud. "But it was part of God's plan after all."

39

TEEYANA

"Girl, you did me wrong. Why didn't you tell me you had been planning to do the *big chop* this whole time?" Amara raises her voice as she tries to talk over Danny's playful shouts in the background.

"Well, I told you I'd been considering it, though, didn't I?" I look up at her.

"Yeah, but *considering* doesn't mean you're going to do it, does it?" She places both hands on her hips. "You didn't even give me the chance to coach you through your journey. I'm offended."

I laugh and shake my head at this best friend of mine, who loves making a big deal out of nothing. "Well, I can see you're not up to par. Do you want me to find someone else to do this job?" I attempt to stand up from my seat.

"Uh, heck no. Girl, sit your butt down. I'm staying right here." Amara holds me down by my shoulders and turns the chair around so I'm facing the mirror in front of us. "I don't know how you were able to hold on to these dead ends for so long, but I'm so glad you're giving up on the creamy crack." Amara runs her fingers through a section of my hair as I smirk.

Even though I've been considering cutting my hair for the

past year, I didn't think I would go through with it. I was excited to tell Grandma that I stopped chemically straightening my hair or using the *creamy crack*—as Amara would put it. But unfortunately, I didn't get the chance.

The past couple of months have paved a way for a new beginning in my life. A fresh start. I want to honour this fresh start by doing something I've never done before. Although it doesn't seem like a big deal to others, I've been scared to cut my hair.

I didn't want anyone's opinion to influence my decision, and I always told Grandma I'll only cut my hair if I want to. Nobody coerced me into making this decision, but I know Grandma would have loved it. So I'm doing this first to embrace this new journey of mine, and also for Grandma.

"Let's do this then." Amara winks at me and then asks Danny for the spray bottle he has been playing with on the floor.

Danny brings the spray bottle over, and I make him sit on my lap. Amara brings out her inner hairdresser persona and puts on a serious face. I stifle a laugh as I stare at her in the mirror.

She adjusts the towel around my neck before parting my hair out into four sections. She then starts with the section at the front right and sprays it with water until she sees the line of demarcation between my chemically straightened hair and my naturally curly hair underneath.

"Girl, are you ready for this? You can still back out now if you want to. Not that I'll let you." Amara asks as she picks up the pair of scissors from the table.

I look at Danny. "Are we ready, Danny?"

He nods and claps his hands. "Yes."

"That's right, boy." I kiss his cheek and turn to Amara. "You heard the man. Let's do this."

Amara cuts off the straight ends, leaving only the curly strands underneath. As the scissors cut the straight pieces off, they fall to the ground, reminding me of all the fear, anxieties and grudges I'd been holding on to all these years. They latched on to me like these straggly dead ends.

But God opened my eyes to see that I needed to let go, and let Him take the scissors and cut them away. Now, just like my natural hair, I can flourish in the life God has called me to live.

When Amara is done cutting the first section, my curls shrink and become shorter. I try to run my hands through my hair, but she slaps it away. "Nuh-uh. You wait till the whole thing is done now, young lady."

"Ouch." I roll my eyes at her and rub my hand. The girl has a heavy hand.

About half an hour later, all the straight pieces of hair end up on the floor and Amara finally gives me permission to touch. "Oh my God." I gasp and run my hands through my natural hair for the first time. It is kinky, curly, and short. I don't remember ever having short hair in my life.

There's a brief moment of silence as I stare at myself in the mirror, running my fingers through my hair non-stop and looking at my head from different angles.

Danny reaches out and runs his hands through my hair too and then through his own hair. "Your hair is short," he points out.

"It sure is, big boy. It looks like yours now." I pinch his cheeks and then turn towards Amara with a big smile on my face.

"So? Do you like it?" Amara presses her lips together.

I shake my head. "Like it? Girl, I love it!!!" I let out a little squeal and turn back to face the mirror. "Are these my curls popping?"

"*Yaaas*, they are." Amara jumps in excitement.

"I can't believe this."

"You better believe it, girl. Your curls are slaying." Amara clicks her fingers.

"I can't wait to show Jayden." I reach for my phone on my bed and click on the FaceTime icon. It opens up, and I click on Jayden's name at the top of the list. The phone starts ringing, and I put it in front of me, getting ready for the video call.

"Okay, I don't care if lover-boy doesn't like it." Amara says. "I know boys can be complicated sometimes. I'll still support you even if he doesn't approve." Amara pats my shoulder.

I playfully shove her hand away. "Don't be so pessimistic. He'll love it. You'll see." I give her a confident smile.

I adjust Danny on my lap when Jayden answers the call, his hands covering his eyes. "So? Is it done? Can I open my eyes now?" He asks.

"Yes, you can." I smile.

Jayden peeks through the spaces between his fingers, then he drops his hands. His jaw drops for a second or two and the only words that come out of his mouth are "Wow. Wow. Wow."

I giggle at the fact that my new look has rendered him speechless. "So...is that a good wow?" I ask.

"A darn good *wow* for sure." His eyes widen as he continues staring at me. "Tee, you look so beautiful."

"I know, right." Amara adds as she squeezes her face next to mine so Jayden can see her. "Shall we take a moment to appreciate the hairdresser, please? I think I deserve some recognition here. Am I right or am I right?" She asks, pointing to herself.

"Yes, definitely. You did a great job Amara, I'll give you that." He turns his attention to Danny sitting on my lap. "And how is the little man doing today?"

"I'm fine, thank you. What's your name?" Danny tilts his head.

"Oh, sorry about my manners. My name is Jayden. And you are?" Jayden asks, even though he knows the answer to that question.

"Danny. My name is Danny." Danny replies. "Are you

Teeyana's boyfriend?" he blurts out, even though I'd never mentioned Jayden to him before.

"Ooohh." Amara chimes in. "Yeah, that's right, Jayden. The little boy wants to know." She wiggles her eyebrows and Jayden gives Danny a nervous laugh.

I try to push Amara away, but the girl won't budge. Jayden smiles at Danny and replies, "Well, would you like me to be her boyfriend, Danny?" He asks.

The little man nods. "Yes. I like you." He points towards Jayden and then looks at me, as if he's asking me to agree with his choice.

"Well, then. I can't say no to you. I'll be her boyfriend." Jayden winks at Danny, who smiles in return.

"Okay, but Danny, you have to promise to keep this a secret between us, okay?" I ask him. "Promise?"

"I promise," he says before sliding down my lap and returning to his toys on the floor.

"He's precious." Jayden says. "I can't wait to meet your parents next week."

"I'm sure they'll love you." I run my fingers over his face on the screen. "It's kinda hard not to."

Amara clears her throat before bursting into a chant. "*Teeyana and Jayden sitting in a tree. K-I-S-S-I-N-G.*"

"*Ugh*, go away. You're *so* annoying." I push her away, and we all burst into laughter.

40

JAYDEN

I tap my feet and rub my palms on my jeans a million times, looking over my shoulder to see if the tall, muscular, dark-skinned man would walk through the door.

What if he doesn't like me? What if I mess up and say something stupid? He'll kick me straight out of his house.

A wave of laughter flows in from the kitchen, which is a few doors away, and Teeyana's voice stands out among them. After dinner with Teeyana's parents and Amara, Mr. Sparks asked to talk with me. I have been looking forward to this meeting all weekend, but now; I feel it'll be an absolute disaster.

The smell of food is still thick in the air, and my stomach is so full from the delicious spaghetti bolognese we had, but I'm so nervous I think I might puke.

Lord, please help me. I have to—

The door bursts open behind me, forcing me to jump in my seat.

"Hey buddy, sorry for keeping you waiting. Here you go." Mr. Sparks places a glass of orange juice in front of me and sits in the chair across the table.

My heart thumps in my chest. "Thank you, sir." I rub my palms together before picking up my glass.

"So, Teeyana tells me you're involved in your youth group at college?" He takes a sip of his juice.

I nod. "Yes, sir. I wanted to stay connected to a Christian community, so I started looking early."

"I see. Do you do anything in the church?"

"Well, sometimes, I lead the small group sessions we have during the week, and occasionally, I play the guitar on Sundays. It's the same thing I do at my home church here in Boston."

Mr. Sparks leans forward and rests his hands on his knees. "So I suppose church, God, and your faith are very important to you?" he raises his brows.

"That's right, sir." I nod.

"And why is that?" He leans back in his seat, crossing his arms over his chest.

Oh God, this is starting to feel like an interview, or better still, an interrogation?

I pick up my glass again and sip, trying to convince myself that this is not an interview. I'm sure he only wants to know more about me, so I have to be genuine.

I straighten my back and lift my head up to look at him. "Because I've realised that I'm nothing without God," I reply. "I lost my brother to suicide five years ago and in the fear of not wanting to end up like him, I started searching for answers and then God drew me close to Him."

"Oh, I'm so sorry to hear about your brother." Mr. Sparks' facial expression softens.

I smile. "It's okay, sir. It's still hard talking about it, but I've been praying that as the years pass and I mature in my faith, I'll learn to lean on God for strength even when I don't understand."

Mr. Sparks nods and rubs his moustache. "Hmm. I'm sure Teeyana told you about my wife losing her mom?"

I nod.

"It's difficult because we invest so much into the relationships we build. It's always hard when we lose someone close to us—especially in such an unexpected way."

"Yes, it's very difficult." I relax more as the conversation progresses. "My brother's death taught me to always think about others and reach out to them. But I've lived the past few years in fear of not doing enough for my loved ones and losing them too."

"Hmm." Mr. Sparks comes in. "As selfless and genuine as that sounds, it's important to remember that we're all humans and we're all broken, son. That's why we all need a Saviour." He picks up his glass and takes another sip of his drink.

Lord, is this the right time to tell him?

"Yes, you're right. I've been learning a lot about that recently, especially since I met Teeyana." I tap my feet again. "It's been a blessing getting to know her over the past year and in fact, I would have never learnt any of the things I told you today if it wasn't for her." I pause and look at him, his face very serious as he looks at me straight in the eyes.

"After praying about this for a while," I continue, "I asked Teeyana to be my girlfriend, and she agreed. I came here to let you guys know that my intentions are pure, and I genuinely care about your daughter."

"You're a good kid, Jayden." Mr. Sparks responds. "This is our first meeting, but it feels like I've known you since Teeyana started talking about you. It's clear that you both have impacted each other's lives and I can see that you care about her."

Why do I have this feeling that there's a "but" coming?

"But..."

Ah, there it is.

"I think it's important for you to understand that the foundation of every relationship is God and He is the unifier." He points upwards. "It's not an easy journey, and it's not one to be taken lightly." He shakes his head.

"If the foundation is not God, trust me, it'll be a recipe for disaster. You can't give something only God can provide. So you both need to love God first, and pray that you love Him more than you love her."

I nod.

"And, you understand that you're the first person I've ever had this conversation with, right? It's a big deal for Teeyana as well as it is for myself and my wife. Teeyana is our baby girl and we love her very much. We will do absolutely anything to protect her and look out for her best interests."

I gulp. "I understand that, sir."

Mr. Sparks stands up and looks down at me. "Well, in that case, I guess there's only one thing left to say." He opens his arms wide. "Welcome to the family, son." I smile and go in for a hug.

"Thank you very much, sir." I smile again, and we head towards the kitchen to join the girls. Amara, Teeyana, and Mrs. Sparks are washing and drying the dishes when we walk in.

"Sorry, honey, for taking your friend away for so long. It's been a pleasure having him around." He looks at me and grins.

We both move out of the way as we let Amara walk past, carrying a stack of plates. "Oh, thank the Lord you are back. Teeyana has been worrying about how much you'd be grilling him." Amara laughs.

"Shhh!!!" Teeyana hushes her best friend as she approaches me. She hugs her dad first before wrapping her arms around my waist.

"Amara is right." Mrs. Sparks gives us a sly smile. "Teeyana hasn't stopped pacing back and forth since you both left for your chat."

"*Ugh*, okay fine." Teeyana buries her head in my chest. "Dad, I thought you were going to scare him away."

"What? Me?" Mr. Sparks laughs. "This man right here will not be scared away easily. He knows what he wants." He pats my back before walking over to his wife.

I look down at Teeyana and grin. "I sure do."

Just then, Danny runs into the kitchen, right past Amara and towards Teeyana and me. I stretch out my arms and pick him up from the ground, letting him wrap his arms around my neck. "So can I tell everyone you're Teeyana's boyfriend now?" Danny shouts, and we all burst into laughter.

Sweat trickles down from my temples and runs underneath my jawline as I keep my gaze fixed on the hoop on the other side. I adjust the sweat-soaked waistband of my trousers and anticipate my next move when a guy from the opposing team approaches me with the ball. It's my first time playing in the men's basketball tournament, and I'm so grateful I'm well enough to be back on the field and enjoying playing ball again.

The boys from Baruch College make a strong team, but it's our first match of the season and we're not going down without a fight. I glance at the clock and there's five minutes left and the scores are fifty for them and forty-six for us.

I shake my head and refocus when Coach Simpson yells at me to move on. There's not much I can hear over the loud cheers which have drowned out everyone else's voice. A rainbow of colours lines Carnesecca Arena—yellow, blue, orange, green, and red.

Among the sea of people, flags wave from side to side, and

large fake thumbs bounce up and down in the front row seats where Mom, Dad, and Teeyana are yelling out my name.

The cheerleaders parade over the edge of the court, waving their pom-poms and jollying out their planned routines, with wide smiles plastered on their faces, and never ending chants escaping their lips.

I wonder how they never lose their voices after all that screaming.

I let out a quick breath and run, aiming to get the ball at all costs. Coming face to face with the opponent, he turns around to evade me, but I smack the ball out of his hands. It bounces away from us and with one quick look at him, we both run towards it.

Diving hands first, I grab the ball and throw it to Warryn who acts quickly, evading all the other opponents and finally throwing the ball through the hoop. Getting up from the floor, I run back to the other side of the court and take my position.

One minute left.

The scoreboards now read fifty for them and forty-eight for us.

"Go on, Jayden. You can do this." Teeyana's faint voice graces my ears from the stands. I send a quick glance in her direction before reaching out my arms and grabbing the ball. Securing it safely in my hands, I run towards the hoop on the other side, bouncing the ball as I go and dodging anyone that comes my way.

Hoping the hoop will be within reach, I halt, bouncing the ball as I get ready to throw.

Bounce.

Lord, please help me.

Bounce.

I'm right here with you, Jayden. I will help you. Trust me.

Bounce.

Stepping back and standing beyond the three point line, I leap and throw the ball towards the hoop. Landing with both feet on the ground, I close my eyes and exhale and the crowd goes silent.

This one's for you, Tyler.

After what seems like the longest second, the crowd erupts in cheers. I open my eyes to see the scoreboard reading fifty for Baruch College and fifty-one for us.

Before I can make sense of what's happening, students run out from the stands and onto the court. The next thing I know is me floating in the air as my teammates jump up and down, chanting.

I sight Teeyana and my parents among the sea of people and I scramble my way down, hugging my parents first before lifting Teeyana and spinning her around.

She plants a kiss on my cheek and whispers in my ear. "You did it, babe. I'm so proud of you."

Kissing her hands, I shake my head. "No, Tee. God did it."

Her mouth curves into a huge smile and I kiss her forehead as my parents go to get us bottles of water.

"Williams." Coach Simpson's hand grips my shoulder and I turn around to face him. "I knew you could do this, son." His eyes sparkle behind his glasses and his grey moustache spreads out across his face as he smiles at me.

"You see those guys over there?" Coach points to two men dressed in suits, sitting in the stands, and talking to each other. "They've been watching you throughout the whole game. If you're interested in furthering your career in basketball after college, they are the ones to impress. From what I know, they are very pleased with your performance so far." He winks at me.

"Really? Me?" My heart thumps in my chest as I think about the possibility.

"Yes, son. You." Coach pokes my shoulder. "I've always known you're capable of doing great things—right from the first time I watched you play basketball."

"Wow. That's an amazing opportunity, Jay." Teeyana says. "This would be huge for your career."

"Yeah it will." I reply, but then pause. "Thanks, Coach. But...I need to pray about it first."

He looks at me for a few seconds and then takes off his glasses. "In my twenty years of coaching, you're the first student I've ever spoken to about an opportunity like this, who has chosen to ask God first." He pats my shoulder. "You inspire me, Jayden Williams. Keep following God. He will never lead you wrong."

For a reason that is unclear to me, tears well up behind my eyelids and, overwhelmed with emotion, I hug Coach Simpson, burying my face in his shoulder. "Thanks, Coach, for always believing in me, and for everything you've done for me."

"I did nothing, son." His eyes water too when he looks at me. "I thank God for causing us to cross paths."

41

TEEYANA

It's been a year since Grandma died, and the entire family is back in Atlanta to spend Christmas with Grandpa. I'm praying this becomes a yearly tradition because I love when my family gets together like this.

I've been looking forward to seeing Aunt Bella who has now moved to Atlanta for her new job. She's still busy, as always, but at least now she's much closer to Grandpa. In fact, things are about to get even busier now because she got engaged last week. I'm excited for the wedding and everything else that will come after, particularly the babies—God willing.

We built a rose garden over Grandma's grave last year and today we've brought flowers to add to it. Even Danny has his own little red rose.

Grandpa takes the first step forward and lays his rose down, saying a silent prayer to himself. He then kisses the tip of his finger and places it on Grandma's name on her gravestone. "You'll forever be in my heart, my love." Grandpa stands up and walks back to us.

Mom and Dad lay down their roses next, followed by Aunt Bella and Danny.

"I love you, Grandma." Danny says. "And I miss you. Say hello to Jesus for me. I speak to Him every day and I know He is looking after you." He turns around and runs back into Mom's arms.

Then it's my turn and I walk forward. The inscriptions on her grave stone remind me of her beautiful name, *Hannah-Grace Elizabeth Thompson.*

"Only a woman as beautiful as you could pull off names like these, Grandma." I kneel and lay down my rose. Then I run my fingers over her name, imagining myself touching her face or stroking her beautiful kinky grey curls.

"I have a boyfriend now, Grandma. His name is Jayden." My lips quiver as the tears run down my face. "He plays basketball, and he even plays the guitar. He loves Jesus and I know you would have loved him too." I smile as tears blur my vision. "Oh, and I cut my hair too." I laugh. "I know. I know. I can't believe I went through with it. You were such an inspiration to me." My voice breaks.

"I thank God for every precious moment He gifted me to spend with you." I palm the tears away. "I only wish that you would have stayed a little longer with us. I miss your smile. I miss your stories. I miss your pies, Grandma." I laugh.

"But, above everything, I miss the way you always encouraged me to be who God has called me to be. You didn't wake up from that coma, but I'm certain that you've woken up in glory." I reach into my bag and bring out a framed drawing I made for her which reads "Be Thou My Vision."

I balance the frame against her gravestone, and pick up a handful of earth as I stand. Looking up at the blue sky, the lyrics to the last verse of the hymn echo in my head, and I sing them out loud.

High King of heaven, my victory won

May I reach heaven's joy, bright heaven's sun
Heart of my own heart, whatever befall
Still be my vision, oh Ruler of all

"I know you are in a peaceful place now, Grandma. And I know that someday, I'll see you again. But until then, may your soul rest in perfect peace. Stay beautiful like this rose. And remember that I'll always love you. The Lord gave, and the Lord has taken away. Blessed be His name." I let the earth slip through my fingers until only dust is left on my palm, and then I turn around and walk away.

Mom hurries towards me, her face soaked in tears like mine. I wrap my arms around her waist and bury my face in her chest. Soon, it turns into a group hug, with Danny almost squished in the middle. After a few minutes, everyone heads to the car.

I turn around to take one last look at Grandma's grave, but I'm distracted by a man sitting in a wheelchair a few yards away. There's a woman standing behind him as he stares at the gravestone in front of him. When she turns the wheelchair around for them to leave, my eyes widen in disbelief. The silvery grey hair, the thick round glasses, and the blue jumper peeking out of his winter coat.

"Rupert?" I whisper as I separate myself from the group. "Rupert? Rupert?" My voice gets louder as I run after the woman pushing the wheelchair. She stops and turns the wheelchair around. "Rupert? Do you remember me?" I come to a halt and lean forward, trying to catch my breath.

He stares at me for a minute and then looks at the nurse, who shrugs at him. A warm smile lines his wrinkled face and he nods. "Ah, you're the young lady from the lift?" His beautiful British accent comes through.

"Yes, that's me. You remember." I grin.

"Of course I remember. I told you I would always remember

a beautiful face like yours. Please meet Martha, the wonderful young lady who has been looking after me." He points to the nurse standing behind him.

"Hello, Martha." I shake her hand and she smiles.

"So what are you doing here, love?" Rupert asks.

My smile fades as I point to grandma's grave. "My grandma never woke up from that coma."

"Neither did my wife, dear." He shakes his head. "Neither did my dear Marjorie."

"Oh, I'm so sorry to hear that, Rupert." I kneel next to him, squeezing his hands.

"It's okay because in every circumstance, good or bad, I'll give thanks to my God. My dear Marjorie and your Grandma are in a much better place now and to be honest, I can't wait to get there someday. God is good, isn't He?" He places his hand on my shoulder.

"He sure is." I hold on to his free hand. "So, what are you going to do now? Do you have family here in the US? Any children?"

"I have a son and daughter living in the UK. They're both married with children and they have families of their own. They're coming over to visit me in the New Year and I'll be going back to the UK with them. You see, Marjorie and I moved here ten years ago to start up the ministry that God wanted us to do together. But I believe my work here is done so I'm going back to England."

"Oh, I see. And what is your ministry about?" I ask.

"It's called *The Chasing Hope Foundation*. We've been travelling around the country, encouraging people who are dealing with grief and telling them about the hope they have in Jesus. Sometimes, we visit schools, orphanages, and some specific families as well. We help families who are struggling financially and give out accessories including books, stationery, and clothes.

We have a well-established team here so I don't need to be here anymore. I'm going back to England to work with the team there, and be closer to my children."

"Wow, that sounds great." I say.

"Yeah, God has been faithful over the last ten years and I trust that He'll continue to be even more faithful in this next chapter of my life." Rupert reaches into his pocket and hands me a small card. "If you ever decide to come to England, particularly to the Southampton, Hampshire area, please call me. I'd be more than happy to have you over for tea." He smiles.

"Thank you, Rupert." I hug him. "When you say tea, do you mean literal tea or will there be food as well?" I tease.

"Well, come on a Sunday and we can add some Sunday roast." He laughs.

"I'll remember that, and I'll keep this safe with me. Thank you so much, Rupert. Goodbye and God bless you."

Rupert waves at me before the nurse turns his wheelchair around and wheels him away. I look down at the card in my hand and put it safely into my jacket pocket before walking back to meet my family.

EPILOGUE

Two Years Later

I pick up my journal lying next to my open Bible before looking out onto the horizon as we sit out on the balcony of Jayden's house. His parents are watching TV in the living room and we've been using the balcony for our Bible studies every week since we came home for spring break.

"What?" I ask when I catch Jayden staring at me.

"You journal now?" he asks.

"Hmm." I nod. "Grandpa got me into it two years ago, and Mary encouraged me to keep going. It's so therapeutic." I clutch the journal against my chest.

Jayden smiles. "I'm happy the counselling is working for you, Tee."

"Me too." I smile back at him. "Do you want to see?" I hand the journal to him.

"Uh...are you sure about this? Aren't journals supposed to have top secrets?" He raises his eyebrows.

I chuckle. "No, not always. Don't worry, you can read this one."

"Yes, Ma'am." He takes the journal from me, turning it over to look at my decorations on the front cover. He smiles and runs his hands over the hand lettered Bible verse—Job 23:10.

"'But He knows the way that I take,'" Jayden reads out loud. "'When He has tested me, I will come forth as gold.'" He continues staring at the verse until his eyes glisten with tears.

"Jay, are you okay?" I place my hand on top of his, dropping my head to meet his gaze.

"Yeah." He wipes his eyes. "I'm fine," he says, and opens the journal. "This verse became my favourite when I was dealing with Tyler's death. I remember sticking up the bold words on the wall in my room and every morning, I read it out loud to remind myself that God knows and sees me." He looks at a few more pages and then looks at me. "It's amazing that God has used this same verse to encourage you too."

I nod. "Hmm, and don't you find it amazing how God works things out His own way?" I ask. "Like how I've lost the desires for some things I used to want before?"

"Oh? Like what?" Jayden raises his eyebrows.

"Like the whole dream about working at Google? I don't want to do that anymore." I shrug.

Jayden's mouth drops open. "For real? But that's literally all you've talked about since we started college. What changed your mind?"

I adjust in my seat. "Well, you know how you prayed and God directed you to becoming a coach for your old high school's basketball team instead of taking up that offer of playing professional basketball?" I ask, and Jayden nods. "And you know how God made everything fall into place? How you were able to get the excellent recommendation from Coach Simpson, which helped you get the sponsorship for your training? And also how your old high school was willing to help you get the experience you need?"

"Yes, I believe God wants me to coach and encourage these young boys the same way Tyler used to encourage me," Jayden replies.

"Exactly. See, you have a purpose in your dream and I don't." I shake my head. "Jay, I've been questioning my motivation behind this whole dream to work at Google. I mean, Google is great, and I loved my internship there, but the only reason I wanted it was because I thought it'll make me sound cool when I tell people I work there. I don't think that's enough motivation to pursue something." I scoff.

"Okay—so what do you want to do now?" Jayden rubs his now grown beard which shapes the corners of his face and makes him look even more handsome.

"Well, I still want to pursue a career in graphic design because I can't imagine myself doing anything else. But there's something I've been praying about and I believe God wants me to do it first. Do you remember Rupert?" I ask.

Jayden squints and tilts his head. "The guy you met at the hospital?"

"Yeah, that guy. So before his wife—Marjorie, sadly died from the accident, they set up an organisation together and it's called *The Chasing Hope Foundation.* They cater for the needs of individuals and families who are dealing with grief, and they tell them about Jesus and the gospel of hope." I reach into my jacket pocket and bring out the card Rupert gave me.

"Jesus healed my broken heart when I thought no one could save me. I want to tell the world about Him so they too can believe in this hope I have found in Him—the same way Heather believed." I smile.

"I've been in touch with Rupert, who is now back in England, and he invited me to volunteer with them this summer. He also said if I like it and want to do more, I can join the next set of volunteers going to Mandritsara, Madagascar, next year." I hand the card over to Jayden. "I was wondering if you would like to come to England with me this summer. It'll be before you start your basketball coach training." I bite my lip.

He stares at the words on the card for about thirty seconds before lifting his head to look at me. "Hmm...well, we'd have to save up for this, but...it sounds like it'll be so much fun. So of course, count me in." He grins.

"Really?" My eyes widen. "Thank you so much, Jay. I don't know what I would do without you."

"Hmm, I know what you'd do without me—crash and burn." He smirks.

"Hey, that's not nice!" I cross my arms and pretend to be mad at him.

"I'm joking, babe. You'll be fine without me." He uncrosses my arms and shuffles closer. "You are very intelligent." He kisses my forehead. "You have a kind heart." He kisses my left cheek. "You are so driven." He kisses my right cheek. "And God has used you to change my life." He kisses my nose and gently tips my head back. "You make me laugh, you chase God with me, and you are beautiful—inside and out."

I stare into his dark brown eyes and follow the lines of the smile on his face—that same smile from the first time we met. It's crazy how far we've come and how close we've become.

"I love you, Tee." His face gets closer and I can feel his fresh minty breath against my face. His beard brushes softly against my skin, and I exhale.

"I love you, Jay." I close my eyes and lean closer, my lips parting in anticipation, and he presses his lips against mine.

The End

A PLEA

Thank you so much for reading this book. I would be very grateful if you could please leave a review online. Reviews are very important because they help the book become more visible to others so they can be blessed by it too. Thank you again and God bless you.

AUTHOR'S NOTE

The inspiration behind this story came to me in September 2017 when I was walking to university. I had an idea to write a story about a girl who has doubts, and who is trying to run away from God. I had just come out of a dark season where I faced rejection, disappointment and failure, and just like Teeeyana, I asked God why He had let bad things happen to me if He truly loved me. But it wasn't until years later that I looked back and smiled at the goodness of God's sovereign love that had been woven into my testimony.

When I started writing this book, God primed my heart to address the false idea that He is not with us when we go through trials. While some of our trials can be consequences of our actions, or something God uses to discipline us, it doesn't mean that because God allows them; He doesn't love us. This was a lesson God helped me learn as I finished the first draft of this book in June 2018. I went into this story without a writing background and not knowing much about the technicalities of storytelling. This was the first novel I ever wrote, and as I worked on the second and third drafts in 2018 and 2019, I made major changes, cut out chapters, and added new scenes. But the message remained the same—nothing can separate us from the love of God—not even the trials we face (Romans 8:31-39).

The central Bible verse for this story is from Job 23:10 and it is actually my favourite Bible verse. Whenever I go through deep waters, God uses this verse to remind me that He knows what I'm going through. Sometimes, when we face trials, we can either live in denial and refuse to face them, or we run away from God and try to handle things on our own. But God didn't create us to be self-sufficient and we can do nothing without Him. The Bible tells us in John 15:5 that Christ is the vine and we are the branches, and just like the branches depend on the vine for life, so do we depend on God for life. This is especially important when we are dealing with suffering.

We may not always see the good purpose for our trials. In fact, often, things won't make sense. But even when we don't see the point, God is still using our suffering to refine us so we can come out as pure gold. The confidence we have when we face trials is knowing that we're not in the fire alone; God is present with us, and He is preventing us from getting consumed. Someday, when we get to the other side of eternity, we will understand why He let the fire burn instead of putting it out. I wanted to capture this message in this story and I hope that Teeyana and Jayden's faith journeys stirred your heart towards the beauty of depending on God as a tactic to triumph over suffering.

Jayden is the character after my heart. He was initially only supposed to be the love interest. But after I got feedback from my first round of beta readers in 2019, God showed me that there was more to Jayden's story that needed to be told. As someone who works in the medical field, I come across patients on a weekly basis who suffer from mental illness—including Christians. I never intended to touch on mental health topics in this book, but it so happened that God wanted it that way.

I believe that mental health needs to be addressed a lot more—especially in the body of Christ. A lot of young people suffer in silence for fear of being misunderstood, but my prayer is that stories like this will point people to the light, and show them that no matter how bleak our circumstances are, Jesus is capable of handling our ailing hearts. Indeed, there is nothing impossible for God to do, and even as we rejoice in our pain, God is comforting us, then using our stories to comfort others. He is drawing us closer to Himself and deepening our faith, so that in the end, His name alone will be glorified.

Mental illness is as real as any physical illness, so please, I hope this story encourages you to educate yourself, to learn the signs, and to reach out to your friends and family members who need your help. If you're reading this and you feel so hopeless that you've thought about harming yourself or ending your life, please don't do it. Suicide is not the answer. You are not alone. Help is available so please stay. If you are in the UK, US or Canada, below are some links you can use to get some help.

Help in the UK: https://www.itv.com/thismorning/articles/suicide-prevention-helplines

Help in the US: https://www.healthline.com/health/mental-health/suicide-resource-guide

Help in Canada: https://www.crisisservicescanada.ca/en/

If you are in other countries and you know suicide prevention helplines, please share this information with friends and family. You never know who might need it.

Finally, if you're reading this and you're yet to surrender your life to Jesus Christ as your Lord and Saviour, here's an open invitation to do so today. It is not too late. The Lord's open arms are waiting, and He is calling you to come home. There's no pain He can't heal. Jesus has already paid the price for you. He wants you to abandon your pride today and run to Him. He has loved you from the beginning of time, and He always will. If you want to take that bold step today, please say this prayer with me;

Dear Jesus, I come before you today with thanksgiving in my heart. I accept that You are God and I am not. I am a sinner, but You alone are the Forgiver of sins. Please come into my heart today. I surrender my all to You as my Lord and Saviour. Make me clean and teach me how to love and obey You. In Jesus' name I've prayed. Amen.

If you've prayed this prayer of faith and are willing to walk into your new life with Jesus, congratulations. Welcome to God's family. Please get plugged into a local church if you haven't already done so. Commit to studying the Bible with fellow believers and find a spiritual mentor you trust who will help you along the journey. If you would like to share a testimony with me, please feel free to reach out to me using the contact form found on my website joanembola.co.uk.

Until the next book,

Lots of love,

Joan.

BOOK TWO

IS GOD SOVEREIGN OVER LOVE STORIES?

Amara Ikezie is a new grad nurse who is thrilled to start her dream job in Atlanta's biggest children's hospital. But when her best friend gets engaged, Amara is faced with the looming pressure from her mom to find her own man. Determined to escape the pressure to marry, Amara takes on a task to find the 'perfect' man who ticks all the boxes on her list.

Raymond Aderinto is a pediatric cardiologist with a wall of accolades and a string of failed relationships. After his fourth girlfriend dumps him, Raymond vows to get confirmation from God first before entering into his next relationship—even though he'd love to find his bride before turning thirty.

When Raymond spills coffee on Amara's scrubs, he becomes certain she's the woman God wants to be his wife. But unfortunately for him, Raymond doesn't tick Amara's boxes, and worst of all, Amara is sure her Igbo mom would never approve of a marriage to a man from the Yoruba tribe.

Despite Amara's efforts to stay away from Raymond and convince herself he is not the one for her, her growing attraction for his character, values, and vision gives her more reasons to wonder if she was wrong about her prejudices towards him. When another doctor walks into Amara's life who ticks all her boxes and shows interest in her, she is caught between running into his 'perfect' arms, or going with Raymond who is turning out to be more perfect than she thought.

The One Who Loves Me, book two in the Sovereign Love series, is a beautiful standalone novel about surrender and learning to take comfort in the sovereign goodness of a loving God who writes the best love stories.

Available Now!!!

Get Your Copy Here

FREE SHORT STORY

Want a free short story? Subscribe to Joan's free author newsletter to download *A Promise To Keep,* which follows a Nigerian couple—Dayo and Dara as they navigate the challenges of life while learning about endurance and what it means to experience the goodness of God.

ACKNOWLEDGMENTS

To say that having this book in your hands was solely my doing would be the biggest lie I've ever told. First of all, I want to thank my Heavenly Father for putting this story in my heart, and then for writing it with me. I would never have done it without Him.

To my parents and brothers, thank you for your support of my writing career over the years. You encouraged me to give it a chance and I appreciate all your love and support for me.

To my love, Oladunni, thank you for staying by my side through the highs and lows of my writing and publishing journey. You listened to all my endless rants and helped me come up with solutions. You encouraged me through my doubts and kept reminding me I could do it. I love you so much.

To my spiritual mentor, Michael Okubote and his wife, Tolu Okubote, thank you for loving me, correcting me and encouraging me through my journey of faith.

To my beta readers- Christi, Feby, Nikki, and Angela. Thank you for your very useful feedback. You have no idea how much it encouraged me and made me excited to make this story better.

To my editors Michaela Bush and Abigayle Claire, thank you for your labour of love, for helping me polish this manuscript, the blurb, and my author bio. It would not be what it is today without your amazing expertise. I appreciate you.

To my cover designer, Elle Maxwell, thank you so much for turning the vision I had in mind into the wonderful masterpiece you created. Seriously, your talent is amazing.

To you reading this book, thank you so much for giving it a chance. I hope it has brought you hope, and that it has reminded you of the Father's sovereign love for you.

Finally, I'll have to go back to my Heavenly Father—the One who knows me. My Lord, I started this journey with You and I'm finishing it with You. To You be all the glory, honour and praise forever and ever. Amen.

ABOUT THE AUTHOR

Joan Embola is a UK-based Cameroonian-Nigerian Christian author who aims to share God's love one word at a time. She writes books about diverse characters whose hope-filled stories point to the love and goodness of God in our broken world. She is a qualified Physician Associate and also the founder of Love Qualified, a ministry dedicated to encouraging others to experience the sovereign love of the one true God who has qualified us to be His beloved ones. She is a passionate lover and teacher of God's Word, as shared on her YouTube channel, blog, and podcast. When she's not writing or curled up with a book, you'll find her watching movies, YouTube videos, or making memories with her family and friends.

You can connect with her at www.joanembola.co.uk and on instagram, YouTube and her podcast. Subscribe to her newsletter to stay up to date with book news, cover reveals, how to sign up for advanced reader copies, and fun giveaways. You will also get access to free books, short stories, deleted scenes from her published books and free writer resources.

DISCUSSION QUESTIONS

1. At the start of the book we see Teeyana in a situation which makes her afraid. How does she respond in this situation? In our own lives, how do we respond in fearful situations?
2. Describe the relationship between Teeyana and her best friend—Amara. What kind of support does Amara offer her friend throughout the book and how does it help Teeyana get to where she needs to be?
3. Describe the relationship between Teeyana and her parents and her grandparents. What role did each of them play in Teeyana's journey of faith?
4. We see throughout the book that Jayden hides his struggles while trying to encourage his loved ones. In what ways does this help or harm him?
5. Describe the relationship between Jayden and Teeyana. Do you think there was a good foundation for their friendship and how does their bond grow stronger with time?
6. This book covers a lot of mental health issues such as anxiety, depression, and suicidal thoughts. How do

Jayden, Teeyana, and Tyler deal with these and how do their actions help or harm them? What actions did Jayden take to help him towards his journey of healing and what role did his faith in God play in this?

7. We see that Jayden and Teeyana have spiritual mentors (Anton and Kevin). How important do you think the role of these characters are in helping Teeyana and Jayden in their faith journey?
8. What lesson did Teeyana have to learn to get her to where God needed her to be?
9. What lesson did Jayden have to learn to get him to where God needed him to be?
10. Does the title of the book make sense to you? Do you get the overall theme that the author was trying to portray?

www.ingramcontent.com/pod-product-compliance
Ingram Content Group UK Ltd.
Pitfield, Milton Keynes, MK11 3LW, UK
UKHW031418100125
453365UK00004B/236

9 781838 450083